Circus

By Sian Rosé

Copyright © 2020 Sian Rosé

All rights reserved.

The characters and events portrayed in this book are fictitious. Any similarity to real persons, living or dead, is coincidental and not intended by the author.

No part of this book may be reproduced, or stored in a retrieval system, or transmitted in any form or by any means, electronic, mechanical, photocopying, recording, or otherwise, without express written permission of the publisher.

A note from the author

Hello readers, and many thanks for choosing this story for your literary consumption. This book is the second in a series and is the sequel to my earlier 2020 novel 'Farm.' For the best experience, I would suggest reading the first book before this one, if you haven't already. You can read it for FREE on Kindle Unlimited here: https://www.amazon.co.uk/dp/B08CF21HZ7

Just a quick disclaimer! This book is **<u>NOT</u>** for the faint of heart or for those who are easily disturbed. In fact, it's more extreme, graphic, and brutal than its predecessor (and *that's* saying something.)

Take note, dear reader, the story is entirely fictional and does not in any way reflect my own personal or religious beliefs. Everything in this book has been wholly fabricated for your entertainment.

If you are offended easily, my advice would be to put the book down and dispose of it accordingly.

If you are still with me, then I hope you enjoy the ride, and please know what you thought by leaving a review!

I am so grateful and delighted that you chose to read my work!

Thank you!

Sian Rose

x

Prologue

Jaws. Thick rows of jagged glass, tearing and ripping mercilessly into abdominal flesh, sending agonising shockwaves surging through my skeleton. I open my mouth, but no sound emerges, too exhausted to do anything but catch my breath.

Blinded by the bright, burning light of a chandelier which dangles from the ceiling above me, my eyelids freeze into place, head paralysed stiff, so I cannot free myself of its scorching glare.

My limbs are substantial as if tied down by heavy anchors, and I've been plunged into dark, murky waters, gasping for air, struggling for safety.

I can't move.

I'm not strong enough.

Somewhere, above the surface, an echoey voice calls out to me. Hot, bitter tears stream down my cheeks, stinging my skin as I resist the overwhelming agony that tightens its vice around me.

"She's here!"

A tiny, barely noticeable release. A small sigh of relief. A momentary escape from my excruciating shackles.

It takes all of my strength, but I jerk my head, desperate to catch a glimpse of her.

But my vision is hazy, obscured by millions of tiny black dots floating in front of my eyes so that the room around me seems to spin, the colours and shapes all blurring into one terrifying mush.

More voices.

I strain to hear, but they're all just distant mumbles to me, just barely tickling my eardrums from somewhere far away.

Suddenly, a rough, sharp force grips me beneath my arms, like iron hooks. I am effortlessly hoisted upwards as if I am just a clumsy-limbed doll, made of paper or rags. The sharp tug in my armpits is instantly drowned out by the vicious pummelling in my stomach, and I finally let my heavy eyelids fall, giving in at last to the exhaustion.

If it wasn't for the sudden screech that shreds the hot, stagnant air, I'm sure I'd pass out, sitting upright in a repulsive pool of my own filth.

But something about that noise- the helpless cry of an infant, my infant, is like a siren from heaven, calling me, summoning some kind of inhuman strength from within my slowly dying body.

The moment that my eyelashes flutter open, my dreamy, blissful few seconds of motherhood are dashed.

Just like that.

In the blink of an eye.

In the slash of a knife.

In a gunshot.

In a snapped spine.

I want to close my eyes again, but it's as though fish hooks have been impaled into my eyelids, holding them open against their will, and the horrifying scene in front of me is slowly branded with a piping hot iron onto my pupils.

Blood.

I could smell it before, that familiar rusty scent. But now I can see it.

Dark red clots of crimson, saturating the bedding beneath me, drowning the lower half of my body, even spattered up the bedroom walls, spraying the headboard of the bed and dripping like raindrops from the ceiling.

A gasp of pure terror gets stuck in the back of my throat, congealing with hot, sickly bile, forming a tacky knot that makes it even harder to exhale.

My disturbed, wide-eyed gaze lingers on my mutilated middle section, where I am finally faced with the source of the ungodly agony that courses through every fibre and cell within my body.

I'm naked from the waist down, my blood-soaked nightdress crudely hiked up, barely concealing my breasts.

My bulging, pregnant stomach has been brutally ripped apart, apparently ravaged by a pack of hungry wolves. A grim, glistening tangle of scarlet innards are exposed to the stuffy air of my bedroom, and loose, dead flaps of skin spill helplessly out to the sides, beyond repair.

Involuntarily, a loud, animal-like groan escapes my lips, draining me of even more of my depleted supplies of energy.

I feel the life, along with the steady stream of blood, trickle out of me, and my consciousness shift in and out of focus as my soul begins to depart my corpse.

"Hey, look."

A familiar, striking face with glittering emerald eyes appears beside me, cradling an off-white bundle of blankets in her arms. Her face is blotchy with tears, features contorted with pure emotion.

As I savour my final breaths, I let my eyes slowly flit downwards.

"My baby…" I muster, though every word is like another dagger plunging through flesh and tearing through the muscle on my stomach.

The green-eyed face gives me a small smile and gently places the lump of fabric and flesh just above my gaping wound of a stomach. I grimace as I notice that she is wearing thick, elbow-length gloves of bloodstains, and grim splatters and dribbles are decorating the front of her nightdress.

"You've not got long left," she whispers softly.

Her words do not soothe me.

I blink back more tears and crane my neck to look down into the face that I cradle weakly in my arms.

Instantly, my grip falls apart, like loose threads in a tapestry, and a horrified croak is stolen from my cracked lips.

Beneath me, its monstrous face writhing, snorting, and grunting like a fully grown pig, the infant throws back its head, searching for milk.

In horror, I absorb the misshapen head, the hideously deformed features, and the alien-like flared slits where a nose should be. Its awful puckered mouth expands, revealing four sharp, pointed teeth already embedded into its blackened gums.

"Aw, she's hungry," the green-eyed face tells me, gushing, cocking her head fondly. "I'm going to name her Beau, for beautiful."

A breathless giggle of hysteria emerges from my throat at the irony. Then more tears slide down my face as the warped features of my daughter leers unpleasantly up into my slowly succumbing eyes.

Without warning, the horrendous creature latches on to my breast, plunging its freakish fangs into my skin and flesh, tearing right through the bloodied fabric of my nightdress until my chest is in shreds.

My final memories of life are a tiny demon gnawing greedily at my teat, feeding on my last unwanted breaths. Sharp stabs of pain force my body into shock. More blood splatters upwards into my face, coating my cheeks, stinging my eyes, invading my mouth and my nostrils.

My final thoughts are, funnily enough, of God.

Does he exist?
What about heaven?
Shit… does hell exist?

Jesus, I fucking hope not.

PART ONE

Faith

6 months ago

I wake up to a heavy, stinking, unfamiliar weight on my body.

I open my mouth to scream, but it is stifled by a thick wad of foul-tasting cloth being shoved into my mouth and the hot, stale stench of frantic breaths congealing on my cheeks.

"You better be quiet bitch," a voice rasps, flecks of spit showering my face. I get an awful flicker of recognition as the voice scratches my ears, and my stomach immediately drops. Tears begin to pool in my eyes as my vision adjusts to the darkness and focuses on the wide figure hovering above me. A small, frightened moan escapes me, and he smacks me roughly around the face. "Be fucking quiet, or I will kill you right now," he warns, hissing venom at me. "Come on, seriously? After all the shit you've pulled, you're really going to start crying on me now?"

Furiously, I shake my head, although I resent that statement.

All the shit I've pulled?

I did him a favour. I've been keeping him fed, haven't I? I'd finally given him a purpose, a chance for him to make people happy, rather than making everyone around him perpetually angry and depressed.

"Right. So, I am going to let you speak. I swear to fucking God if you call out or scream, I will murder you here. If I'm dying, you're coming with me. You understand?"

I nod, and he rips the material from my mouth. I cough, and he hits me again. My cheek burns loudly with the pain, my entire skull vibrating from the collision. "Shut up!"

"Sorry," I mumble, my voice barely even a buried whisper, but still broken.

I'm in total shock, but I remember to pray. A deep breath escapes my lips, and I allow my eyelids to close.

How the fuck did he get out?

He's been locked up all safe and sound in his cage in the stables outdoors. How could he have broken out?

…unless… no, it's unthinkable. Could one of my own have betrayed me? Conspired to let him out?

I know that I must keep calm.

It's all going to be okay.

"I want to get out of here. Now," he whispers sharply. "Now," he repeats, almost hysterical. "And you are going to come with me. Understand? No waking up any of your fucked up little mates, alright?"

"I understand," I reply, although I don't appreciate him referring to my family as 'fucked up little mates.'

He releases his vice-like grip on me, allowing me to sit up. The cool, jagged edge of a kitchen knife is pressed to the front of my throat. I gulp.

"Pull any funny shit, and you're dead," he warns me.

Awkwardly, he helps me to stand up, never freeing me from the threatening embrace of the knife. I tremble uncontrollably, despite my breathing exercises. He guides me out of the pitch blackness of my bedroom and back out into the corridor of the house. We're pressed tightly together, my back to his front. The stench of infection and rot radiate off of him and mercilessly attack my nostrils until I'm silently retching.

I hate myself for being so frightened.

Why should I be?

I'm God, for fuck's sake.

This will all blow over any moment now.

He forces me down the silent, brightly-lit staircase, down into the central part of the house. I can see that the sun is starting to come up.

"Car keys?" he growls.

Wordlessly I nod and lift a shaking hand to point towards an old oak bookcase where the spare set is concealed. He nudges me forwards, and I obediently go over and retrieve the keys from their hiding place.

Any moment now.

Any moment now, everything will be okay.

I force myself to smile, a technique I learned to do whenever I am feeling irrationally anxious. Because this is irrational. Why should I be worried? After all of the shit that has happened to me in my life, this scum is the very least of my concerns. I was raised by a drug-addicted lowlife of a mother and a father who never wanted me. I brought up my little brother, Sundance, practically single-handedly. I did badly in school, and the other kids were horrible to me.

Everything bad happened to me.

But it all turned out good. I built my family, my business. Now, I never worry because I know that I am different.

I will always be okay.

I am God.

"Come on," the bunny grunts, digging me sharply in the ribs and nodding towards the front door. It's ironic, really, that he should be exercising power over me. When I met him, he was nothing but an ignorant, pig-headed piece of shit. I transformed him. I made him better. I made him into something good. Blinking, I try to focus on my handiwork, the elegant rabbit ears tastefully woven into his scalp. The amount of joy he has brought to us all. Our little pet bunny. Now, it appears he has turned against us.

That's very sad.

I unlock the front door and pull it towards me, ignoring the loud creak it makes. The cool night air floods in from outside, and swarms around me, clinging tightly to my skin like an icy-cold cloak. Bunny digs me in the small of my back, forcing me to move forwards towards one of the vehicles parked out front.

"You're driving," he hisses roughly.

Nancy

"No… yes… yes, of course… well *no*… look, a couple of days tops."

I absent-mindedly kick stones in the towering blades of grass that surround them, watching little clouds of dust explode at the toe of my right trainer. Sighing, I listen to my mother continue her concerned rant down the phone. I don't bother to interject for a while. Sometimes it's better just to let her go… get it all off of her chest.

I wait for a promising pause in her speech.

"It's fine. I just need to know the truth Mum," I reply earnestly, rubbing my temples. I glance upwards at the sun that is setting slowly over the miles and miles of countryside that surround us and wistfully wish that the trip wasn't planned under more pleasant circumstances.

Mum goes quiet, then groans, defeated.

"How's Fred and Stella?" I ask, taking the opportunity to change the subject.

"They're fine. Both tucked up in bed, sleeping soundly."

I smile, imagining their peaceful little faces, their enviously long, fluffy eyelashes fluttering angelically over their snowy white cheeks.

"Thanks for taking care of them, Mum."

She scoffs, and I envision her rolling her eyes.

"I'm good to you, missy. Now, promise me a couple of days, and if you have no luck, you'll come home?"

"I promise. I love you, Mum. Night."

"Night, night, sweetheart. I'll call you tomorrow. Love you."

I hang up and slip my phone into the back pocket of my denim shorts, then take in a long, deep breath of fresh country air.

It's a far cry from our hometown, the grimy jungle of concrete, with its towering buildings and floods of grey-faced clones in suits.

In fact, this place- the quiet, British countryside- is precisely the kind of place I had always imagined living.

As a teenager, I fantasized about owning a cute country cottage with a thatched roof and ivy climbing all over the walls. Maybe we'd have a few chickens in the back garden, and we'd be within walking distance of a quaint little village where everyone knows each other's names. Plenty of hills, and trees, and fields for the children to explore, with little use for tablets or computer games.

"What are you daydreaming about?"

I turn, cruelly torn from my blissful delusion by a voice that comes from behind me.

"A simpler life," I reply honestly to the brown-eyed girl who stands a few feet away from me. She tosses long, shiny brunette hair over an olive-skinned shoulder and takes a few steps closer.

We're standing out the back of a desolate but gorgeous bed and breakfast. On the outside, it is a shabby, distressed barn, but on the inside, it is decorated beautifully, with fresh flowers in glass vases and old, endearing antiques lining every wall and surface.

"You and me both," sighs Violet, "but let's stay positive."

I nod, letting a comfortable silence fall upon us so that only the light sound of the wind making the grass dance can be heard.

The quiet is short-lived.

From the back of the building, out of a pair of whitewashed French doors, emerges the other three members of our party, also staying in the charming, rural hotel. Two of them are linking arms, giggling stupidly to one another, staggering on top of each other, clearly drunk on the complimentary house wine we were offered at dinner. Trailing behind them is a disgruntled comrade who has a face like death, clearly completely fucked off at having been left to babysit them.

"You okay, Addie?" I ask, letting a small smirk creep up onto my lips as the trio approaches us.

"Peachy," snaps Addison, the tall, skinny girl with the pinched features and the stern lines staining her forehead. "I think these two have forgotten the reason we're here," she stares after the drunken pair disdainfully as they begin to fumble with lighters and cigarettes.

Violet and I exchange amused glances.

"*Mate*," protests one of the drunk girls, a petite, brown-skinned teenager with intense eyes and a scarlet red headscarf covering her sleek, black hair. "I've been to hell and back recently. I think a few drinks is what we *all* need."

Addison rolls her eyes, folding her arms. "And I suppose a few drinks is going to make you extra alert for tomorrow, Priya?"

"Look, mind your business," interjects Magda, swaying slightly on her high heels. She lifts a lit cigarette to her mouth and hungrily inhales. "Just get off our backs, okay? We all deal with this differently."

Just over half a year ago, none of us knew each other. But, although we have nothing in common, we are all connected, bound tightly together by the thick, constrictive vines of the same dark and unexplained event.

"I set up the group so that we could find our respective family members," argues Addison snippily, "not so we could all go on a jolly-up to the countryside and get shit-faced."

This comment seems to smack the silly grin right off of Priya's face, and suddenly her expression crumples, no doubt as she thinks of her cousin. Addison is cut from a different cloth to the rest of us, slightly older, raised in the posh part of London, a Cambridge graduate, and now a high-profile scientist.

I'm not sure I've ever seen the woman smile or do or say anything that hasn't made her come across as a total ice queen. Needless to say, I find myself wanting to defend naïve little Priya, who is only eighteen-years-old and appears to be severely lacking in basic common sense.

"That's what we're doing, Addie," I cut in, "tomorrow, first thing, we're going to the retreat. We'll find them, okay?"

"And we'll do a better fucking job than the bloody police," mutters Violet, sling bitterly.

Just over half a year ago, a police investigation was opened into the mysterious circumstances surrounding the disappearance of my husband, Kevin. He was on one of his annual work retreats with four of his employees. Violet's sister Hollie, Priya's cousin, Abdul, Addison's brother, Bobby, and Magda's best friend, Prue.

Magda laughs at Violet's resentful comment, her high-pitched, inappropriately jubilant cackle echoing around the otherwise peaceful landscape like a siren.

"Can you imagine if it turns out that they really *did* all just fuck off and abandon us?" she jokes, flicking her cigarette onto the grass, then stubbing it out with her foot.

Much to our dismay, the case was closed sooner than we'd have hoped since all five of the missing colleagues sent text messages, explaining they'd moved away for a new business venture. Apparently, the local force had gone a thorough search of the area but ultimately found nothing suspicious or of interest.

No-one in the police seemed to want to push it further, and they probably wouldn't have, had I not dug my heels in and made them. So far, I've shelled out thousands on private investigators, religiously bombarded police detectives with phone calls three times a day. My mother, and most of my friends, can't understand why I'd go to all the effort. They can't fathom why I can't just accept that Kevin abandoned us.

Don't get me wrong, Kevin is *precisely* the type of husband who would walk out on his wife and children.

I don't question my husband's moral compass.

Not even one bit.

The bloke has had affair after affair, disappears for nights on end, then turns up reeking of booze, gurning his jaw off from a cocaine-bender, having emptied half of our savings account to gamble, and rent prostitutes.

But still, my husband is wealthy, and he provides a standard of living that I want for myself and the children.

So I'll put up with his bullshit, time and time again.

Swings and roundabouts, you know?

And besides, I *know* him.

Kevin might be a druggie, and a liar, and a cheat, and a feeble, cowardly man hiding behind a tall, muscular, business-savvy exterior, but he always comes back.

Like a boomerang.

A very fucking annoying boomerang, with an alcohol problem and a disturbing sex addiction.

He wouldn't just take off of his own accord.

That is the only thing I am sure of.

"That won't happen," I tell Magda firmly. "We know them better than anyone else, right?"

The other women nod.

Addison set up the group, initially as support. A place to chat. When detectives decided to give up, and all of the practically non-existent leads dried up, our group evolved from girls grieving missing persons into feisty women on a mission to find them.

"They didn't just abandon us," I continue, "something isn't right here. And we are going to find out what that is."

Kevin

6 months ago

As she drives through the countryside, I keep the harsh, jagged blade resting on her bare, slender thigh. I keep my eyes fixed tightly on her, studying her face for any minute signs of weakness.

She has stopped crying, and her skinny wrists no longer tremble at the wheel. Her big eyes stare straight ahead, the emerald green irises shimmering in the dashboard lights. It's fucking infuriating. The adrenaline that coursed so powerfully through my veins when I jumped on her sleeping frame is melting quickly away, leaving nothing but the agonising pain that sears in my scalp. That little bitch.

Fury bubbles and simmers beneath the surface of my skin, and I feel hot all over. I know I'm ill. My wounds are infected. I only hope it's not fatal.

More than anything, I want her to cry again. I want her to be shaking all over, screaming out for help, wincing with pain every time I prod the side of her flesh with the point of my weapon. I want to do to her what she did to me.

Every time I close my eyes, vibrant, colourful images flash before my eyes of that moment. That horrifying moment when I woke up in that grimy basement, my arms and legs strapped painfully into iron vices, keeping my entire body paralysed by my shackles. All around me, I could see rows and rows of rusty weapons, chainsaws, swords, daggers, knives, and fuck knows what else hanging from racks on the gloomy cellar walls.

I was so afraid; I pissed myself.

Then, she came.

My throat had finally closed up from all of my screaming, and suddenly I heard a door being released and then slow, teasing footsteps descending a black, metal staircase. She appeared, looking as fiendishly beautiful as she did before, batting her eyelashes, that intoxicating smile still dancing on her lips.

At first, I thought she was coming to help me.

When she saw the puddle of acidic urine beneath my chair, she threw back her head and cackled so loudly that the sound of it makes my blood curdle. "You're disgusting," she smirked, appearing to take some form of delight in my shame.

What followed was the stuff of nightmares, and trust me; this is no fucking exaggeration.

As much as I try to block out the memories, my bald scalp sizzles with the pain as the wound demands tirelessly to be acknowledged. I blink away hot, blistering tears and feel the various lacerations that streak my limbs burn.

"Why did you do it?" I ask suddenly before I have time to think. My voice comes out in a choked-up squeak, which makes me feel pathetic. I hate myself for it.

She flinches at the noise, clearly surprised to hear me speak. Her eyes stay clasped on the winding country road ahead, but her lips open.

"It's God's work," she says, in a voice that is so shamelessly self-assured, it makes me want to scream.

"What?" I gasp incredulously. A shallow laugh of disbelief escapes my lips. "Are you fucking serious?"

"God wasn't very happy with you," Faith says icily, tossing long black curls over her shoulder.

I study her side profile for a moment, my brain hurting as I try to even fathom what I am hearing. "And I suppose you think he's happy with you?" I demand. "Mutilating people for the fun of it?"

She shrugs and sighs. "I know it's difficult for you to understand. But just trust me when I say I was put on this earth to do an important job. I saved you."

Then, I laugh. I throw my head back and let out a huge roar of laughter that vibrates in my throat and causes my injuries to sting.

"Well, thank you so much. That's very generous of you. Now, please let me return the favour. Pull over if you please."

I watch her face drop and then contort with confusion. "Pardon?"

Fist trembling with rage, I scratch the top of her thigh with the knife, ripping open the flesh. She lets out a yelp of pain and swerves the car.

"I said pull over," I snarl, my eyebrows knitting together.

And there it is, a small, subtle grimace on her face. Fear. It radiates off of her like a strong cologne, and I inhale it hungrily like a smoker breathing in nicotine. Obediently she slows the car to a stop and parks up on the side of the deserted, dusty road. When she switches off the engine, the overhead light flashes on, filling the card with bright, yellow light.

I swing my body over so that I am straddling her skinny body on the driver's seat and swiftly collect up both her wrists in just one of my hands, clamping down on them so tightly that she winces beneath my touch.

"Do you remember what you did to me?" I whisper, pressing my forehead hard against hers, staring deep and menacingly into her frightened eyes.

She squeaks.

"Do you?" I thunder, screaming into her face.

"Yes, I do," she moans desperately.

I withdraw and yank her arms outright so that the long, frail sticks are stretched out in front of me. "First, you cut me. Do you remember that?"

She nods, closing her eyes, and pursing her lips. She knows what is coming.

"Open your eyes, or I'll cut your fucking eyelids off," I punch her hard in the stomach with my free hand. "I want you to remember every moment of this. I want it permanently branded into your brain, tattooed onto your skull so that every time you close my eyes, you see my face, and remember what a fucking piece of shit you are."

To my surprise, she obeys. She stares up at me stonily, grey-faced, and sober. I curse myself for still somehow finding her to be beautiful, even knowing what an ugly, monstrous soul lurks behind her delicate features.

I take the knife and carefully carve the first wound into the top of her arm. It's neat and premeditated, a perfect narrow slit, which obligingly starts to bleed scarlet. She takes it well, her face barely even moving an inch. I see it as a challenge.

"Tough girl, eh?"

I start to swipe harder, rougher through her flesh. The lacerations become deeper, more jagged, skinning the surface of her limb. I only mean to do a few cuts, like she did to me, but I get caught up in a mad, bloodthirsty frenzy. I can't stop my wrists, chopping and cutting, slicing, and skimming. She starts to cry then. Low, pained moans come from deep in her throat, but the more I cut, the louder they get, until she is producing high-pitched shrieks. I laugh when she does that because she laughed at me when I was making those noises. Blood is spurting everywhere, it drenches her body, and is splattering all over my face, and it gets into my mouth and lingers in my nostrils so that my senses are totally overwhelmed with it. Blood. But not just any blood.

An enemy's blood. The taste and stench of revenge. It's better than booze, or cocaine, or sex, or money.

I want to bathe in it, I want to feel it all over me, I want to cut her open and shower myself in her pain and suffering.

Finally, I stop because my arms are hurting.

My breaths are hard and ragged, and I return to my seat, my lungs struggling to keep up. I'm on such a high, I buzz. I look over to Faith, just sitting there, upright in her own bloody mess. I chuckle satisfied.

"Now, what do you think God would make of that, eh?"

Faith turns her head and narrows her eyes at me, her dark pupils shooting daggers that somehow penetrate my skin like bullets. I shudder. Her entire body is covered in blood, her arms saturated with thick, dark red paint. The seat is ruined.

I sit back and catch my breath, my entire body heaving. A sudden wave of unwelcome exhaustion comes over me.

I can't stop now.

Abdul

When Rowan wakes me up, it is pitch black outside. It's unnerving to me because the outside world has become a foreign concept, and I have lost all sense of day and night. I do my work, and then I sleep and wait to be awoken again, preferring to spend my days ignoring my existence.

As usual, a sharp boot between the shoulder blades jerks me into consciousness, and I instinctively sit bolt-upright on top of the filthy, stagnant bed sheets. My eyes snap open, and I fix my pupils on Rowan, a tall man who always appears to have a large gun superglued into the crook of his muscular arm.

"Come on," he grunts at me, turning his back and leading me towards the narrow exit to my grim abode.

Obediently, I get up, blinking sleep from my eye, trying not to focus on the graphic, blood-splattered images that decorate the walls. I've gotten better at ignoring the pictures and avoiding the wide, frightened eyes of the beautiful, helpless woman within them.

Prue.

Every time I think of her, a hard knot of grief forms in my throat. There's no way for me to tell how much time has passed, but the pain is still as raw and fresh as if it were just yesterday that they tore her away from me.

Swallowing, I trail after Rowan, out of my box bedroom and back through the thick, sickening atmosphere that lingers in the slaughterhouse. No matter how much time I spend here, I never get used to the stench of thick, rusty clots of blood and still find it sitting unpleasantly at the back of my tongue, forming a vile, ruthless taste.

Wordlessly, Rowan guides me in and out of the metal tables and the blood-spattered wooden posts, apparently oblivious to the gruesomeness of it all.

I follow him out of the warehouse and into the gloomy courtyard of the farm outside, relishing the wave of cold, fresh air that washes over me. As if I have been starved of oxygen, I inhale deeply, filling my lungs. It feels good to breathe without ingesting the vile stench of pain and suffering.

Fortunately, because it's dark, I can walk past the sea of cramped cages without having to meet the eye of any of their prisoners. But I still feel them there. I still sense their shivering, naked presence, trembling with fear, weeping with hopelessness, praying to a God that they maybe never believed in before. I'm grateful to leave them behind as I traipse around the side of the house and obligingly clamber into the back of an open van, which is parked on the gravel out the front.

With no kind of explanation, Rowan slams the double metal doors shut behind me, and I sit in the darkness, hugging my knees to my chest. Soon, I hear the harsh slam of the driver's door, then the sound of the engine being switched on and rumbling to life.

Maybe, some time ago, I'd have been paralysed with fear, just sitting there in the black shadows of the van, unknowing what the fuck lay ahead. I'd have been terrified, wondering what the hell my sick, demented captors had in store for me next.

Now, I feel strangely at peace.

Now, I'm not so worried about being killed.

After all, the most important lesson that I have learned here is that there are far far worse things than death in this world.

I know, because I have seen them.

We aren't driving for long when the vehicle swerves, presumably into a driveway or car park of some description, and then comes to an abrupt halt. Rowan kills the engine so that once again, I plummet into a deathly silence.

Instinctively, my limbs seize up.

I am tense, from the cold gnawing viciously at my fingertips, as well as the unsettling anxiety that sits uncomfortably at the base of my spine. It seems like a long eternity before the doors to the back of the van are ripped open, exposing me again to the fresh, dark sea of the inky blue night outside. I shiver as the cold chill floods the compacted space, and before I can properly catch my breath, Rowan's rough, beefy forearm is lunging forwards, fishing me out from its grim depths.

Once my feet are back on the ground in their oversized, clammy work boots, I strain my eyes and glance around at our surroundings. It's difficult to see in the gloom, but I notice the large, faint edge of a wide dark-bricked building towering over us to the left. Although it is impossible to know for sure, I sense that similarly to the farm, our location is remote, likely bordered either by dense forest or abandoned fields for miles and miles around. Shivering, I pull my smelly coat tighter around me.

"Come on," Rowan grunts, slamming the van doors shut, the heavy clang of the metal erupting into the chilling evening air. He hooks his arm through mine and pulls me roughly along towards the building, so forcefully that the ball in my arm socket aches.

"What is this place?" I ask, bracing myself for a smack around the back of the head.

Nowadays, Rowan is the boss man at the farm and is, therefore, the one I have the most contact with.

Sometimes, he's okay. Sometimes, he tells me about when a new intake is coming and about the changes Faith is making to the business. One time, he sat and explained the sorting process to me: who, out of the new recruits, gets to be a worker, who gets to be a test subject, and who gets to be mincemeat. A few times, we've even had private, passing jokes. For example, when a hysterical new recruit jumped me in the slaughterhouse and almost strangled me to death. Rowan sliced one of his arms off before shooting the man in the head. After my initial shock had faded, I'd let out a manic cackle of laughter. You see, aside from being spattered in blood, I realised I was still holding onto the bloke's severed hand.

I'd held the surprisingly heavy chunk of flesh out to Rowan.

"Need a hand?" I'd asked, just before we both fell about in hugely fucked-up bouts of laughter. That night I'd cried myself to sleep because, for the first time, I had thought to myself, *well shit, I'm turning into one of them.*

But still, the point is that Rowan isn't made of stone... not all the time anyway.

With that said, sometimes he is one nasty fucker. Depends on his mood.

One moment he'll sneak you a cube of chocolate, the next, he'll boot you in the face simply because you didn't get up from scrubbing blood off the floor quick enough.

So asking Rowan a simple question about the menacing brick fortress in front of us is quite a gamble on my part.

"You'll see," he responds gruffly, taking me up to a small, inconspicuous brown door. Upon closer inspection, I see that it's not that all of the lights are out, but that all of the windows are boarded up, glass panes replaced with heavy planks of wood.

He releases me briefly to raise a hand and rap his knuckles against the panels of the door, each knock somehow making my skeleton flinch. I try to swallow back the dread that rises in the pit of my stomach and try to exhale the unease that grips my lungs.

Whatever it is cannot possibly be any worse than the farm.

My only comfort these days is knowing that things truly cannot get any worse. I've been confined to a tiny cage, squashed up against hundreds of sweating, filthy bodies, like an animal. I've watched men be shot dead right in front of me. I've been forced to slice and chop up rotting corpses.

I watched a friend and the woman that I loved be killed, right in front of me. For fuck's sake, I live in a tiny box room, where the walls are plastered with photos of her mutilated body.

Nothing can be worse.

The door opens, and a gust of warm, stuffy heat rushes out, along with a strange smell, sort of like burning plastic. A dim light illuminates the doorway, and I see one of the other men, also armed, standing there, stern-faced as always. He steps back, allowing Rowan and me to pass, then I shudder as I hear the door thud shut behind us.

Nothing can be worse.

It's like entering one of those extreme haunted houses, where you walk up a long, narrow hallway that instils claustrophobia in even the bravest of thrill-seekers. Even though you can see the badly disguised fire escape signs, fear prickles up and down your spine. You know that at any moment now, an actor in a cheap, shitty costume will jump out at you. You know that, somewhere in the shadows, something is lurking, ready to catch you out. No matter how much I pretend to be brave and how much I tell myself that *nothing can be worse,* my body is tight and rigid with unadulterated terror.

Rowan presses on down the corridor, and I traipse behind him. Thick and smoky, the humid atmosphere is like a plastic bag smothering my airways, clinging tightly to the air. As we progress, the passage seems to grow skinnier and skinnier, darker and darker, right up until we reach the end, where a medieval bookcase conceals the end wall, from ceiling to floor.

"Turn around," Rowan orders.

I do as I am told.

I stare back down the passage, now unable to see the front door which we entered through or the man who let us in. Anxiously, I chew my bottom lip and eye the random assortment of doors that are staggers either sides of the corridor. For a moment, I wonder what lingers beneath them. And then I realise that I don't even want to know.

A loud *DING!* noise startles me, and I'm twisted around by Rowan's hand on my shoulder. To my surprise, when I turn back, the bookcase has opened out, like a secret door in a murder house, and what appears to be a tiny room made of metal is exposed just beyond the opening.

Rowan pulls me in, and as a pair of metal doors clang shut behind us, I realise that we are in a lift. I stand anxiously in the corner, watching Rowan's stocky fingers tap something in on a tiny keypad. A rickety jolt nearly knocks me off my feet and is then followed by a loud, painful screech as the lift begins to move on presumably ancient mechanisms.

"It's alright, Pig," Rowan chuckles, seeing the terrified expression on my face, "it's all safe. Don't you worry about that."

Maybe if I wasn't almost shitting myself, I might laugh at the irony of his assurance.

A few seconds later, the lift grinds to a halt, and another rickety jolt of the minuscule metal square alerts us to its arrival. Rowan taps something else into the keypad, and the doors re-open. This time, he doesn't grab my arm but instead gestures for me to step out, nodding towards a brightly lit room beyond the iron doors.

"On your own from here, Pig," he tells me with a nasty smile.

Nodding, I take a deep breath and force my heavy feet to drag their way out of the lift. The fact that Rowan won't be joining me makes me feel extremely uneasy. Well, more so than usual.

I envision a terrifying monster lurking down here, ready to rip me apart and promptly devour me.

Oh well.

At least it'd be a quick death.

Not exactly painless, but over in a jiffy.

As soon as I set foot out of the lift, the doors close behind me, and I truly am alone.

I glance around the well-lit space and am briefly teleported back to a period of time that feels like forever ago. Back when I was taking A-Levels, and I had a friend who was studying music technology. Some days I'd go with him to the recording studio in the college. There was always a carpeted room with a huge panel of complicated dials, buttons, and switches, positioned in front of a long glass window through which there was a room with instruments and microphones.

The room I find myself in reminds me of the music studio, but without the complex control panel. Just a set of plush leather sofas facing the huge pane of glass in an otherwise empty room.

Curiously, I move forwards, looking around for any sign of life.

It smells new, like a fresh building down here. It's a welcome change of odour from the usual concoction of blood and rot that I have grown so accustomed to.

Stupidly, I let myself relax.

I wander over to the leather couches and marvel wistfully at the generously padded fabric cushions that are splayed over them. Six months without a decent pillow, sure makes you appreciate the little things. I smirk at myself, and at how totally absurd it is of me to be thinking about fucking sofa cushions, given that I am the prisoner of a deranged cult of murderers.

That's when a prickle on the back of my neck forces me to look up, and I finally clock what lies beyond the huge pane of glass.

I freeze, the soles of my feet rooting themselves to the ground beneath me. My knees wobble dangerously, but my brain is screaming so loudly that I hardly notice.

My instinct is to run, but I am stuck.

I feel my eyes bulge out of my skull.

It is then that a harrowing realisation dawns on me.

No... it doesn't dawn on me... it smacks me hard across the face, with the force of a metal-studded wrecking ball.

Something can be worse.

Something can *always* be worse.

6 months ago

Faith

My wounds are not as bad as they appear. In fact, the discomfort of my blood-soaked pyjamas and the saturated fabric of the seat beneath me bothers me more than the sting of the cuts that now streak my arms like crimson tiger stripes. I wince and reluctantly start up the car engine again at Bunny's orders. It feels as though I've expelled an entire decade's worth of periods all at once.

I don't speak as the car rolls forwards, and we set off again into the foggy, early morning. I'm tired from the rude awakening and need to keep my wits about me. Still, I have full faith that it'll all be okay. Sure, it doesn't exactly look promising right now, me sitting here drenched in my own blood, sat next to a being who clearly despises me. But then I think of all the other hopeless situations I have ever been in before. When Prue ran out on us and released all of the livestock at the farm.

That was the scariest time of my life.

I thought that everything good was going to come crashing down on top of me, but low and behold, it all came right. It always does.

I am God.

Then, of course, there were the times where my abusive, drug-addicted mother forced me to spend freezing cold nights at a time out in the animal enclosures of our farmyard. There was one occasion when I was just a little girl, and I was trying to sleep in the pigsty, and one of the pigs almost crushed me. At first, I was just trying to cuddle up to it, but the poor thing passed away, and my frail little arms couldn't move it off me.

I thought I was going to die that night.

Most children would have died.

But not me.

Then, my father came to see me, drove up to our farm in his big, posh car, and found me out there, barely breathing, covered in mud and shit, freezing out in the enclosure. I begged him to take me with him that time.

But he didn't.

That broke my heart.

Although, that's not the worst memory I remember from my childhood.

The worst one, the one that chills me to the core without fail, absurdly, is one that I can't properly remember. It is more broken fragments of memory; sharp, jagged pieces of a mutilated image; a chaotic swirl of the senses made up of my mother's loud, pitiful cries; the harrowing sound of crunching bones; dark, glistening red splatters; and the stench of rust and rot. With it always comes a feeling like a sharpened dagger impaling my ribcage, being thrust roughly into my heart, and being twisted tighter and tighter, until I'm doubled over on a cold, clammy floor, sobbing so hard that I cannot breathe or see.

I never tell people these things, except my best friend and my brother, Sundance. See, you don't get shit from sympathy. Fuck, Daddy taught me that more than anyone. He felt so, so sorry for me, and yet he let it continue.

The point is this: no matter what life has thrown at me, I've always gotten through it, and look at me now. I made the perfect family, I made a successful business, and I'm the leader of a movement which is making our planet, and our world, and our people, better and better every single day.

My lips involuntarily stretch out into a smile as I remember this, and I think of all of my beautiful family back home.

No doubt they'll already be out searching for me.

"What are you smiling about?" grumbles Bunny. His voice is harsh and rips through the quiet atmosphere that hangs between us. I resist the urge to gloat because I can't afford any more slashings. Next time he might hit a nerve or an artery.

"You just surprised me," I tell him honestly.

He did surprise me. Of course, I'm not exactly pleased about it. The cold air from outside is now seeping in through the windows, and I'm shivering uncontrollably from being soaked through.

"Sorry?" he asks.

He has a thick, common accent. I like it because it reminds me of Prue.

Oh, Prue. I did really like her.

If only things could have been different.

"I was wrong about you," I reply. "I thought you were a pussy."

Silence. Then, after a few moments, he laughs.

I laugh too, fuck knows why.

"My God," he shakes his head in disbelief, "you really are one crazy bitch, aren't you?"

My face falls into a frown. "I'm not crazy. The world is crazy."

Bunny goes quiet again. I hold my breath, unsure whether to expect another brutal altercation.

"You really believe you're doing God's work, don't you?" he asks me, bemused.

I clear my throat then and turn the wheel to go around a bend in the road, "no," I admit, "I have recently discovered that I am God."

He breaks out into loud, hysterical laughter, which seems to go on for an eternity. My face crumples with annoyance, and without thinking, I pull over into a layby and park up. Indignantly, I turn to face him, ignoring the sharp sensation that aches in my fresh, bloodied wounds.

"What's so funny?" I snap, glaring at him.

I'm not accustomed to being laughed at or made a fool of. Fuck, I think I'd rather die here and let the fucker go to prison for murder than have him take the piss out of me.

Bunny looks unwell. Majorly so. His skin is clammy and grey, and his eyes are disorientated and out of focus. It's a shame because otherwise, he might be attractive.

"Nothing," chuckles Bunny, holding his big, bloodied hands up. "Shit, you've got a lot of nerve, haven't you?"

Defiantly I fold my arms, groaning as the slices across my flesh stretch and sting. "Laugh all you want. Look at my life, then look at yours. Are you making the world a better place?" I ask.

He lifts his eyebrows, and I realise that I need to speak a language he understands.

"Do you own a multi-million-pound business? Do you live in a mansion and own several other properties across the country, outright?"

It does the trick. His face falls.

"I'm guessing not," I continue, "so maybe you shouldn't scoff and turn your nose up at our way of life."

Bunny opens his mouth, then closes it again. He gawps like a gormless fish. Inspiration strikes. This... man. I smelled him from a mile off, back on that first night we met.

The typical CEO of a small business.

Moderately rich, arrogant, cocky, thinks he's God's gift to women, ignorant, greedy, materialistic. No moral compass of any kind, but willing to overlook any personal ideologies in the name of making money.

I've slaughtered many in my time. I know how to play them.

"I have a proposition," I announce.
Strike whilst the iron is hot and all that.

Addison

"Here, Addie, this is the place." I glance to my left and follow Nancy's gesture out of the passenger window, towards a big wooden sign that has 'Luxury Work Retreats' engraved crudely into its surface. Swallowing, I indicate and change gear, turning neatly onto a dirt road lined with trees.

"So much for luxury," scoffs Magda from the backseat.

I bite my tongue.

As predicted, Magda and Priya aren't feeling too chipper this morning. Well, I hate to say I told them so.

"I am surprised," admits Nancy, squinting down at the map that blares from her phone screen. She pushes a curtain of fair, wavy hair back behind her ear, "normally Kevin splurges. I'd have thought he'd invest in something a bit more lavish."

Priya groans, "God, I hope they have a decent bathroom."

I don't realise I am scowling until I check the rearview mirror.

The main base for 'Luxury Work Retreats' is just as simple and humble as it's entrance sign. In fact, it doesn't look much like a base at all. As the car creeps further into the thick mass of trees, I peer through the branches and can just about see modest wood cabins peeking through the gaps. Well, they could probably pass as oversized sheds, to be honest.

"It doesn't look very safe, does it?" Violet asks, nibbling anxiously on her thumbnail. "Anyone could just waltz in and go up to one of the doors…"

No-one says anything then because her words leave an unpleasant image in each of our minds.

Eventually, the car approaches a large, circular clearing, in the midst of which is a rectangular cabin which has a slanted roof and a wooden porch that reminds me of old western movies. Beside the building is another poorly carved wooden sign that reads *Reception*.

I park up, and we all exit the car, Priya dashing the fastest as she sprints towards the nearest tree, then promptly bends over and begins vomiting all over the roots.

Repulsed, I wrinkle my nose.

Fucking teenagers.

As if on cue, a rickety door swings open out onto the porch, creaking loudly, and sending rusty bells jangling. All of our heads, excluding Priya's, snap towards the sudden noise in the otherwise peaceful glade, just in time to see the lanky figure of a man exiting the doorway. As he steps out from under the porch, he reveals himself to be skinny and tall, with a receding hairline and thin-rimmed glasses that perch on a pointed nose.

"Hi, there!" he waves jauntily, beaming from ear to ear as he comes forward to greet us. "I'm Baz. Welcome to Luxury Work Retreats."

The other girls murmur their greetings, then all turn to look at me, their pupils watching me expectantly. I'm the leader of the group. The sensible, proactive one. Clearing my throat, I return his pleasant smile and move towards him to shake his hand.

"Hi Baz, my name is Addison. These are my..." a brief, uncomfortable pause, "... friends."

Baz's eyes shine delightedly as if I have just told him an incredibly funny joke. "That's fab! Now guys, do you have a book with us for yourselves today?"

"Uh... no, actually, we're not looking to book a retreat," I explain, tripping awkwardly on my words. "We were actually wondering if we could just ask you some questions... you see, a group of colleagues came here last July..."

Instantly, I watch Baz's face darken. His eyebrows knit together. "In the terms and conditions on our website, it *clearly* states that we cannot be liable for the badgers or the damage that they may cause," he informs me coldly.

My face creases into a frown, and I turn to exchange confused glances with the other girls.

"No... sorry, it's nothing to do with badgers. A group came here last July and well, they went missing. I know that the police have already spoken to you..."

Now it's Baz's turn to look confused. He scratches his chin. "We've not had any police come around here since a few years back, back when a horse got run over down the road…" he shakes his head and tuts sadly to himself, "… nasty business that."

"No, that can't be right…" Nancy steps forwards, shaking her head in disbelief. "The police specifically said that they were dispatching the local force to come and talk to you about it and look at your CCTV systems… I even hired a private investigator to do the same."

Baz shrugs, "nope. No police have come down here. Heck, I don't even have CCTV. Maybe you've got the wrong place?" he suggests.

"Are there any other work retreat places around here?" Violet asks doubtfully.

"No, sir," chimes Baz, puffing out his skinny chest proudly, "only ones around."

The hopeless fug that surrounds us must be noticeable because Baz's smile quickly falls. "Tell you what, do you want to come in, and I can check the reservations on the system? See if your work colleagues checked in here?"

Ten minutes later, and we are all squashed onto uncomfortable sofas in the small reception area of the cabin, Priya clutching a glass of water tightly in her petite hands. Baz perches on a high stool and adjusts his glasses as he studies the screen of an outdated looking computer.

"Ah yes… under the name Kevin, due to arrive 15th of July 2018…"

"So they were here?" Nancy asks, hopefully.

"Hmm…" Baz purses his lips tightly together and rubs his head. "Apparently, they never checked in."

"Why bother booking it if they weren't planning on coming?" Magda asks.

"Can't think why they wouldn't want to," Baz comments huffily, clearly offended.

I shake my head and sigh, frankly far too stressed to be dealing with anyone who calls themselves 'Baz.' "The group sent us messages saying that they were moving away," I explain impatiently to him. "But something feels off. She's saying that if their plan all along was to run away somewhere, why bother booking a cabin here?"

The thick, dark cloud that has circled my head for the last six months only seems to intensify until my brain is aching, and my thoughts are impossibly fuzzy.

Violet stands up and goes through the images of the missing people, on the off chance that Baz recognises them.

"Nope, sorry. Never met any of them in my life," he says with an annoyingly indifferent shrug.

"Does anyone else work here, who might have seen them?" Priya asks, her voice quieter and raspier than usual from projectile vomiting over the tree.

Baz shakes his head. "Just me, myself, and I!" he explains cheerily, though his smile is soon wiped clean as he clocks our disappointed faces. "Look, girls," he says gently, "have you ever thought that maybe your friends did just up sticks and leave? Maybe you're overcomplicating this..."

Anger surges through me, and I feel my cheeks burn red. I resist the urge to stand up and punch Baz in the nose, instead tightening my fists by my sides.

I am so fucking sick of being told that I am overcomplicating this.

We all are, and that's the only reason I can bear to put up with the likes of Magda and Priya.

They're amongst the only four in the world who get it besides me, that there is something clearly not right. The investigation should never have been closed, and by the sound of it, it was never properly carried out in the first place.

"My brother is a skinny, materialistic gay, who likes to wear Louboutins at the weekends," I say through gritted teeth. "He had only just managed to save up enough for a pair of his own. There is no way on this earth he'd have left home, leaving them behind."

Stunned silence follows my passive-aggressive outburst, and in that moment, I realise how ridiculous I sound.

Furiously, I blink back bitter tears and get to my feet, pushing through the door and storming across the wooden porch.

Coughing back sad sobs, I hastily wipe my face and stride back over to the car.

I can't let them see me cry.

If other people know that I'm sad or weak, it becomes true.

And I can't be sad or weak.

Not until I find Bobby.

I fumble with the car keys and let myself in, breathing deeply as I attempt to compose myself.

If... *when*... I find Bobby; I'll have all the time in the world to cry and be as sad and weak as I want.

But until then, I need to be strong.

I need to be my brother's hero.

For the first time in my sorry life.

6 months ago

Kevin

I must be delirious.

This realisation sinks in as I slowly get out of one of my captor's cars, the one I had hijacked just a few hours prior. I feel the heavy weight of at least a dozen sets of suspicious eyes resting on me, their pupils boring hard into my skin, like bullets embedding themselves into my flesh.

How the crazy bitch managed to persuade me it was a good idea to come back to this godforsaken place, I have no clue.

I must be turning just as mad as them. Or she's just a real master of manipulation. Even drenched in blood, and even after she tortured me to within an inch of my life, she's like the Pied Piper, able to switch on the seduction at any given moment, lulling me into trusting her.

And I guess I was just trying to look at it from a financial angle.

Why shouldn't I reap some benefit from this otherwise dire situation?

Besides, the girl is stained totally red. Her arms are basically skinned, and she is probably smaller than half the size of me, even after days of being starved. When she gave me her proposition, all I could think as I absorbed her words was that no court in the world would believe she was the attacker, and I was the victim.

So I took a chance.

After all, that's what being a business man is all about. Taking risks. Doing the unthinkable. Going to places where others are afraid to. Taking a few lines of coke to take the edge off. Then enjoying an almighty payout at the end of the day.

But as I lower myself from the car and stumble foolishly across the gravel, Faith's shredded arm weaved through mine; it occurs to me how truly fucking stupid I have been.

At any moment now, she could say the word, and they'll all turn on me.

I'd be back in that stable, or worse, I'd be dead.

"House meeting- kitchen- now!" Faith repeats, her voice sharpening as she brings us to a firm halt and gestures for her cronies to go back inside the house. They all obey her without question or so much as a muttered word.

My mouth falls open. I'm speechless as I watch them follow her orders as if they are nothing but light, wooden puppets dangling from thin wires entwined on her fingers. Even without saying anything, Faith appears to sense my disbelief.

"They are my disciples," she whispers.

I smirk, and she glares up at me. It's comical, really, how such a petite woman, no taller than five feet, holds so much power.

Once everyone is in, she guides me towards the front door, wincing as the bitter morning air chills her raw, meaty wounds. Whilst we go, my brain burns with questions. All of the panic that gnawed at my stomach just a few moments ago has dissolved into pure, unadulterated bewilderment.

How did this one woman round up so many men and women and somehow convince them to carry out her evil, deranged deeds? How did she come to own such a fuck-off massive house? How has she not been caught? Why isn't she rotting away in some high-security prison cell somewhere, or better still, festering in the darkest recesses of an insane asylum?

I fully expect to be brutally murdered the moment the heavy front door closes behind us. I envision an iron shower of arrows pummelling me, or a congregation of axes and knives flying through the air, straight for my head. I can't stop thinking about that dingy cellar she held me in and how the four walls were covered from top to bottom with an array of grisly weapons.

However, as she leads me over the threshold into the deadly mansion, I can see that Faith's strange colony are all still trailing like braindead zombies in through a wide-open door which leads into a kitchen.

How completely and utterly bizarre for this murderous tribe of lunatics to reside in such a neat and tidy home. When I made my escape from the stables, I had prepared myself for the interior of the building to resemble one giant dungeon of death and torture, and instead, I found that it looked more like something from an IKEA showroom.

One of Faith's followers, a woman I recognise from the night she poached me at the pub, holds open the door, her face saturated with confusion as her eyes absorb me.

Clearly, victims don't often escape from their shackles alive.

Nancy

Back in the car, we drive along in silence for some time, all of us feeling horribly empty and deflated.

So the police haven't even been taking us seriously. They haven't found any CCTV from Luxury Work Retreats or even done any interviews.

My skin prickles with rage every time I think about it.

"So, what now?" Magda asks, finally breaking the tense quiet that engulfs the car. "We came all this way. There must be something else that we can do."

"Like what?" grumbles Addie, scowling like a petulant toddler. I notice that her eyes are a little pinker and puffier than usual.

Priya shuffles with something in her handbag, then withdraws a stack of colourful, glossy papers. Addie tuts loudly, glaring at the girl disapprovingly in the mirror.

"Oh yes, *Heat* magazine will definitely be a useful resource in this situation," she says sarcastically.

"For your information," Priya interrupts indignantly, "these are tourist magazines. I picked them up from the hotel. They have places of interest in them. We can find places nearest to the retreat, and go have a look round, ask some of the locals."

Violet licks her lower lip thoughtfully, "that's actually not a bad idea. It's just a shame the car they rented couldn't be tracked; then we'd know for sure where they stopped."

This was another suspicious factor in the case that sounded alarm bells in my head. Why would the group rent a minibus and then dismantle the tracking device if they planned to run away? Surely they wouldn't risk having to pay the costs? Kevin's casino company ended up shelling out thousands to the car rental place.

Besides, would any of them even know how to dismantle a car tracker? It seems doubtful. We're talking about a group of office workers, not a ring of criminal masterminds.

"Are there any bars or pubs there, Priya?" I ask.

"Tonnes," she replies, her pretty brown eyes scanning one of the pages. "Although, if I know my cousin, I doubt he'd have gone to a bar.." she pauses then, and a flicker of memory passes her face. At first, she smirks to herself, and then she lets out a small, sad sigh. "Out of all the cousins, he's the sensible one. Whenever we would go out together, we'd all joke and call him dad... he'd rather go to a bloody museum than a nightclub."

Magda smiles sympathetically and gently rests her hand on top of Priya's.

"My Kevin is pretty much the opposite," I tell them grimly, "I think he spent more of his time drunk than he did sober..." a pang of guilt hits me in the chest then. I feel bad for talking badly about my husband, but it's nothing but the truth. I choose to ignore the feeling, shoving it into the back of my head. "And I also know that he was the kind of boss who didn't exactly take a democratical approach... if he wanted to go for a drink, that's where they would've gone."

The others mutter their agreements in low voices.

I wince.

I don't know what's worse, the fact that my husband's faults are so glaringly obvious to me or the fact that his colleagues clearly all thought the same.

Chewing my lip, I turn back in my seat, suddenly not wanting to be around the rest of the girls anymore. I picture myself at home, cuddled up in bed with my babies. Maybe Mum was right, and I should've just left things. Why would I go to all this trouble for a bloke who would never do the same for me?

"There's a pub nearby called The Cock Inn," Priya finally says, cutting through the cold, miserable silence. "According to my phone, it should take five minutes to drive there. Then there are quite a few others in the town centre, but that's more like twenty-five minutes away."

"Really?" Violet sounds surprised, "God, we really must be out in the sticks."

Magda laughs, slapping her palm to her forehead. "Fucking hell Vi, you make out like we're hiking up the bloody highlands or something, just because we're twenty minutes away from a pub!"

Violet and Priya laugh as well then, and I even see a brief glimpse of a chuckle dance at the corners of Addie's mouth. I let myself smile.

"So, The Cock Inn here we come," I announce, unable to even try to force any sort of optimism into my voice.

Sundance

The pub, as usual, is dead.

Dawn and I sit behind the ring-stained bar. Her with a baby attached to her in a sling, me gripping on to a grimy rag that I occasionally swish over the surface in a half-arsed attempt to look busy.

A few of the regulars are dotted up and down, old and decrepit as ever, staring listlessly down into the same pint they've been nursing for the last hour. Even just looking at them makes my stomach turn. How the fuck anyone can drink beer at this time in the morning is anyone's guess.

Daddy whimpers in his sling. I glance over at his tiny wrinkled face, squashed up against Dawn's chest like a particularly irritated, miniature old man.

Yes, you heard, right.

Faith, my older sister, named the kid Daddy.

After our Daddy.

That Faith held hostage for years.

And tortured.

And eventually killed and buried in our back garden.

Maybe there *is* a reason to drink beer in the morning, especially if you come from a family like mine.

Clearly, Dawn didn't want her precious little boy to be named Daddy, but Faith makes all of the rules.

Period.

No questions asked, and absolutely no form of deliberation.

"I'm going to go and feed him," Dawn says, speaking in a whisper as if anything louder in this bar would be wildly inappropriate.

"Oh, Dawn, no. You can't leave me now. We're positively heaving with custom," I reply drily.

Dawn smirks and rolls her eyes, getting up off of her barstool. "I'll be back."

She waddles slightly under the weight of the bundle strapped to her torso and disappears into the backroom, understandably reluctant to whip her tit out in front of the strange, smelly old men in front of us.

Maybe if this were an ordinary pub, seeing how empty the place is might be disheartening.

But it's not fit for ordinary purposes. My sister didn't buy the place to make money, or to sell fine ales, or to provide any kind of service to the public. At least not the kind of service that they would actually appreciate. Needless to say, our business isn't suffering on account of the bar's emptiness. In fact, strangely enough, I think it's better this way.

So it is startling to suddenly hear the doors to the entrance swing open. After all, it isn't a noise that we hear too often.

All heads, the ancient punters' included, snap to the creaky double doors located somewhere to my right, eyes straining to see the opening, which is concealed by the shadows and gloom of the dismal place. Instinctively, my nose twitches and a twinge of dread stirs in the pit of my stomach.

I swallow, my throat uncomfortably dry. Maybe this reaction to something so normal and casual sounds irrational, but whenever there are new visitors to the pub, my body always behaves the same way. In an instant, I go from being bored but comfortable to feeling as though I am teetering madly on top of a dangerously high cliff top.

It's probably Faith, I reason.

I picture my sister strolling into the bar any moment now, her usual smug smile dancing on her lips, emerald green eyes twinkling charmingly as she lunges into yet another update of her newest business venture.

It's been going really well, and boy, don't we fucking know about it. These days, it's all she ever wants to talk about, besides Beau and Kevin… how things change. More often than not, I find myself escaping from the house to this tedious, dull place, just to get away from it all.

But, as a group of five unfamiliar women emerge from the dark, dustiness of the pub, immediately I find myself wishing that I had just stayed at home and that today, The Cock Inn had remained shut.

My heart plummets into my chest, and I absent-mindedly lose my grip on the dirty cloth in my hand, which floats weightlessly to the stained carpet. I glance all around.

Right. Stay calm. Just stay fucking calm.

Clearing my throat, I offer a weak smile to the newcomers who are approaching the bar with an air of uncertainty, clearly unimpressed with the grimy interior of the pub.

Swallowing, I awkwardly raise my now empty hand and do a weird half-wave. "Hi," I muster.

Inside my head, sirens are wailing, red and blue lights flashing chaotically as I rifle through my mind, frantically searching it for a scapegoat… an excuse… just anything that will get them out of this place as quickly as possible.

A tall, lanky woman with a face that looks as though it is perpetually pissed off strides ahead of the others. She eyes me from behind spectacles and wrinkles her pointed, freckled nose at her unagreeable surroundings.

"Hello," she says, "my name is Addison."

I suck my front teeth and involuntarily begin drumming my fingers on the bar top. Quickly, I glance around to make sure that Dawn is still safely out of earshot, tucked away in the backroom. I lean forward and lower my voice.

"You know that in the town, there are lots of lovely restaurants," I say.

Addison's face crumples into a sharp frown, and she lifts an eyebrow. The other girls join her, each of them looking just as confused as if I am some kind of lunatic.

I guess they aren't far off.

"And pubs and bars," I add, my eyes flitting around nervously as if my sister is going to jump out of nowhere at any moment and catch me in the act.

"Are you trying to get rid of us?" one of the other women asks, folding her arms. She looks amused. As I take in her face, I feel a strange flicker of recognition, as if we have already met. Maybe somebody I knew from school?

"No… of course not," I reply hurriedly, "it's just… well…" now I am whispering, "come on… this is hardly a place for young people to hang out…" I am trying to make it sound as though I am one of the cool kids, just a friendly guy trying to make a decent recommendation to a group of holidaymakers.

"We aren't looking to eat, or even get a drink," Addison interrupts, "we're looking for some people who came to the area about six months ago… they were supposed to be staying at one of the cabins at Luxury Work Retreats, but apparently they never turned up."

"And the police haven't been any help," chimes in a pretty blonde woman, who looks as though she has been cut straight out of a fashion magazine.

Shit.

My face freezes as I slowly try and process their words, with very little success.

A crazy, mad, lunatic part of my brain screams at me that this is finally my chance. My golden opportunity. I can tell these girls the truth, subtly give them an address, tell them to get the fuck out of here as quickly as they can to get help.

Like I have wanted to do so many times before.

Too many times to count.

Bobby's face, dead, contorted with pain, clammy with suffering appears in my head, and a sharp stab of guilt winds me.

"Excuse me?" Addison pulls me out of my thoughts, her expression sharp and impatient.

I blink.

When I hear the door behind me opening, I know that I have waited far too long.

I've fucked it up.

Again.

Addison

Trust Priya to get sidetracked.

As soon as the pretty woman with the baby appears behind the socially challenged barman, Priya is gushing loudly. "Oh my god, what an adorable little baby!"

I sigh and resist the urge to roll my eyes.

Not that I have an issue against babies, but there are just more pressing matters at hand. And I don't want to spend any more time here than absolutely necessary.

"Thanks," the woman beams proudly. She skirts around the edge of the bar, so she is standing on the same side of it as us. She has long, wavy blonde hair that looks as though it could do with a comb. Her face is bare of makeup, giving her a beachy look like if you kissed her, your lips would taste like sea salt. Along with the strange sling, she carries the baby in and the long tie-dye skirt, she looks like some kind of gypsy woman. "Do you want to hold him?"

I open my mouth, about to politely decline and purposefully steer the conversation back on track, but before I can make a sound, Priya is cooing, "oh, could I?"

"Of course," the woman expertly unravels the cloth wrap with just a few swift movements, "my name is Dawn, by the way. This is Sundance," she nods towards her awkward counterpart, whose face is deathly white, a stark contrast from the flaming ginger mop on his head.

She carefully hands Priya the baby, the peaceful little being swaddled in the fabric from the wrap. "Ah, he's lovely," gasps Priya. "I'm Priya; these are my friends, Magda, Nancy, Violet, and Addison."

"So great to meet you," Dawn winks, showing a row of pearly white teeth as she flashes a dazzling grin.

"He really is *so* cute," Violet admits shyly, with a wistful smile.

Nancy and Magda nod in agreement, whilst Priya cradles him carefully, her face instantly besotted by the miniature human.

Not particularly caring if I spoil the moment, I clear my throat.

"Nice to meet you, Dawn," I say, not trying too hard to conceal the sarcasm in my voice, "but we're actually here because of five people that came to the area about half a year ago."

Dawn cocks her head, "okay…"

"They went missing," I clarify. "They were supposed to be staying at Luxury Work Retreat cabins but never turned up. We're searching all nearby places to see if we can find anyone who might know where they are."

Frowning, Dawn rests her elbow on the bar, "sounds like you ought to get the police involved…"

"We did," I reply impatiently. "But they've been useless… won't investigate it any further because they all sent texts saying they'd run off to start a new life…"

The barman and Dawn exchange looks. Something passes between them, though I cannot quite put my finger on what it is. He looks helpless, as though he is anticipating something dreadful happening… but what? A sickly feeling of unease begins to settle somewhere deep inside my chest.

"So, why are you worried then?" Dawn asks. Maybe I'm wrong, but I'm sure I can detect a hint of playful defiance, dancing mischievously on her full lips. As if she is teasing or making fun of me. I brush it off. My brother always did say to me that I look too far into things, always assuming the worst of other people. Social anxiety it's called.

I look around at the others for support, but they appear to be too consumed by the baby to come to my aid.

"It's just suspicious…" I reply feebly.

Dawn lifts an eyebrow. She folds her arms over her stomach, which is still slightly cushioned, presumably from where she only recently gave birth.

"Look, can you just look at these pictures and tell me if you've seen any of them?" I ask, forcing myself to sound braver than I feel.

Since the very beginning, I've been the leader of the group, doing all the research, questioning the police, going to the media. I'm not a cowardly woman. But there's something about Dawn, and the way her intense eyes bore into me as if her pupils are lasering every inch of my body, analysing every fibre and molecule of my person.

"Go on then," Dawn says eventually, after just long enough for the atmosphere to plummet even further into uncomfortable territory.

Clumsily, I fumble in my pocket for my phone. Still, the others are totally oblivious, still chuckling over the kid.

"What is his name?" Nancy asks Dawn as I'm loading up the images on the touch screen. "I remember my little boy being this tiny… it just goes so quick…"

"Daddy," Dawn replies proudly.

Involuntarily, I smirk. Who wouldn't? What sort of name is that for a baby? But as soon as the chuckle escapes my lips, I feel my face burning bright red. All eyes are on me.

"Sorry… I was just laughing at a meme on my phone…" I explain hurriedly, then scramble to get the pictures up, unable to look Dawn in the eye.

Painful silence follows, and I feel goosebumps erupt out over my upper arms beneath my jacket as my thumbs slide across the screen until the photo of Bobby flashes up at me. I turn the phone around and position it so that Dawn and Sundance can see.

"This is my brother Bobby," I cough, doing my best to brush off the embarrassment of my outburst.

Out of the corner of my eye, I catch a subtle but definite flicker of something on Sundance's face. Somehow, his already pasty cheeks seem to drain even more, and his lower lip falls slightly open, revealing crooked, yellowing teeth.

"Oh yes," Dawn smiles, nodding. "Yeah, we've seen him. Haven't we, Sun?"

"Oh my god, really?" I practically yelp with excitement, "when? Where? Do you know where he is now?"

"He's fine and dandy," Dawn says, her eyes twinkling. "He's joined our movement… we're like a little family."

Magda steps forwards, "what, you mean like a cult?"

"What about the others? Show the other pictures, Addison!" demands Violet.

Typical that now they're all suddenly interested. I scroll quickly through the other four pictures, and Dawn continues to nod until she resembles one of those bobble-head dogs you can keep on your dashboard. "Uh-huh, yeah, they all decided to join us."

Nancy's face falls, "so you mean they're all fine? They all just decided to leave us?" her voice is tinged with hurt and disbelief.

"Why the hell didn't they call?" Violet grumbles, "we've been so bloody worried about them."

Dawn shrugs, never dropping the almost smug grin stretched out across her cheeks, "we don't believe in technology as such. They'll have thrown away their phones and devices."

Violet's anger is infectious. I feel it bubbling in the pit of my own stomach now and find my fingernails digging in painfully to my palms as I tense my fists.

"Where can we find them?" I ask.

At last, Sundance chimes in, "it's a secret location, sorry," he says quickly, guiltily almost.

I exchange appalled glances with the rest of the girls. Even Priya's jet black eyebrows knit together. She hands the baby back to Dawn. "I really need to see my cousin," she says, her voice suddenly as hard as a newly sharpened blade. "There's been a death in the family."

A pang of guilt wallops me in the chest.

Priya hadn't mentioned that anyone in her family had passed away. And this whole trip, all I've been doing is criticising her every chance I get.

"I'm so sorry, Priya," I blurt out. She ignores me, keeping her intense brown gaze fixed tightly on Dawn and Sundance.

"Please, can you take us to visit them? she asks, her tone softening, pleading.

Dawn and Sundance look at one another. As she bobs about, Dawn rhythmically pats the baby's back and kisses his tufty head, seemingly deep in thought. "Well, if there's been a death in the family, I think we can make an exception," she says after a while. "I'm sorry for your loss," she says to Priya, smiling smugly in a way that indicates that she isn't sorry at all.

"Thank you," Nancy says grimly.

I turn to look at her. Her pleasant features have tightened, her lips a thin, unhappy line, the sparkle missing from her eyes. Maybe she was happier believing that something terrible had happened to Kevin. Somehow, perhaps, that is a less painful truth than having to face that he abandoned her and left his own kids without a second look.

"Can you give us the postcode, please?" I ask, suddenly desperate to get out of the vile pub and away from these two strange, shady characters.

"Don't know it, unfortunately," Dawn shrugs, "but if you give me a ride back, I can direct you."

Her suggestion is met with quiet.

Already, I know that the other girls have firmly decided. Of course, we should give this strange woman a lift. But still, there's that unspoken rule that every decision made in our little search team needs my stamp of approval. I feel four pairs of eyes ogling me and realise then that I don't have a choice.

I swallow and force myself to nod.

As Dawn thanks us and says goodbye to her brother, that awful feeling of unease continues to gnaw away at my senses, and the back of my neck prickles nervously. Something tells me that something here is not right. It's not just telling me; it's screaming at me. But what can I do?

With feet that are as heavy as lead, I force myself to trail out behind the group. I see that the others are bombarding Dawn with questions, trying not to come across as pushy or impatient, and failing miserably.

What's worse, when I glance behind me to bid farewell to the barman, I see that his face is still frozen, his eyes wide and full of fear as he stares after us.

It's your anxiety. It's all in your head.

Bobby's voice in the taxi to a nightclub echoes around my mind. Whenever I got nervous or worried, he'd be the one talking me down, sharply forcing me to snap out of it.

It's all in my head.

Wordlessly, I follow the group out of the pub, my shoes sticking to the diabolical carpet beneath us, as if the grimy thing is trying to force me to stay. As we emerge back out into the cold, white day and cross the gravel car park, I force myself to take deep breaths.

When I see Bobby, no doubt he'll laugh at how silly I've been. I imagine him flicking back the shiny curtain of hair out of his eyes, putting his hands on his hips, and sassily telling me to get a grip. "Seriously, Addie? I texted you. I literally told you I was safe. You are *so* paranoid," he'll say.

And I don't think I'll even protest my brother's sassiness. I'll just laugh and force him into a cuddle, and be grateful that he really is safe and well.

There's no way in hell I am leaving without him, though, whatever the fuck this bloody place is. A movement? *A family?*

I wrinkle my nose and roll my eyes. I've heard about these sort of things before. Religious cults where people get sucked in and end up living like savages, smoking cannabis cigarettes all day, sleeping in filthy caravans. No doubt, my brother was seduced by some sexy hippy man with a beard.

We'll see.

It's only then, as I open the driver's seat door and slide into my seat, that a bewildering thought dawns on me. The conversation of the other women around me has faded into a hum, distant background music to the steady beating of my heart.

They all pile in, and I listen to the metal clicking of seat belts and slamming of car doors. I put the key into the ignition and turn it, then listen for the familiar rumble of the engine.

Sundance said that the house was a secret location.

But, if it was a secret location…

…how did Bobby and the others get there in the first place?

Nancy

My brain is buzzing with questions. It feels as though my thoughts are bubbling furiously, like a stew in a pot, overspilling out of my skull through my ears, scorching my skin until I blister and burn.

And yet, I find myself the quietest I have been since we came on this trip.

I take up my usual seat in the front of the car, beside Addie.

As she starts up the engine, I glimpse Dawn in the rearview mirror and feel compelled to mention to her about the baby needing a car seat. But it's as if my lips have gone stiff. Every time I go to open my mouth to speak my mind, something holds me back. So I just keep quiet and try to think about what I will say to my so-called husband.

Of course, I will never admit it out loud, but knowing now that he is alive is disappointing.

I don't mean it in a sick, sadistic, murderous way. I just mean it's disappointing to know that he really did leave us. Mum was right. My friends were right. The police were right.

And I've made a complete and utter fool of myself, ranting on about how something was up. Something wasn't right.

How stupid must everyone think me?

I visualise seeing his face. That handsome, rugged face, with his chiselled features and his intense eyes that seem to stare right into your soul. When he looks at you, he can make you feel like the most beautiful, interesting person in the world. I suppose that's why he finds it so easy. Perhaps it's naïve to assume that a man like that can stay faithful to one woman.

The reunion will go one of two ways, although the conclusion must be the same.

Either I'll break down and be the pathetic scorned wife. I'll see him, and it'll hit me that I'll never sleep beside him again or inhale the warm, familiar scent that lingers on his neck. Tears will flow freely from my eyes, and I'll make ugly animal-sounding moans. I'll make a fool of myself. Kevin will realise even more why he left me.

Or alternatively, almost a decade of bullshit will come to a head, and I'll punch the stupid dick head right in the nose. Hopefully, it breaks.

No matter what, it's the end of us.

Being cheated on, lied to, and disrespected is one thing. Being abandoned was my limit. And he went there.

Sighing, I press my forehead up against the cool glass of the window. I watch the blur of countryside speeding past until my eyes sting. When I blink, I realise that pools of hot, salty tears have formed beneath my lashes. I swallow them back and try to focus on the conversation in the back of the car.

Anything to temporarily take my mind off of my deceitful swine of a husband.

"I just don't understand… it's just so crazy…" Priya is saying. I don't turn around, but I can hear her disbelief. "I know Abs wasn't like… hardcore Muslim… but I just thought that meant he was sceptical of all religion."

"And who can blame him?" Dawn asks, "in order to be awoken and enlightened by God, truly, you need to see the power first hand."

Magda scoffs. "Isn't that defeating the object of faith a little bit?" she points out.

It's a fair argument, but I wince at her condescending tone. Dawn seems like a nice enough lady, and I always naturally assume that mothers can be trusted. But still, the way she was looking at Addie back in the pub was a little intimidating. I'm not sure I'd want to be in an altercation of any kind with her.

To my relief, Dawn just laughs in response. "Why would you believe in something that there is no proof of? It doesn't make sense."

"So why do you believe in God?" Violet asks curiously.

Part of me feels the urge, as the motherly one of the group, to turn around and hiss at Violet to stop asking such personal questions. But I'm still rigid and find myself wanting to hear Dawn's answer.

"I was a drug addict and a prostitute. I had no family, no real friends, nothing," she says. "I was homeless, regularly being told I was the scum of the earth. My life was nothing. *I* was nothing." She pauses a moment, and I hear the tiny sound of the baby gurgling.

"But my life has changed now. Now, I have a family and friends, a beautiful home, a gorgeous son, a wonderful life. And best of all, I have a purpose," she finishes, "and that's all thanks to God."

I turn to see Addie's reaction, but her face is fixed firmly ahead, her eyes glassy and distant, as if she is buried deep within her own thoughts.

"That's a really inspiring story and all," Priya says, "but don't you take credit for your own success? I mean, you must have worked really hard to get away from addiction and rebuild your life."

"I didn't work hard at all," Dawn says bluntly. "I found Faith, and that's when everything changed."

I suspect that this response would have stirred even more questions, but before anyone can ask, Dawn is leaning forward in her head. "Turn off here," she says, jerking a finger to the left.

At the last minute, Addie slows and swerves the car. Her fingers are white as they tightly grip on to the steering wheel. It feels as though the tension is physically leaking out of her, stirring into the atmosphere in the car.

I blink curiously out of the windscreen as the car creeps forward across a wide deserted space, surrounded by a thick border of trees. Surely there is enough greenery in this place to supply the entire planet with oxygen. Everywhere you look, there are bushes, branches, blades of grass stretching out over vast expanses of the countryside.

"Guys, I was just wondering, for dinner tonight, does anyone have any special dietary requirements?" Dawn asks suddenly, although I am temporarily distracted from answering by the huge, towering brick building that stands above us.

In amidst all of the surrounding woodland and fields, it sticks out like a sore thumb. A miserable, dreary prison block with boarded-up windows and dirty brown bricks.

"I'm allergic to nuts, and I don't eat pork," says Priya.

Violet gasps playfully in feign horror, "how can you live without bacon, Priya?"

"Nothing better than a bacon sarnie in the morning," agrees Magda.

As Addison parks, she leans forward over the steering wheel and frowns up at the dismal looking place. "Is this your house?" she asks doubtfully. "Is this where Bobby is staying?"

Dawn ignores her. "How about you two girls? Are you bacon lovers as well?"

Addie shrugs, pupils still fixed uncertainly on the building in front of us, "it's alright, I guess."

I turn around in my seat, "you don't need to make us dinner, Dawn, though thanks so much for the offer. We are staying at a hotel, and food is included…"

"I insist," Dawn smiles sweetly. "Come on then, let's get inside!"

As I exit the car, I notice that a sharp chill now lingers in the air, and instinctively pull my jacket tighter around my body. A forceful, unfriendly wind slams the car door shut behind me, the clang of the metal echoing in the chilly breeze. I hug my arms tighter still and wish I'd thought to bring gloves as the icy fingers of winter creep in through my sleeves and pinch mercilessly at my skin.

"Shit, it's gotten really cold all of a sudden," Magda comments, making her teeth chatter.

"It's warm indoors," Dawn announces, pulling the baby close to her chest so that it's face is practically buried in between her breasts. She strides quickly away from the car, presumably keen to protect her infant from the sudden plummet in temperature.

I remain rooted to the spot until I can see that the other girls are standing around me, and we are all gazing up at the unsuspecting building.

"It looks like a factory," Addie whispers uneasily.

"Definitely *doesn't* look like a commune," agrees Violet.

We're silent for a moment, somehow able to sense each other's apprehension.

"Maybe they're squatters. Sometimes people do that…they move into abandoned buildings. I watched it in a documentary once," Priya says finally, low enough that Dawn can't hear.

It seems like a plausible explanation. After all, most cults that you read about are hardly rolling in cash. In fact, I'm pretty sure that most of the time, they are infamously broke, living in poverty, sleeping in rundown caravans, and stealing food just to survive.

Apparently, Priya's rational words also comfort the other girls, because next, I hear the sound of movement on top of the gravel. Addie is moving forwards, her face stony and solemn, filled with her usual purposeful demeanour. "Come on. Let's just get this over with," she says.

Abdul

Every part of me aches.

I haul myself up onto my knees, my joints cracking in protest as if I am five times my actual age. With a sigh of exhaustion, I glance around, blinking my sagging eyelids in a vain attempt to unblur my vision.

Done. At last.

Wincing at the pain stirring in my muscles, I push myself up onto one of the rounded plastic benches and gently massage my thighs and calves as they sweat through the material of my trousers. Sullenly, I examine the overspilling, industrial-sized rubbish bag that sits to the right of me. It is the sixth one I have filled cleaning the place. Then, to my left, right beside my boot, is a vile bucket filled with a glistening red mass of lumps and shreds. The foul concoction is composed partially of bleach and cleaning chemicals, and partially of the crimson pools of blood I scrubbed tirelessly from the floors, as well as the smaller shreds of flesh and muscle that got tangled up within the end of the mop.

I've been so busy for the last few hours, deep cleaning and sanitising the brightly lit, miniature stadium, and so distracted by the soreness of my poor, overworked muscles, I'd not had the time to absorb the enormity of the situation. But now I'm sitting here, just staring into a bucket of partially dissolved human remains, the sting of chemicals niggling at my nostrils, it finally hits me.

Months of watching innocent people suffer in tiny, congested cages in their own filth, be forced to slice bloody flesh from the bones of their friends, and then eventually be shot dead and turned into mincemeat had convinced me that they couldn't *possibly* think of anything anywhere near as cruel.

How naïve of me.

"Pig!"

The sudden voice interrupts my thoughts, and I tear my eyes from the bloody bucket to glance into the centre of the main ring. It's one of those horseshoes stages, where rows of seats curve around in a semi-circle in front of the stage.

My blood runs cold when I catch sight of her. Ignoring the painful protests of my joints, I immediately stand up.

Faith has her hands on her hips, her petite body swamped by the expanse of the underground big top. She flicks her long black hair over her shoulder and flashes me one of her unsettling smirks.

"How you getting on?" she calls to me, taking a few steps forward.

"Fine…" I mumble, gesturing half-heartedly to each of the bags.

Fiery green eyes sparkling, she glances around at my handiwork. The place isn't exactly gleaming, and I don't think the stench of pain and suffering will ever be able to be fully scrubbed away, but I've done my best. She seems to appreciate this and nods, satisfied.

"Good job," she says approvingly, "we've already got another new intake, so I'm re-opening the ticket queue for a show tonight."

I stifle a groan of exhaustion.

Another show means another heavy-duty clean-up operation.

"Since you've done such a good job, Rowan is going to take you back to the main house. You can have a proper bath, a decent meal, and a clean bed so that you're all fit and rested for clean-up early tomorrow morning," she tells me graciously as if she is granting me a huge favour. I have to resist the urge to respond sarcastically.

Gee, thanks.

"Thanks a lot," I reply instead, behind gritted teeth. I pick up the rubbish bag in one hand, the mop and bucket in the other, attempting in vain to ignore the stagnant taste of blood on my tongue.

A bath *does* sound good. Food and a bed will be nice as well. The last time I had a proper wash was the morning we set off on the work retreat, well over six months ago.

Who knows? Maybe if I act grateful, this crazy bitch will start trusting me to come back to the main house more often. I won't be constantly stranded, locked away at the farm. Maybe, if they trust me enough, I'll have a better chance of planning and making my escape…

Sundance

I close the pub at half-past six. Normally, I'd stay much longer, but my sister calls to say that I am needed.

I was *really* hoping that she wouldn't say that.

As I turn away from the bolted back doors and face the dark, inky blanket of winter night, I pull my jacket tighter around my scrawny, pale arms and strain my eyes to search for the car. Trudging around the side of the pub, I catch sight of a rusty, battered old range rover in the otherwise deserted front car park, it's gritty yellow headlights on, casting two glowing beams across the gravel.

Swallowing, I continue forward, every step growing heavier and heavier, the three or four vodka shots I've just downed already burning the pit of my stomach and making my head feel foggy and off-balance.

"What's the matter with you?" Faith asks me as I open the passenger side door and reluctantly slip inside the car beside her. "Jesus Sun, you stink of booze."

"I know, mad that, isn't it? Smelling like booze when you work in a pub." I say sarcastically, to which she smirks and nudges me playfully in the side. I slam the door shut and slump back in my seat. In her usual erratic fashion, Faith steps on the gas and swerves blindly out of the car park, then hurtles way too fast down the long country road.

"I just don't think I'm the best choice to help out," I reply feebly.

Although I'm aware of the 'work' the family does, I've always stuck to running the pub. I don't have the stomach, or the heart, for the farm work. Let alone... *this*.

"Relax, you're just going to be on the door," Faith says cheerily. "You check the ID, send them in, sound the alarm if you see anything suspicious. Nothing too strenuous…"

I lick my lower lip slowly and nod. "Those women… they were looking for Prue's group…"

I sense Faith stiffen at the mention of Prue's name. Faith basically fell in platonic love with the girl at first sight and had her heart set on getting her to join the family…

"So?" she scoffs.

My sister is still sour about the fact that Prue escaped and set free a tonne of the others from the farm. Obviously, they didn't get far at all. As much as Faith liked Prue, once she has been scorned, she is a very dangerous woman. She murdered Prue, although this is actually an understatement.

She ripped Prue to shreds.

Sometimes I wonder what Faith would do if she found out that it was me who helped Prue to escape. Really, it was the ultimate betrayal.

Clearing my throat, I shrug, feigning indifference. I don't know why I said anything.

Faith drives us back to the new building. The place is so dark and gloomy that it is practically camouflaged by the night's sky. Fit for purpose.

I follow my sister out of the car, and she strides confidently over to the entrance. I dither weakly by the car.

"What are you doing?" she asks sharply, as she digs around in the pocket for the keys.

"I'm on the door, right?"

She rolls her eyes and tuts loudly so that a puff of smoke escapes her lips in the frostiness of the early evening. I watch her shove the correct key into a concealed lock on the door, then roughly twist it, the sound of the metal scraping abnormally loud in the vast space.

Once she has pushed the door open, she glances back at me over her shoulder, "you'll freeze. Showtime isn't for another half an hour or so."

Although she says it as though I have a choice, I know that I don't. I last approximately half a second underneath her hard stare before I reluctantly follow her across the drive, towards the orange glow emitting from the narrow doorway. Every step is like being on an insanely, terrifyingly steep incline of a rollercoaster, slowly inching further and further upwards, knowing that any moment you're going to plummet downwards.

My heart pounds as my palms begin to sweat, my insides being pounded by the insatiable jaws of dread in my chest.

Inside, I close the door behind us and follow Faith down the long, thin corridor to the secret elevator at the back of the building.

The ground floor and the upper storeys are cleverly disguised as a warehouse- I know because I helped to move the boxes and the machinery into the various rooms. I also helped to install the bookcase with the concealed door; however, I've never been into the cellar before.

I really don't want to see what is down there.

I mean, I know what is down there. But seeing it on a computer screen somehow makes it feel as though it might all be pretend. An act. A trick of computer animation.

If I see it in person, it all becomes real.

Once again, I hover awkwardly at the sliding metal doors whilst my sister walks straight into the shoddy tin elevator. This time, she doesn't speak or question me. Instead, she cocks her head and widens her beady green eyes at me expectantly.

Despite myself, I press on and join her in the lift.

Silence falls over us as she taps in instructions on the keypad, and the box jolts into life and begins to move downwards.

I blink away tears and turn my head so that she cannot see.

Addison

I wake up with a start as if I am having one of those nightmares where you're plummeting from a scarily big height, and you regain consciousness just as you collide with the ground.

As I sit up, the back of my head smacks into something hard, and a deafening clang rattles my ears, causing a painful vibration to sear the back of my skull.

Thousands of fuzzy black spots cloud my vision, and the unmistakable stench of urine stings my nostrils.

I crouch, keeping my body still, fixed firmly into place as I try to blink away the ache behind my forehead.

The ringing in my eardrums gradually fades into what at first sounds like the low hum of an engine but soon transitions into something more reminiscent of animal, pitiful groans of exhaustion.

My eyes snap open, and I take a few seconds to absorb my surroundings. Beneath me is a black, plastic square with hard ridges that dig into the flesh on my knees and palms.

Bewildered, I glance up, wincing as the sudden movement of my flitting pupils causes another wave of nausea to course through my brain. More black dots dance before my eyes before quickly fading away to reveal hundreds of little black iron squares.

A horrified gasp catches in the back of my throat.

My heart plummets to the pit of my stomach.

I press my hands up against the wall of a tiny dog cage, threading my fingertips into the squares.

In my ears, my pulse pounds loudly like a death drum, ticking rhythmically like a bomb about to detonate.

Desperately, I press my face closer to the wall of the cage and peer out, straining my eyes to focus.

Across from me is another black dog's cage, but it's a good five metres or so opposite me. A small figure hugs it's knees in one of the far corners, it's naked back vibrating and quivering.

"H-h-hello?" I croak, lips trembling as I frantically glance around, desperate to catch a glimpse of the rest of the room. If I force myself into the corner nearest the wall, I can see that we are in a high-ceilinged basement, with no windows, just dismal, oily grey walls, and flooring. There are more cages, but only one of the ones I can see appears to have a person inside.

"Hello?" I repeat, louder this time, much to my overworked lungs' dismay.

Frozen with fear, my fingers become rigid on the bars of the cage, and a single tear wells up in one of my eyes.

Where the fuck am I?

"Addie?"

More tears follow, spilling down my cheeks now as I sigh a breath of relief to hear a familiar voice.

"Violet?" I call back, pressing my face into the bars in a vain attempt to see where the voice is coming from. She must be in the cage directly beside me or a few cages down.

"Addie, where are we?" Violet replies, her words breaking. I know that she must be crying too. "I can't remember anything."

It strikes me then that neither do I.

My last memory is following Dawn from the pub down a humid, stuffy corridor… entering a small, tiled kitchen… another woman… maybe a cup of tea?

"Me neither," I squeak, hopelessly.

"You've been drugged."

Another voice interrupts, then the solemn harshness of the words slicing through the air.

I glance back at the cage opposite me and decide that the girl with her back to me is the one who is talking.

"Drugged?" I repeat.

"Yes. They lured you here, drugged you, and now you're stuck."

A small rasp of laughter escapes my dry, chapped lips.

I'm thirsty, I realise.

"No…" I say, shaking my head.

The woman across from me lets out a sigh but doesn't say anything else.

"Violet, what can you see?" I shout.

"Cages… I can see Priya in the cage opposite me, but she's passed out. It looks like she's been sick…" she trails off, and then I hear her sniff loudly, "… Addie, what should we do?"

I rub the tears from my eyes and force my brain into gear.

What should we do?

Heart racing, I scramble about inside the tiny confines of my enclosure, wildly scanning every nook and cranny for a padlock or a mechanism to release us. I run my fingers along every surface until I find the catch, a little door that is secured in place with two separate locks.

My hands move instinctively to my chest, and I feel a tiny flicker of hope as I realise that I am still wearing a bra underneath my clothes.

Fingers trembling clumsily, I lift my top up and grab the bottom of one of the cups. I take hold of the left wire and try to force it through the fabric.

"Violet, are you wearing a bra?" I ask, as I desperately will the wire to poke through.

She pauses.

"Violet?"

"No, I'm naked," she replies hopelessly, humiliation wracking her words.

I stop then, more tears pooling in my eyes. I don't want to think about why she's naked or who would do such a thing to her. Is this some sort of trafficking scheme? I brush the thought to the back of my mind and furiously continue working at the task at hand.

I've seen it in movies before, people picking locks with thin pieces of metal wire.

"You're wasting your energy," the woman across from me says, without looking up.

Her mousey brown hair is short and matted, her bare skin grey, clammy, and stained with streaks of dirt. I grimace.

"It's worth a try."

"No, it's not."

Frustrated, I grab the bars of the cage and angrily shake them with tight, white fists. "If you aren't going to be helpful, why don't you just shut up?" I demand, flecks of spit erupting from my mouth.

The woman across from me shifts slightly, although she keeps her head bowed. "I've been here a while now. I've tried everything…" she says. Her words are muffled slightly, although there's no mistaking the hopelessness in her voice.

"Who did this? What is this place?" my eyes widen searchingly as I press my face up to the bars, and I strain to get a better look at the mysterious individual who speaks to me. "How long have you been here?"

She sighs at that. "I can't know for sure; it feels like forever. A week or so?"

"Addie… it was Dawn…" I hear Violet croak, "I remember seeing her; she watched a man bring us down here…"

Fucking Dawn. I knew that woman could not be trusted.

"But why?" my heart sinks as it occurs to me that Dawn was either lying about seeing my brother or else he is trapped in a cage somewhere as well. Either way, fresh tears well up in my eyes. "Why would she do this?"

"No idea," the woman replies. "Every so often, someone comes and takes one or two of us… they never come back…"

Maybe if I wasn't so wrapped up in my own fear, I might've felt a stab of sympathy for her. It sounds as though she is speaking from experience. I wonder if she was with friends, and they got taken away. The woman must be terrified.

"What is your name?" I ask her.

She pauses before answering as if considering the risks of this simple action. "I'm Jade."

"How do you know picking the lock with metal won't work?" I press her, zero patience for pleasantries or formal greetings.

Jade smirks a low, eerie chuckle that sounds like darkness. It makes the skin prickle up and down my arms.

"Even if it did," she eventually answers, "it would be a very bad idea. On one of my first days, I managed to snap a part of the mechanism on the padlock. It opened, and I managed to get out. I tried to run, but we're locked into this room by a thick metal door. They must have cameras because some of them came running straight away…"

"What happened?" Violet wonders out loud, although the dread in her voice indicates that she would rather not know at all.

Jade pauses then, ensuing a brief but horrific, deafening sort of silence that makes my blood run cold. Instead of speaking, eventually, she lets out a small sigh and slowly lifts her head out of the nest she has made with her arms. The curtain of matted hair falls dramatically away from her features as she leans forward onto all fours and crawls clumsily towards the bars of her cage.

I freeze as she comes into the light, and my eyes register what they are seeing.

The woman's face is caked in blood- two thick, dried splashes covering her gaunt cheeks, then lighter, sporadic patches stain her forehead and chin.

Her eye sockets are torn messily at the seams, the skin of her eyelids nasty and rigid, as though they have been mauled from the inside by sharp-toothed rats. Searching through the crimson tangle, I'm unable to meet Jade's sad gaze and find myself staring aimlessly into two empty abysses where her eyeballs should be.

I cock my head as the sound of Violet's terrified gasp tears me out of my trance. "W-w-what happened to your eyes?"

Manically, Jade laughs then. She slumps up against the side of the cage, still chuckling to herself under her breath. "They pinned me down, then gouged them out, so I wouldn't be able to run away," she replies bitterly. "And *that* is why breaking out is a bad idea."

Nancy

I wake up to ice-cold water cascading over my head, scalding and scorching the red skin on my cheeks, and roughly pulling me from unconsciousness. Flickering, orange light stings my eyes as I blink and strain my neck to glance around at my unfamiliar surroundings. In front of me, a fuzzy face comes into focus and soon takes up most of my vision, exhaling warm, stagnant breath that congeals on my flesh.

Instinctively, in my disorientated state, I attempt to stretch the strained muscles in my limbs, only to find that I am shackled or paralysed. Dead weights are attached to each of my joints, dragging me beneath the murky depths of a water bed, or making me sink into a thick sludge of mud. Either way, I cannot move.

A cracked groan escapes my lips.

The sudden noise brings the face into sharper focus all of a sudden. An ugly man with distorted features stands in front of me, puckered nostrils flaring as he takes deep, wheezy breaths.

Panic begins to hammer like a warning siren in my chest, and I glance down to see that my wrists and ankles are strapped to the spindly arms and legs of a metal wheelchair. Frantically I jerk and writhe in the chair in a vain attempt to move.

"What the fuck is this?" I demand, trying to sound braver than I feel. But my voice rasps and wobbles violently, and my eyeballs bulge out of my head as pure dread gnaws like a vicious beast on my insides.

Wordlessly, the man spins me around, causing a horrific groan in the mechanisms of the chair. I'm forced forwards, the wheels scratching like scrabbling rats on the grimy tiled floor beneath me. My trembling mouth opens to let out a scream, but the sound gets trapped in my throat, forming a tight knot that makes it hard to breathe.

"P-p-please? What is this?" I'm sobbing now, my pupils flitting around the small, grimy room, beads of sweat and water glistening as they quiver on my bare arms and legs. "Please let me go; I have money… I can get you anything," I beg, just as he plunges me through a curtain of wooden beads.

I'm wheeled through to a gloomy corridor, my terrified cries echoing against the grey, windowless chamber.

As we progress, I hear a rumble of applause which grows louder and louder with every step, background noise to the squeaky echo of a microphone, and a few high-pitched whistles and cheers. When my captor pushes me roughly through a set of double doors, sending a sharp spike of pain into my kneecaps, the noise amplifies by about a hundred.

In fact, the thunderous clapping and delighted shrieks are now so deafeningly loud that they drown out the agonising scream that rips like a jagged shard of glass through my already raw throat.

My eyes are fixed, rooted to the horrific scene in the centre of a circular circus ring.

Everything else fades into an indistinguishable blur; the roaring sea of people; the colourful, striped backdrop; and even the vice-like shackles that grip at my bones.

At that moment, I feel the life drain from my blood, and rapidly I descend into stone-cold shock.

Drenched in the white glow of a spotlight, a naked woman is crouched on the ground before a large hoop, her entire body quaking with fear, her face red, blotchy, and contorted with pain. A man dressed as a ringleader with a crimson jacket and a top hat digs the heel of his boot into the base of her spine. He's talking into a headset, his deep, booming voice shaking the entire room. Draped in one of his white-gloved hands is a long, floppy whip that he traces teasingly over the woman's back.

I stare into his face, my head spinning as I analyse his features.

It can't be.

But it is.

It's Kevin.

Abdul

I almost threw up when I first saw Kevin alive.

He's become one of *them*.

After all of the shit I have seen, you'd think nothing would surprise me, but I honestly did not see that one coming.

"Oi, make sure you're watching!" hisses Rowan, digging me sharply in the side with his elbow.

The two of us are sitting on the plush sofas in front of the control panel, staring out of the wide pane of glass down at the moderately-sized circus stadium that Faith is so proud of. From up here, Rowan controls the spotlights and sound. He is teaching me the ropes.

Aren't I lucky?

Swallowing, I force my pupils away from the dark sea of people settled in the seats and look at the illuminated circus ring, where my former boss is tormenting a poor, hopeless woman. I blink away tears as I watch her naked body quiver and shake beneath the cruel slither of the whip on her skin and wish that I could trade places with her.

My heart sinks as Kevin jabs his foot into her spine, knocking her to the ground so that her chin collides with the ground. A horrendous chorus of laughter from the audience follows.

Fucking sickos.

Fucking rich sickos.

"Now, my lovely assistant, Miss Lacey, will you do the honours?" Kevin thunders into his microphone, extending a long arm and gesturing to the hoop.

Obediently, Karma strides confidently out of her corner, her sparkly green corset shimmering chaotically in the lights. Wolf whistles erupt into the stadium as she totters forwards on ridiculously tall platform heels, then pauses to pull a box of matches out of her cleavage. Grinning flirtatiously at the audience, she strikes the match and holds up the orange flame in the air, just before setting alight the hoop, which immediately becomes a crackling, fiery ring.

I hold my breath as the audience applauds her, the fingers of fire dancing madly in my irises.

"And now," Kevin shouts, silencing the room, "for the first trick of tonight's show. Our subject will leap gallantly through the flaming hoop!"

"WAIT!" another voice booms. The crowd goes hysterical as a second ring leader, a female in tall, spiky, thigh-high black boots, appears and crosses the stage. She wears tight, tiny shorts and a sparkly red jacket, her big green eyes glittering wickedly. My face falls as I strain to see what Faith is carrying under her arm. I groan helplessly as I realise it's a metal canister with a fire hazard sticker plastered to the side of it.

Oh my god.

"Ladies and gentlemen," Faith announces, "here at the circus, we do nothing by halves. Shall we make the act a little more interesting?"

"YEAH!"

"DOUSE HER!"

"FUCK HER UP!"

I shudder at the manic screams from the audience; my stomach churning at their cruelty.

Faith slowly unscrews the lid of the canister and then carelessly tips the entire contents of gasoline over the poor woman's naked flesh, who screeches in agony as the flammable substance leaks into her wounds. "Now, *that's* a trick!"

From beside me, Rowan chuckles under his breath, scratching his head in amazement. "Bloody hell. That's insane, even for Faith."

Hatred simmers beneath my skin, and I resist the urge to hit him. Instead, I force my eyes to turn back to the horrific show of sadism that continues in the ring below us.

"Thank you very much, my queen," Kevin smiles at Faith, sickening adoration shining in his irises as he watches her slink back off of the stage. Then, standing well back, he poises his whip in the air, teasing the audience as he positions it above the unfortunate victim.

"Now, on the count of three, our volunteer will perform the trick… one… two… three!"

A bead of sweat trickles down the side of my head. The woman lifts her face, her skin glistening, smeared all over with a vile paste of blood, tears, and snot. Before she can move, Kevin strikes her hard across the back, the deafening crack of the whip chilling me to my core as it collides with her spine.

The girl screams and smashes down to the ground again, more tears leaking from her puffy eyes.

"Too slow!" shrieks Kevin, lifting the whip again, this time slashing her at a different angle so that an angry red cross now glares from her quivering back. "Come on! Go!" He hits her again, on the back of her calves, even harder this time.

"Now, I'll give you another count of three!" Kevin barks, folding his arms. "Three seconds to jump through the hoop, or the next time, I think we'll have to turn you over…"

The crowd goes wild at this despicable suggestion. I clutch a hand to my mouth and swallow back vomit, furiously blinking away tears out of blind fear that Rowan will turn and see.

This time, the woman shakily forces herself back up, protectively clutching her chest. Crimson blood leaks from her gaping wounds and trickles down her legs.

"One…"

Crying uncontrollably, she staggers forwards, her eyes widening as she absorbs the furious circle of fire.

"Two…"

I watch her lips purse, and her eyes squint shut. She knows that she is about to die. You can see it splashed across her face, etched into her horrified features.

"Three!"

Opening her mouth, the woman propels herself forward, her injured legs stretching wide as she leaps over the convulsing flames. For a brief moment, I think she will succeed. She is skinny and petite enough to fit through the hoop and musters all of her energy for the jump.

But it takes only a split second… just a tiny, brief moment for her efforts to crumble.

As one foot lands through the hoop, the other knee becomes stuck and is quickly embraced by a tangle of fire.

She falls, and soon the orange flames are engulfing her entire leg, and she is writhing about on the ground, legs up in the air, convulsing and fitting in agony.

Unable to tear my eyes away, I watch the young woman burn to death, whilst an entire audience watches her horrendous demise with glee. Their laughter chills my bones as the lashings of fire char her flesh, blackening her blood-stained skin.

Her eyes roll into the back of her head, bulging out of her skull as all of the nerve endings in her body are sizzled and severed, the flesh on her skeleton melting like wax beneath a flame.

I feel my heartbreak.

She can't be any older than her mid-twenties, just like Prue.

Fresh tears well up in my eyes.

I wonder what her last thoughts are. I wonder if she thinks about her family, her friends… if she had a boyfriend. Maybe she even had children- who are now motherless and alone in a world where this kind of vile cruelty goes on unnoticed behind closed doors.

At the last moment, a manic grin on her face, Karma reappears with a fire extinguisher and quickly murders the flames. Thick clouds of white foam are blasted onto the girl's roasted brown limbs, like drops of snow landing on a desolate forest floor.

Sundance

It's dark by the time I arrive home.

I stumble across the threshold of the house and firmly close the front door behind me, my head on fire as I feel about for the light switch. Groaning, I rub the tension that collects beneath my forehead and moves quickly towards the living room, not bothering to remove my shoes or coat.

There's only one thing on my mind, and I *have* to have it.

Now.

I slip inside the living room and collapse into my usual armchair with a heavy sigh, then hastily reach into the cabinet beside it for the little wooden box where I keep my drugs.

It's nothing heavy. Just weed.

And I don't think that any sane person could blame me for wanting to inhale a substance that makes it almost impossible to care about anyone or anything.

Because that's just what my life has come to.

An existence where every waking moment is a constant reminder of other people's essentially unnecessary and avoidable pain and suffering.

I'll do anything to shift the guilt that constantly weighs down on me, like a tonne of bricks crushing me slowly to death. If I'm out of weed, I'll drink myself into oblivion or knock myself out on sleeping pills.

Apparently, slowly but surely murdering my own body is preferable to doing what I know is right, but somehow feels so morbidly, unfathomably wrong.

Greedily, I snatch up a pre-rolled joint from inside the container, shove it into my mouth, and light the end. The familiar scent of the pungent herb floats instantly into my nostrils, and straight away, a sense of calm washes blissfully over me like a wave. I breathe out and lay back, letting my eyes close as I savour the sweet relief.

It's short-lived.

"Sun, you're on Beau duty."

The words cruelly rip me away from my moment of peace.

I open my eyes and glare accusingly at the door, where Dawn is poking her head out, an apologetic look on her face.

"Are you kidding me?" I grumble, although I already know full well that this is not a joke.

"Look, I'll give you five minutes to finish that," she replies softly, gesturing towards the spliff that is balanced between my fingers, "but then I've really got to get back to Daddy. I've left him upstairs alone…"

I laugh humourlessly at that and shake my head in disbelief, taking another generous drag of the joint. "How about *I* see to Daddy, and *you* take care of Beau?"

Dawn says nothing and just shakes her head, letting out an exhausted sigh, which tells me she is not in the mood for jokes. "Five minutes, alright? We're in the kitchen."

She disappears behind the door again, and I lean further back into the plushness of the armchair.

I knew this would happen.

Faith has been hellbent on expanding our family, not just with new recruits who are few and far between, but by pro-creating more little creatures with brains like sponges, which will easily succumb to Faith's bizarre way of thinking.

But then again, wasn't that just what I was?

I was just a baby myself when Faith took me from my birth mother. She raised me to be just like her. So how is it that my entire life, I've always secretly questioned her, hating myself for harbouring any kind of doubt.

After all, she's my big sister. She loves me more than the others. Fuck, I get away with a lot more than them. Because she is so fiercely defensive over me.

I stub out the joint when I get about halfway down and leave it balanced inside the box on the arm of the chair.

My head swims pleasantly, a peaceful, slowly swirling blur of thoughts and colours. Breathing out, I force myself up to my feet and finally shrug off my coat and kick off my shoes.

It would all be so much easier if I was just like the others, hanging on to every word Faith says. I swear, they'd even believe Faith if she told them that rabbits could fly. They'd probably hacksaw their own feet off if Faith told them that it was all in the name of 'God's work.'

Another good thing I find about being high is that I'm able to be even remotely optimistic. As I pad out of the living room and head towards the kitchen, I find myself feeling grateful that at least I am here and not at the circus anymore. Calling it that makes my skin crawl, as if the place is somewhere you'd take your children to eat popcorn and marvel at contortionists. I've watched snippets from the live streams, only when I really had to. I can't think of anything worse than actually sitting there in that stuffy, underground stadium, the stench of blood and decomposition attacking my nostrils, my brain permanently scarred by the appalling acts of cruelty that go on in the ring.

Beau, thankfully, is not crying when I slip into the kitchen.

Dawn is tiredly rubbing her eyes, her hands dark and glistening, stained with blood. In front of her is a highchair where the oversized baby sits, her back to me.

"Surely she's not still hungry?" I groan weakly.

"We're going to run out at this rate," Dawn nods grimly. She stands up and hurriedly picks up a tea towel from the kitchen side, wiping her hands. "You've got a few more slivers there." I nervously follow her gaze towards a bowl from another surface.

I wince, and my stomach churns. You'd think, after all this time, I'd have gotten used to it. But no. It turns out you never grow immune to the foul stench of severed flesh.

We exchange our goodnights just before Dawn darts off out of the kitchen, clearly eager to get back to her son, as well as escape the monstrous little creature she leaves behind.

Gritting my teeth, I force myself forwards across the tiles, my limbs tensing as the deformed infant's features come into view. As guilty as I feel for the poor baby, an involuntary gasp of horror escapes me as I catch sight of it.

Her wrinkled, puckered mouth opens, exposing the dark, rotten-looking gums and the jagged blades of teeth that stick unevenly out of them. She projects a disgusting noise that reminds me of rubber boots squelching in mud, followed by an animal-sounding rasp that chills my bones.

"Oh God… please don't cry," I plead quietly, rushing to the infant's side. "What's up, honey? Do you need more food?"

The strangely shaped slits where her nose should be flare and gape as she takes sharp intakes of breath, and the random mounds of swollen flesh that coat her skull contort.

"Here…" grimacing, I gingerly slip my fingertips into the bowl that Dawn has left and pick up a juicy, crimson shred of flesh. "Oh shit…" I gag, bile knotting uncomfortably in my throat. "Oh god…" before I can vomit, I toss the scrap of meat onto the white tray in front of the baby. Like some kind of wild predator, she pounces on it, gobbling the entire thing at once. I stare at her in horror, watching her contentedly lick her lips with a stumpy tongue, and shiny dribbles of blood trail down her chin.

Covering my mouth, I close my eyes and attempt to calm the chaotic storm that rages in my gut and teases my esophagus.

When I open my eyes again, I'm delighted to find that the child's jet black eyes are drooping, puffy eyelids falling, and her misshapen head is leaning into the side of the high chair.

For a moment, as I watch her finally descend into slumber, I can kid myself into thinking there's something cute about her. Then again, I only have to remind myself that the little monster devoured her own mother's breasts at less than a minute old to realise I'd be stupid to be fooled.

Dismally, my pupils flit from the blood-soaked infant to the half-empty ceramic bowl full of chopped up breasts.

Chopped up human breast, no less.

When it comes to rearing children, *Netmums* and *Babycentre* sure don't prepare you for everything.

Addison

It feels as though hours have passed by the time I am able to somehow manipulate the padlock into opening. Barely able to see, and my wrists feeling as though they are about to snap, I let out a hysterical cry of laughter as the mechanism finally clicks.

"Oh my god! I did it!" fresh tears of desperation blur my eyes as the wire from my bra falls to the floor of the cage with a light clatter, and my fingers hurriedly begin untangling the noisy chain.

"Shut up!" hisses Jade from her shadowy corner. I don't look up, but I sense her crawl forwards and tighten her grip around the bars of her own jail, the emptiness of her eye sockets boring into me. "They'll hear you!"

Ignoring her, I wordlessly continue to fumble, until eventually, the padlock falls free with a heavy clunk to the ground, sending a deafening echo resounding around the dismal cellar.

Adrenaline pounds manically through my veins as I realise that the other lock is just for show and isn't even properly connected, the thing springing apart easily in my fingers.

"Violet, I'm coming!"

Frantically, I tug at the latch until it releases and then stand up too fast, clumsily banging my head on the top of the cage in the process. Pain searing at the top of my skull, I scramble out of the iron confines, then accidentally shove my knee into the solid metal wall. From the impact, I tumble ungracefully out onto the concrete on the other side, landing in a pathetic, quivering tumble with skinned and bleeding elbows.

But still… I'm out.

"Addie!"

I glance up and see that Violet's head is pressed against the bars of her own cage, and she is staring out at me, hopefully, her face chalky white like a ghost. My heart swells to see a familiar face, and instantly I haul myself back up onto my feet.

"Get the bra wire!" she says, pointing a finger through her bars, back towards my cage.

I do as she says, and within seconds I am craning over her cage, jabbing the end of the wire into the padlock that enslaves her. I pretend not to notice that she's naked, even as she flushes bright red and attempts to conceal herself with her hands.

"Shit…" I curse under my breath, beads of sweat dripping down my forehead whilst my pulse hammers loudly in my eardrums. "Shit, it's not going…"

"It will!" Violet insists, "please keep trying, Addie…"

"I will," I promise, although the wire slips awkwardly between the clammy pads of my fingertips, "come on!" I hiss impatiently, partly at myself and partly at the flimsy piece of wire I attempt to maneuver into the lock.

The air goes cold and silent as each of us holds our breaths, even Jade included. But in my hurry, I keep dropping the wire, or the stupid thing keeps getting stuck or going in at the wrong angle.

My heart rate quickens, thundering hard inside my rib cage like the persistent ticking of a time bomb, a constant reminder that a pendulum on our eyes… maybe even our lives is swinging back and forth…

Then suddenly, a loud thud in the distance sends a jolt of electricity down my spine.

I freeze.

"Shit!" I hear Jade whisper, "shit! Move Addie, hide! Quick!"

I let the wire drop from my fingers and clatter on the floor of Violet's cage, then I spring into action, giving the poor woman one final apologetic grimace as I glance frantically around the room.

"Addie, no… please, don't leave me…" Violet shrieks, raising her voice, suddenly as her voice breaks into loud, heartbreaking pleads.

"I'll come back for you," I whisper, my own eyes growing foggy with yet more tears. I stand up on wobbly legs and rub my eyes, straining them to study my gloomy surroundings. As I suspected, it is a rectangle, with about eight dog cages, most of which are empty and are lining the opposing walls.

My eyes flit to the heavy door in the corner of the room, then back towards my former prison at the opposite end of the room. Swallowing, I run back towards it and desperately untangle the heavy, metal chain, then wrap it around my wrist as I sprint back towards the door.

When I get close enough, I shrink down as small as I can against the wall, crouching down beside the exit, hopefully where I won't be seen straight away.

Incoming footsteps grow louder and faster, each thud making my blood curdle inside my veins.

Violet continues to cry, long, agonising wails of fear that are branded forever into my brain. She shakes the bars, her petite hands dainty and weak against the thick, black metal.

A terrified sob gets stuck in my throat as I think of Jade's gaunt face and the horrific empty windows where her eyes should be.

Will I be next?

Desperate not to reveal myself, I plunge my teeth into my tongue until I taste blood and tighten my grip on the chain to stop my frightened whimpers and trembles exposing me.

It occurs to me at that moment that the chain might be made of sturdy iron, but it's nowhere near large enough to cause any kind of damage. I consider throwing it around my enemy's throat, but I know I'll easily be thrown off.

I'm not strong.

I just like to pretend I am.

How completely fucking stupid of me to come searching for my brother in this strange place that I don't even know. How naïve of me to trust those freaks from that disgusting pub.

If I die today, I deserve it for being such a total idiot.

The sound of the footsteps get louder and louder in my eardrums until each one feels like a vibration in an earthquake. I envision a crack in the ceiling, then huge lumps of jagged concrete falling down on top of me, slowly crushing us all to death.

I squint my eyes shut and find myself praying.

Dear God, please help me.

And then, just like that, the footsteps stop.

The tiny scrape of a lock makes all of the hairs on my back stand up on end.

I hold my breath, my lungs on fire as I try to control my shaking legs.

Slowly, the huge door swings open, causing a painful creak of protest to flood the room.

Violet screams.

My face falls as I watch a man stride into the room, straight over towards Violet, his back to me.

Suddenly rooted to the spot with fear, my eyes widen, and I look from Violet to Jade.

Time slows down.

The man is wearing dirty work boots and tatty trousers covered in dark, unsavoury stains. I hear his low grunts, although his words are unfathomable over the loud, rasping cries that come from Violet's red, blotchy face. I notice, in one of his trouser pockets, there is a rusty, gnarly-looking bread knife, the metal poking out of the top.

I watch him lean down and pull a thread of Violet's hair through one of the holes in the cage, then yank roughly on it so that her contorted face is smacked against the bars. She screams even louder then, but he does it again, and again.

Shakily, I force myself to stand up. My head feels so heavy that I can barely even see or walk straight.

What happens next is a blur, over and done within a hot, white flash. Just like a dream, the events run too quickly through my head to comprehend.

Seeing the agony in her eyes spurs me on, and I lunge forwards before I can stop myself. In one swift movement, I tear the knife away from his pocket, just as he turns.

My mouth falls wide open, and a horrified gasp that drains my chest leaves me breathless.

The knife clatters to the floor, and I stagger backwards as I absorb the hideously deformed mash of a face that stares back at me. Bulbous, bloodshot eyes glare at me from within mottled sockets, and open, oozing sores dot the swollen skin.

"Addie!" Violet sobs, knocking me out of my daze.

Without thinking, I whack the monstrous creature in front of me with the chain, hard enough to temporarily stun him and knock it out of my grip.

He groans and holds his bald head in his hands.

Crying, I fall down to my knees and frantically feel about on the ground for the knife, which I swiftly grip with my right hand. Blinded by the hot, stinging blur of my own tears, I lash out, aimlessly plunging the blade into the air until it finally meets flesh. I stab again, and again, for as long as I can, until there is suddenly a deafening crack, and the weapon sticks.

My attacker lets out a roar of pain and crashes down onto his knees, grabbing the handle of the knife, twisting it out of my grip.

Before he can act, I sprawl backward and clumsily scramble to my feet.

"RUN ADDIE, RUN!" I hear Violet behind me.

I do as she says.

My feet pound the dank floor of the basement as I pelt out of the door and hurtle down a long, narrow corridor, propelling myself further into a stretch of pitch-black nothingness.

Nancy

I'll always remember the first time that I found out my husband was cheating on me.

It was long, long ago, before we even had children or had gotten married.

It was back in high school.

My best friend at the time, Clara was having a birthday party.

I couldn't go because I'd come down with the flu, but I didn't want Kevin to miss out, so I said that he could go ahead without me.

Well, halfway into the night, I decided I'd just get up and go anyway.

You see, I couldn't stand the idea of missing out on all the fun of getting drunk on cheap cider, smoking shitty roll-ups, and pretending to genuinely enjoy terrible garage music.

When I arrived at the party, I was let into Clara's house by a guy I didn't even know. I remember weaving through the hordes of drunken teenagers, searching for a friend or, even better, for Kevin.

It didn't take me long to find both.

Clara and Kevin were in the garden, having sex over a wheelie bin.

I always used to think that that pain was a hundred, a million times worse than anything anyone could ever physically inflict on me. Over the years, that theory was proven right. Every time Kevin cheated, lied, let me down, nothing ever hurt as much as that night at Clara's birthday party.

Childbirth, breaking an ankle, getting a personal trainer, a concussion… all of these things never seemed to match up.

But as I sat there, watching my husband… the father of my children… the man who'd one day walk our daughter down the aisle… the man who'd be my son's role model…the man I'd grown up with... torturing an innocent woman... laughing at her agony... forcing her into her own long, painful death...

Now, I just don't know.

What hurts more, being whipped to within an inch of your life, then being burned alive whilst a stadium of people watch, and somehow find hilarity in your suffering...

...or knowing that your missing husband is the one holding the whip?

The lights have been blacked out over the ring, whilst a group of figures dressed in black hurriedly haul the props and the still sizzling corpse onto a wagon, then out of sight.

Thunderous applause and the roar of the audience blares loudly in my ears, barely audible over the jaunty carnival music that blasts from speakers. Lips frozen stiff, I'm rendered speechless, too traumatised to make a sound.

It feels as though somebody with razor-sharp nails shoved their fist into my mouth and ripped out my vocal chords, leaving me helplessly silent.

Somewhere, in amongst all the noise, as if down the opposite end of a tunnel, I think I can hear my name being called, though I am sure it's just an undercurrent in the music, playing cruel tricks on me.

Nancy!

My eyes blur, and my chest tightens.

Nancy!

I know that wherever I am and whatever the fuck is going on, it's extremely likely that I am about to die. And all I can think of is my children.

Nancy!

I know that my mum will take care of them. But a hot, salty tear forms in my eye nevertheless as I think of how little time we had together.

I'd always dreamed of watching my kids grow up.

I'd always dream of Kevin and I doing it together, the perfect nuclear family that I never had... and now what?

At best, they'll grow up believing that both of their parents walked out on them, and worst-case scenario, they someday discover the truth- that their father left to become a psychotic piece of shit, and their mother was burned alive in some kind of fucked up circus show.

Nancy!

Finally, I cock my head to the left, my fingers scrabbling madly with fear over the arms of the chair. I notice another wheelchair a few metres away, the figure strapped inside it partially concealed by shadow, partially illuminated by the spotlights that travel over the noisy, leering audience.

"Magda…" I croak, although the words are instantly drowned in the ruckus of the stadium.

Like me, she is forced to sit bolt upright, her limbs rigid in their restraints as though she has been electrocuted. Tears streak her face, glistening in the sporadic lighting, her features pinched and frozen in terror.

She doesn't say anything, and neither do I. Even if we could hear each other, what would we say? But there's a narrow sliver of comfort in seeing her there beside me, in the same place, living the same hellish nightmare.

"Ladies and gentlemen!" my husband's voice startles me, and I avert my watery-eyed gaze back to the ring in front of me. My top row of teeth pierces my lower lip, and a hot, sickly feeling congeals on my tongue.

The lights flash back on, and I see his tall side profile, standing charismatically at the front of the stage, a freakishly brilliant grin smeared across his face. "It is now time for our second act!" he announces, "and that means time for another volunteer!"

A loud drum roll begins. I tremble uncontrollably as the red-headed woman, the alleged 'lovely' assistant, appears and strides towards Magda and me. Her eyes sparkle greedily, straight past me, fixing purposefully on my friend.

No…

"No!" I scream as loud as I can so that it feels like the sharp point of a dagger is piercing my throat. Frantically, I jerk my limbs and try to move in my chair, but it's no good. The woman doesn't even bat an eyelid, probably can't even hear me. All I can do is writhe and twist helplessly in my seat, watching desperately as she snaps the break on Magda's wheelchair and pushes her slender, half-naked frame forwards into the ring. Two men dressed in black help her to hoist Magda over the raised, stripy edge, and she totters forwards the rest of the way.

"Ladies and gentlemen, a round of applause for our next volunteer!" Kevin shouts, causing the room to explode into more vigorous claps and cheers.

My heart rips in two as I watch Magda shiver, squinting as she is taken into the bright white light, and one-by-one, the woman removes her ties.

"Our next act is an old family favourite," explains Kevin, as the two men reappear a few seconds later, pushing what I first assume is a fish tank on wheels. "The classic woman in the box trick, but… with a twist…"

He is interrupted by a sudden crack then, as Magda's final ankle tie is removed, and she swiftly lifts a barefoot and kicks the woman in the face.

"Fuck!" groans the assistant, falling backward onto her backside in surprise.

Magda stands up, wobbling madly like a baby deer, and starts to dash away. Of course, she doesn't get very far.

One of the men grabs her by the band of her bra strap and effortlessly yanks her backwards so that she crashes down to the floor, and the cups of the bra are twisted, revealing her breasts.

"Someone's excited!" laughs Kevin, "well, I guess we'll just get straight into it then!"

I bow my head, but even when I close my eyes, it's impossible for me not to realise what is going on. There must be amplifiers on the stage because I can suddenly hear Magda's voice, her broken wails, and her desperate pleas. I hear the slap of skin wrenching her body into place, and the sound of her frantic struggle as they lift her up as though she is nothing and shove her into the box. I don't look up until Kevin speaks again.

"And now, for the twist!"

When I look back up, the sight before me is so shocking that it feels as though a wrecking ball has been thrown into my chest, cracking my sternum into shattered fragments.

Magda has been locked into what I first assumed was a fish tank, her sobbing face sticking out one end, and her feet, streaked with blood from her shackles, sticking out of the other. She continues to struggle, causing the entire thing to jolt and wobble on its metal wheels, but it's no good. She's well and truly stuck.

Beside her, a long, metal table on wheels has been left- the kind you see in operating theatres, holding all of the surgical instruments.

My blood runs cold.

On top of the table, glinting evilly in the lights, are all different kinds of blades. A huge kitchen knife, a dagger, an axe, a saw… the image runs miserably like a sordid water painting in front of me as more tears form in my eyes and dribble miserably down my face.

"On top of the base price for the performance ticket…" Kevin continues, "which, by the way, can be purchased either to watch here in our underground theatre or on a *very* discreet live stream online…"

Something slides into place at that moment. My husband has that familiar gleam of excitement in his eye, the kind when he wins big at the casino or the business has a particularly good month.

My husband loves money, perhaps even more than he loves sex, drugs, booze, and his own children.

"…here at the circus, we also offer you the opportunity to come down and be a part of the action…" he takes a step towards Magda and sticks his hand through the top of the transparent box so that his meaty fingers can be seen tracing her flat stomach.

"No! *Please*!" Magda shrieks, her voice like nails on a chalkboard, the blood-curding horror in her plead bouncing sharply off of the walls.

"With a selection of instruments, *you* can be the magician… the star of your own act!"

Excited applause thunders through the audience, and Kevin grins.

"On the app, you were asked to download prior to the show; you may now enter the live auction… bids starting at £10,000! Thirty minutes on the clock starting… *now!!*"

Abdul

When the elevator doors suddenly pinged open, and the heavy thud of frantic footsteps tore mine and Rowan's attention from the bidding app on one of the computer screens, it was an enormous relief.

Immediately, I spun, temporarily pleased to be able to look away from the rapidly increasing figures on the monitor. In a way, the changing numbers were even more disturbing than watching the actual show itself.

I know blood and guts. I've learned all about the limitless boundaries of cruelty humans can unleash upon one another. Pain and suffering are now like my second language. But watching the eye-watering amounts of cash that these people are willing to spend flash up right in front of my eyes is a harrowing, ungodly experience in its own right.

I mean, who in the fiery depths of hell would voluntarily pay £25,000 to kill a person? To inflict excruciating pain upon them, for no apparent reason?

It makes me fucking sick.

So taking a break from the despicable image was a relief, albeit a short-lived one.

It was Fern who thundered into the room, sweat beading down his horrifically scarred forehead, his deformed lips sharply inhaling and exhaling breath as if he had been running a marathon.

I don't bother learning most of the names of the family unless there is a reason why they stick out in my mind or if I am forced into dealing with them on a regular basis.

Everyone knows Fern because of the horrendous injuries he sustained from an altercation with Faith. Rowan told me once, on one of his nice days. He said that Faith has a habit of dousing people in a scalding hot liquid when they disappoint her.

Needless to say, his face is not one that you forget in a hurry.

"What are you doing up here?" Rowan had snapped, clearly irritated by his presence.

"One... one... one of them's... escaped..." Fern had mustered, leaning forward to put his hands on his knees as he attempted to get back his breath.

"What?" Rowan demanded then, getting up from his seat, clutching his gun between his thick, meaty fingers. "From where?"

"The... the... cellar..."

"For fuck's sake," Rowan had grunted in disgusting under his breath, poising his gun in his hands. He stomped past Fern, nudging the overweight man hard with his shoulder. Just as he reached the elevator doors, he turned back towards me, lifting an eyebrow and eyeing me threateningly. "Don't get any funny ideas, Pig," he hissed. "Or you'll be down there with the rest of them," he nodded towards the screen, and I felt my heart sink. The two of them left me alone in the control room, just sitting there, heart racing as my brain whirred with possibilities.

Five minutes have passed, and I'm still glued to my seat, staring wistfully at the exit.

Part of me wants to run. In fact, there is a voice- Prue's voice- at the back of my head, screaming at me to get up and go.

But the fear is paralysing, keeping me frozen in place, my limbs locked tightly so that all I can do is sit and wait.

I could get in the elevator, but what would I do if one of them were inside? Even if there wasn't, how would I know what buttons to press on the control panel? How would I know where to go or how to get out? I've been watching as carefully as I can when Rowan brings me back and forth, but the system still confuses me.

Then, I glance to the left, at the door a few metres down from the control panel. That's the door I go through when I'm on cleaning duty. It leads directly into the stadium, where hundreds of psychotic lunatics are bidding ludicrous amounts of money to literally tear some poor, innocent woman apart.

Neither of my options seems particularly promising.

The choice is taken out of my hands when I hear the sound of the lift stopping again, and hastily I turn back around to glance at the computer screen. The last thing I want is to arouse any sort of suspicion about my loyalties.

That's my only real hope at ever escaping.

Gaining their full trust.

On the monitor, £39,218 blares back at me.

I blink.

Fucking hell.

More than what I used to earn in a year.

At that moment, a loud, frightened gasp startles me.

Slowly, I take my eyes off the screen and turn around in my seat.

My own mouth omits a low cry of shock.

Behind me stands a tall woman, blood streaking her hands and wrists, her clothes dishevelled, her face grey and clammy, her face wretched and distorted in sheer terror. I've grown to recognise this expression well, on what feels like a million different faces.

Immediately, I know that this must be the escapee.

If she were one of them, she wouldn't look so traumatised.

My brain kicks start into action, and I spring to my feet, suddenly powered on pure adrenaline. Too focused to speak, I lunge forward and grab one of her skinny, blood-stained forearms.

Big, huge, massive, fucking mistake.

"GET OFF ME!" she shrieks, lashing out, fresh tears pouring out of her face like waterfalls.

"Shut up! Shut up!" I hiss, tightening my grip on her, "shut up, I want to help you for fuck's sake!" Roughly, I smack the palm of my hand over her mouth, silencing her. I'd have never dreamed of treating of man-handling a woman like this in my old life, but she leaves me no choice.

I'm surprised at my own strength as I manage to keep her lips clamped shut and her arms wrenched still. Her eyeballs bulge out of her skull, glassy with tears, her pupils dilating and twitching madly with fear.

When I see her looking at me like that, as if she is just a small, vulnerable animal, trapped by a vicious predator, my heart breaks a little. I soften, and all I want to do is hold her in my arms and comfort her.

But I don't.

The last time I did that, I lost Prue.

So instead, I think on my feet.

I twist her body towards the door that leads out into the stadium.

"Your only hope is to get out there, mingle with the audience…" I whisper, trying to keep a low, calm tone. "Most of them are drunk. Ask them to get you a drink and clean off your hands. Go home with one of them. Then get out of here and get help. Do *not* go to the local police."

I release her, glancing behind me as I push her forwards, propelling her towards the door. She staggers backwards, her face crumpling, her bloodied hands clasping around her lips.

"But… why… why can't I just ask one of them for help?" she mutters, presumably referring to one of the members of the audience.

"Do that," I warn, "and you're a dead woman. They're all just as sick and twisted. Now, go! Open the door quickly before anyone sees you!"

Wordlessly, the woman turns and scrambles frantically with the bolts on the door. Every inch of my body tingles as I watch her, silently willing her to hurry the fuck up.

She hauls open the door, her arms visibly trembling, and then doesn't look back as she quickly slips out of the small gap. I hurry forwards and hastily re-adjust the locks, then go straight back to my seat, my right leg bouncing uncontrollably as I try to calm myself down by looking at the screen.

Did I do the right thing?

If she gets caught, and she grasses me up, they'll kill me. And it won't be quick and merciful, on account of my many months of service. They'll make it painful.

Very fucking painful.

But what if she doesn't get caught?

My heart flutters, hopefully.

Time for the auction is running out.

£42,392

Mad.

Nancy

£44,520

This is the final bid. The total cost of Magda's life.

My throat feels as though it is splitting apart as I scream and shout as loudly as my lungs will allow, writhing uncontrollably in my seat, pulling hopelessly at the tight, wretched restraints. My vision is totally obscured by the tears so that the world becomes just a brightly coloured blur in front of me.

This can't be it.

Magda surely isn't going to die.

Any moment now, there will be a police raid. A thousand armed officers will rush in and save us. There will be cups of hot, sweet tea, foil blankets, sirens, and flashing lights. In a few hours, I'll be safely tucked up in some hospital bed.

I'll get the best lawyer in town and screw my sick fuck of a husband for every penny he is worth.

But most importantly, Magda will be safe.

I've not known Magda long, but she, along with the other three girls, has become my ally in what has been the hardest time of my entire life.

No-one else ever understood my persistence to find out about Kevin. They reminded me of what a total arse he has always been and how much better off me, and the kids are without him.

Well, that was all very well for them to say, but that didn't stop me from missing him and being so very frightened for him.

During the last six months, such a dark, cold, and lonely time, Magda, Addie, Priya, and Violet have become friends I never knew that I needed. All of us so different on the outside and yet, the same on the inside.

Just five stubborn women on a mission to find the truth, for the sake of someone that they love.

A mission that has gone epically, catastrophically wrong.

"No…" I murmur, jerking my hands as a spotlight flits into the audience and highlights a smartly dressed woman descending the short flight of steps to the ring. She has shiny black hair slicked back into a high ponytail, her face perfectly made up, a tight, glittery dress covering her toned, slender figure. At first, I don't even consider that this can be the highest bidder.

Surely not a woman?

I stand corrected.

She strides across the ring confidently in her stilettos, a red-lipsticked smile spreading across her shapely cheeks.

My stomach flips. I continue to pull at my restraints, to no avail. I stare desperately at Magda, who appears to have run out of tears. Her face is still and grim; all colour drained from her cheeks.

I zone out of what Kevin and the woman are talking about and the hideous bursts of laughter that come from the audience.

I focus on Magda's face, a wave of sadness falling over me as I continue to wait for the cops to arrive. I wait, and I wait, and I wait.

No-one is coming.

"Now, would you like a gown?" Kevin asks, "we have a selection of medical-standard overcoats and suits here at the circus, in order to retain complete client security," he directs this statement at the audience as if he is giving a pitch to one of his business partners.

As if Magda isn't laying behind him, about to be chopped and brutalised into shreds.

My blood curdles.

I want to rip his face off.

"That won't be necessary," the woman says, in a strong, eastern-European accent. Her eyes gleam.

"A woman who doesn't mind getting her hands dirty… I love it," Kevin winks, giving her that familiar smile that I always used to find so charming. That's the smile he gave me whenever he was winning me over. He'd always follow it up with kisses down my neck- the kind that made me quiver with excitement and feel weak at the knees.

"Without further ado, ladies and gentlemen," Kevin continues, waving a long arm in a grand gesture, "I bring to you, the…"

I don't know what it is that makes him suddenly look at me.

Maybe it's just the way he side-steps to clear the stage and tilts his head so that his eyes flit into my direction, a movement that is frozen stiff as his gaze falls upon me.

A low hum of chatter ensues from the audience. The sleek-haired woman frowns in confusion.

"…sorry, ladies and gents, I just…" Kevin trails off uncertainly, never taking his eyes off of me. "Just… just enjoy the act…" he hastily rushes off of the stage towards me, to yet another roar of vile, sickening applause and cheers.

My chest tightens, my body rigid as I watch the woman grin evilly and select the long, shiny kitchen knife from the table. More tears pool in my eyes and a sharp pang of pain winds me straight in the stomach as I hear the first of my friend's agonising screams.

Without a word, Kevin roughly takes the handles of my wheelchair and pushes me back out the way I came, away from Magda's blood-curdling shrieks and the delighted squeals of the audience.

I begin to struggle again, my wrists and ankles jerking, my heart thundering hard and fast inside my chest.

When we get outside of the doors again, I can finally hear my own voice. It has been reduced to a pathetic, gravelly scratch of a croak, but it doesn't stop me from sobbing, pleading, and begging for him to do something, to save Magda.

The corridor is empty. Kevin wheels me down a short way, then turns me, kneeling down in front of me. Bewildered, I frantically scan his face, my pupils flitting madly across every inch and crevice of his features. Upon closer inspection, I notice silvery scars across his eyebrow and his chin, hidden underneath a thin sheen of glistening sweat. He is wearing that ridiculous top hat, but even with his head concealed, I can see that his hair has been shaven.

"What the fuck is this, Kevin?" I try to scream, but once again, my vocal chords are strained. He places his hands on my upper arms, and I recoil at his touch as if his palms are made of molten lava. I'm not even shocked when he manages to look hurt at this response.

"Nancy… what are you doing here?" he asks, his face and voice softening with concern. He glances around him, and his eyes become glassy with tears. Just like that, within seconds, it's as though I am staring at a different man. I wonder if my brain is playing tricks on me, and I'm confused. Surely this isn't that same evil, nasty fucker I just witnessed out in the ring.

"I came looking for you," I rasp, my chest aching with every breath. "I thought something awful had happened to you…"

Kevin stares at me and chews his lip as if something is worrying him. As if there is something he wants to say but can't.

"You have to save my friend," I sob. "Out there… that's my friend, she's been helping me find you… please…"

As I plead, he is shaking his head slowly. He bows his head.

"I can't help her, Nance…"

For a split second, I stare at him, my eyes wide. I expect him to burst out laughing, tell me it's all a sick joke, or smooth it over with another of his bullshit excuses.

But it never comes.

Another agonising scream echoes from within the stadium, the sound of it bouncing off the walls of the corridor.

My face falls. "No… no, you have to Kevin… you have to…" I cry, "please…" I don't think I've ever cried so hard. Every inch of me hurts.

Kevin purses his lips. He pushes his hand behind my head and strokes the base of my neck with a thumb. "I can't save her, Nance…" he whispers, "but I can save you. Just like I saved myself."

I scream then, and this time the noise comes out as a deafening wail, tearing through the grimy corridor.

My husband stands up then and continues wheeling me back down the passage, quickening his pace. I continue to shout until I'm sure I'll pass out. But he never stops, his echoing footsteps drumming rhythmically across the floor like a pulsing heartbeat.

He never turns back.

Not even when an earth-shattering shriek blasts down the hall towards us, piercing my ears like razor blades, sending a cold shiver down my spine so that goosebumps erupt out over my clammy skin.

Something tells me that it's Magda.

My blood runs cold.

Magda is dead.

I feel it in my bones.

But I have no time to grieve, as a thick, jagged metal blade is suddenly pulled out from nowhere and pushed to the side of my neck, nicking the skin.

My mouth shuts, and silence falls upon me.

I open my puffy, sodden eyes.

The black-haired girl, the other ring-leader from earlier, is standing in front of me, a stern look on her face. But she doesn't look directly at me, just poises her knife against my flesh, her pale hand gripping onto the hilt so tightly that her knuckles are a bright white. Instead, she looks over me, glaring indignantly at Kevin, a sight which might be comical in other circumstances, given that they are both dressed as circus ring leaders.

Shivering, I chew my lip nervously and blink away painful tears, digging my fingernails into my palms, my neck quivering against the sharp metal point.

"What is going on, Kevin?" the woman asks him, lowering her voice.

Kevin doesn't speak at first, as he usually does when he has been caught out.

Never did I ever imagine I'd ever be on the other end of it, though.

I almost giggle maniacally at the idea.

Me? The other woman?

Hysterical.

He whispers something then that I cannot make out. Every part of my body tenses up tightly, and I hold my breath, unable to focus on anything else apart from the knife that threatens my jugular. As always, Kevin appears to have wormed his way out of whatever the hell is going on because the woman reluctantly withdraws the blade.

I exhale.

Sundance

My sister has always told me that siblings are the closest family you can have. She says that brothers and sisters have psychic abilities and have this deep-rooted spiritual connection that can withstand anything. Apparently, it's something to do with being the most genetically similar (even though we technically have different mothers.) Naturally, as a kid, I always believed her. But it's as though, the older I get, the more sceptical I grow of Faith and all of her weird superstitions.

However, there are moments when I see a glimmer of truth in her theory.

It's about midnight, and I can sense it in my bones that my sister is angry. That's an understatement- Faith doesn't get angry- she gets enraged, furious…

As I cradle Beau, my skinny forearms straining under her weight, I feel tension stirring in the air, like the atmosphere warning a storm. I glance at the clock on the wall.

Almost 12 am.

Anxiously I nibble on my lower lip and stare back down into the baby's face. Drool glistens like a slug trail over her misshapen chin.

I grimace.

The child is still awake, and I know from experience that she will screech the house down if I even attempt to put her into bed… so it looks like there is absolutely no hope of slipping off upstairs to escape whatever rage my sister will bring home with her.

Fantastic.

As predicted, just a few moments later, I hear the front door swing open with such force that the wooden panels smack hard into the wall. The noise startles me, and I almost drop Beau, who furrows her brow at the disturbance.

"I know the feeling, kid…" I mutter under my breath with a sigh, shifting uncomfortably on my bar stool.

Her voice blurred slightly through the kitchen wall where I sit; Faith's voice crashes through the quiet of the house.

"YOU TELL HIM THAT IF HE DOESN'T FIND HER, THAT'S IT. HE'LL BE IN THE SHOW, AND I'LL KILL HIM MYSELF."

Wincing, Beau, and I exchange looks.

Two seconds later, the kitchen door blasts open, and Faith stomps in, still dressed in her sparkly circus outfit, her thigh-high boots clicking furiously against the tiles. Her bright green eyes twinkle angrily, her fists balled tightly by her sides. Kevin trails behind her, his face pale as though he has seen a ghost.

"What the hell is going on?" I wonder out loud.

Faith comes straight up to me and effortlessly snatches Beau out of my arms. Her face softens as she holds her up to her face and plants a soft kiss on her head. "Oh my beautiful girl, mummy has missed you so much…"

Beau babbles back, clearly overjoyed.

The two of them have a bizarrely unbreakable bond, despite Beau only being born a few weeks ago and the fact that Faith isn't actually her mother at all. In fact, I was wrong about my sister. I could never imagine her as a motherly figure, even though she raised me since she was just a teenager. But yet, here she is, her anger instantly dissolved, replaced instead by pure adoration for a raw-meat-eating, mutant infant.

I turn to Kevin and raise an eyebrow searchingly, waiting for an answer to my question. He groans and takes off his ridiculous top hat, revealing the thick, ugly scar that covers his scalp. The sight of it turns my stomach.

"Well?" I push on, folding my arms.

Before Kevin can speak, Faith cuts in. "Kevin here is having second thoughts," she snaps indignantly, bouncing Beau on her hip.

"I'm not having second thoughts for God's sake!" he protests in reply, rubbing his forehead, "she's the mother of my kids, Faith…"

Faith throws her hair back and laughs sarcastically, "oh, so, therefore, because she is the great and wonderful Kevin's wife, she is an exception to the rule? You'll risk ruining our work, ruining our family for one woman from your old life?"

Suddenly, it clicks in my head what must have happened. One of the women at the pub… who went off with Dawn… that must have been Kevin's wife… and Kevin must have seen her at the circus.

"I did tell you about this earlier," I remind Faith curtly, "in the car."

"This is a true test of your loyalty Kevin," Faith says, ignoring me, flashing him a piercing glare. "If you really are as dedicated to our work, building our family, making this world a better place by ridding it of vicious monsters who abuse animals…"

"I am!" he shouts suddenly, irritation flashing in his pupils.

Frosty silence.

No-one shouts at Faith and gets away with it.

But then again, I've never seen Faith warm to anyone the way she has warmed to Kevin over the last half a year. It's strange to think of how badly she used to abuse him. Now, I wouldn't even be surprised if she loved him as much as she loves me.

"Then you know what you need to do," Faith hisses under her breath. "Tomorrow, she *will* be on the show. You understand?"

Kevin swallows uncomfortably and slowly shakes his head. "There must be another way…"

I'm not Kevin's biggest fan by any stretch of the imagination; however, when I see the sadness reflected in his eyes, I find myself feeling sorry for him.

That's what separates Faith and me. That's what severs our so-called spiritual connection.

I can't help but have empathy for other people, whereas my sister is stone cold.

"What do you suggest? We let her go?" barks Faith. "She'll go to the police, and we'll all go down. Is that what you want?"

Wordlessly, Kevin shakes his head. "No…"

"Or shall we let her live here, in our home? How's that going to work exactly?" she demands, "I thought you wanted to be with me?"

My mouth falls open then.

Rumours have been circulating the walls of the house, and I had a hunch that there was something more between Faith and Kevin, but it has never been admitted out loud.

Faith has never been romantic with anybody.

Not because she can't.

She's extremely beautiful and can hypnotise men with a mere bat of her eyelashes. But underneath the hard exterior, she's also very broken.

She never wanted to fall in love or feel for anyone.

Until Kevin broke out of his cage, held her at knife-point, then proceeded to slash her half to death. Long, silvery scars still stain her arms and shoulders like tiger stripes.

Only my sister could convince someone she'd brutally tortured and imprisoned to reconsider going to the police. Only my sister could fall for a man who had practically skinned one of her forearms.

"I *do*," Kevin insists then, stepping toward her. "But Nancy is my wife… how can I just stand by and let her die?"

Faith looks stung.

"Look," I intervene then, putting my arm around my sister and stroking her shoulder comfortingly, "maybe there is another alternative…"

Both of their heads snap towards me then, their eyes gazing at me expectantly.

"Pig could use an assistant, especially now we have the farm and the circus," I offer. "He could train her up. That way, she isn't dead, she's helping the cause…"

Although he doesn't say anything, I register a flicker of hope crossing Kevin's expression. He glances back at Faith, waiting to gauge her reaction.

My suggestion is a long shot, and I am fully expecting her to have one of her infamous meltdowns. If it was anybody else, I'm sure that's exactly what would happen. Kevin would be a dead man walking.

So, I'm completely flabbergasted when, to my shock and surprise, she simply scoffs and rolls her eyes. "Fine, whatever."

Kevin smiles and wraps her tightly in an embrace.

I stand back and take in the scene for a moment.

The perfect fucked-up family.

My murderous sister, her batshit crazy lover, and the deformed baby. And if you think it can't get any more twisted, it's highly likely that the reason Beau is so… distorted is that Kevin kicked the shit out of her biological mother when she was pregnant.

Dysfunctional is an understatement.

"Get on the phone to Fern now," Faith instructs Kevin sharply, stubbornly refusing to hug him back, even though I'm sure I detect the slight quiver of a smile in the corners of her mouth.

"On it," Kevin replies softly, pecking her on the forehead.

As he obediently trots off out of the room, I turn to my sister and cock my head. "What's Fern done now?" I sigh.

She laughs humourlessly and lowers Beau so that she is laying in the perfect nest of her arms. I see that the child is finally, at long last, sound asleep.

"We had an escape," Faith says bitterly. "All Fern's fault."

I visualise the hideous scars that warp Fern's face and grimace. He was already on his last strike.

Faith seems to read my mind.

"He's got until morning to sort it out," she growls under her breath, "or I'm going to kill the useless fucker myself."

Addison

I've been running on pure adrenaline for the last few hours, but it's finally beginning to peter out. Now, all I can do is blink desperately, repeatedly, certain that this is all just one horrific nightmare, and if I can only wake myself up, it'll all be over. I'll wake up, twisted hopelessly in sweat-soaked sheets, my heart pounding, my arms covered in goosebumps.

Maybe one of the scariest things was the fact that I didn't have a fucking clue what the hell was going on. One moment, I was pelting down a hallway, running as fast as I could from the distant thud of oncoming footsteps. The next, I was in a lift, praying to God for any kind of mercy.

And, extremely briefly, I'd thought my prayers were answered when I stumbled into that control room, and I came across the handsome Indian boy with the frightened eyes. He'd let me go. I thought I'd found an ally.

Now, of course, I realise that he was practically feeding me to the wolves.

As I slipped out of the room, I was immediately hit with the thick stench of sweat, mixed with booze, mixed with something much more sinister… burnt hair…burnt flesh.

I strained my eyes to see into the packed space, although it was desperately dark.

The entire place was flooded with the loud hum of chatter, laughter, cheers, and an eerily jaunty circus track that made bile crawl up my throat.

I followed the Indian boy's instructions and shrank down against the walls, hoping to somehow blend in, desperately scanning the pitch blackness for even a shadow of a vacant seat.

That's when I saw it.

At first, I'd just assumed the audience was watching some kind of performance, but I'd been too focused on hiding to actually look at what it was down in the ring.

I had to slap a hand to my mouth to stop myself from screaming, although I don't think anyone would have heard me over the ruckus anyway. My legs unsteady, wobbling beneath me, I staggered forwards like a baby deer, my lungs pregnant with dread.

Magda.

It was definitely her; I could spot her distinctive features from a mile away. After all, I'd spent much of the last six months with the girl. She looked as though she were locked in an incubator- the kind they put premature babies inside, her feet and head hanging limply out the ends.

Her face was screwed up like a newborn baby's too, filled with horror.

Then I noticed the tray beside her and the faint glint of the metal blades that lay across them.

Desperately, I wracked my brain. Magda and I hadn't always seen eye to eye, but when you spend so much time with someone, you can't help but grow attached. But what could I do? It was me, apparently up against a sea of humans who apparently had no moral query with what was going on in the ring.

I wondered then if it was a play. A prank, or a joke of some sort. Albeit a pretty fucked up one, but why else would there be so many people just sitting there, watching?

"Have you placed your bet?"

A sudden, low purr of a voice tickled my ear then, hot, stale steam resting in the crook of my neck. Startled, I spun around, my fingers trembling madly as I caught sight of the tall, skinny man standing behind me.

In each hand, he held a plastic cup of amber liquid, a thin layer of foam topping each.

Unable to form any kind of coherent sentence, I shook my head.

The man shrugged and smiled, "it *is* pricey. Considering you spend so much on the ticket alone," he paused and licked his lip. I didn't like how close he was to me, although I supposed I wouldn't hear him over the crowd if he was any further away.

"Want a beer?" he asked with a smile.

I swallowed and forced myself to nod, even though I couldn't think of anything worse. I told myself that I'd only pretend to drink it. That's what the Indian man in the control room told me to do, and I had no other option but to trust him.

"I'm Marcus," he said, handing me one of the plastic cups, which I took, trying hard to conceal my shaking hands. He nodded to his right, into the hot, stagnant sea of bodies sitting on the seats surrounding the ring. "Why don't we sit down?"

Obediently I followed him.

Finally, my eyes were beginning to adjust to the darkness as I entered the pulsing crowd and eventually slumped down into the seat that Marcus indicated.

At that moment, at the front of the stage, a man with a familiar face dressed as a circus ring leader boomed through a microphone attached to a headset, proudly announcing the winner of some sort of auction.

My face twisted into an uneasy frown, and I felt my stomach churn. Instinctively, I lifted the cup to my lips and took just a gulp of the beer. Once I'd had that first taste, it's as though my senses all caught up at once, and I realised just how thirsty I was.

"I like a woman who can drink," Marcus chuckled in my ear, nudging me. He nodded towards my cup, which I noticed, with much dismay, was now completely empty. As I stared, a floating spotlight cast a glow over my bloodied hands, which I jerked quickly to my sides, out of Marcus's sight.

But I was too late.

"Hey… what's your name?" he asked, cocking his head.

A roar of applause erupted then, and a tall, pretty woman waded through the audience towards the staircase that led down to the ring. My gaze was roughly torn away from her though, as I felt Marcus's hand on my elbow. When I turned back, he was staring at me intently, his eyes wide and sincere.

"What happened to your hands?" he asked, lowering his voice, gently lifting my fingers up into the light.

I opened my mouth, but no words would come.

Before I could stop them, my eyes filled with tears, and a huge, ugly sob formed in my throat, suffocating me.

To my surprise, he hooked an arm around me and pulled me close to him. The pleasant scent of his aftershave filtered up into my nostrils, and I found myself grow rigid and stiff in his unwelcome embrace.

"You're one of the girls, aren't you?" he whispered in my ear.

I didn't move, frozen with fear.

"Listen to me," he whispered, "we can't make it too obvious..." he lifted his head and glanced around suspiciously. The people surrounding us were all glued to the ring, transfixed. He lifted his hands to his tie and straightened it, I suppose in an attempt to appear casual, before he leaned his head towards mine again. "Listen, my name is not really Marcus. I am Detective Elliot Taylor, undercover... suspicious things have been going down around here for a long time... I can help you."

I pursed my lips. The booming voice of the ringleader continued somewhere in the background, blurring with the noise of the rowdy audience to form one obnoxious blur of sound.

Elliot delved into his pocket and pulled out an ID badge, discreetly positioning it so that I could see the face. I squinted down at the surface of the card. Sure enough, there was a picture of the guy alongside the name Elliot Taylor.

A sharp breath of relief escaped me, just as a horrific scream tore through the air.

My heart skipped a beat.

My head snapped forwards. My eyes fell upon the stage.

Instantly, I was filled with monumentous regret.

Blood.

A dark crimson stream poured from one of Magda's bare feet, whilst her naked body convulsed madly in the incubator type box, her face warped, eyes rolling into the back of her head.

Vomit surged up through my chest and erupted from my lips, spilling onto my already filthy lap.

The pretty woman from the audience stood proudly, a bloodied knife in one hand, the other holding something tiny up in the air.

No... surely not.

But my fears were quickly confirmed as I watched on in horror. The woman dropped the small object onto the top of the glass box, in plain sight where Magda could see. Then, slowly, clearly savouring the frantic cheers from the audience, the sadistic woman knelt down, picked up Magda's other foot, and began sawing, this time at the ankle.

"NO!" I shrieked, the residue of vomit left on my lips dribbling down my chin. Elliot grabbed my elbow then and lifted me up. People around us were starting to stare, apparently repulsed by a bit of puke, as opposed to the innocent woman being mutilated on the stage in front of them.

"Put this on," Elliot whispered, taking off his suit jacket and draping it around my shoulders.

"We have to help her; you need to get back up!" I sobbed inaudibly into his ear as he pulled me along like a helium-filled balloon on a string.

Elliot turned to me grimly as we reached the aisle beside the rows of seats and gripped both of my arms. "What is your name?" he asked firmly.

"Addie…" I gasped, hardly able to breathe through my tears.

"Addie, you need to get your shit together, or we are both in deep crap," he hissed. "Let's just get to the car; then we can save your friend, okay?"

I nodded and sniffed back the tears as best I could, roughly wiping my face with the sleeve of his jacket.

Elliot entwined his hand in mine, threading our fingers together, gripping onto me tightly. Shakily, I followed closely behind him up the staircase, gnawing hard on the insides of my mouth as I desperately tried not to burst into fresh floods of tears. The sounds of Magda's agonised screams continued to rip through the unbearably stuffy atmosphere, chilling me to my bones, drilling hard into my core.

We reached the top of the stairs, where a couple of tall, armed men guarded a set of double doors. Elliot quickly nodded at one of them, who grunted in response and moved aside to let us past.

Even as we slipped out into a wide corridor, and Elliot had briskly marched me a good few metres down the passage, the sounds of Magda's cries taunted me. Her screams echoed like ghosts floating round and round in my head, even as we finally reached the end of the hall and got to another set of double doors.

More men stood there, both of them armed as well.

This time, neither of them moved aside.

"The wife's had too much," Elliot said apologetically, "had too much beer, didn't you, love?" he turned to me, nudging my arm fondly. I kept my head bowed and pulled the jacket tighter around me as I felt the heavy stares of the guards boring into the top of my head.

"We need to see of both of your IDs," one of the armed men responded, his voice flat, bored almost as if he was working the graveyard shift at a supermarket.

Elliot slipped his hand into his pocket, and I felt my body tense.

"Oh shit… sweetheart, do you have your circus ID?"

Circus ID? What the fuck is that?

I shook my head, hoping my withdrawn behaviour would convince the men that I was indeed completely wasted.

"She must've dropped it inside, sorry about that," Elliot tutted, rubbing my back. "But we do really need to get home; she's been throwing up all over the…"

"Sir, we can't let her go without seeing her ID," one of the men interrupted curtly.

A wave of upset wracked my body, and I felt a thick knot of a sob get stuck in my throat.

Don't cry. Don't cry.

"Maybe we can settle this another way," Elliot suggested cooly.

Briefly, I looked up through the curtain of my hair, expecting to see Elliot hand over a wad of cash. Instead, he withdrew something small, too small to be money from his shirt pocket, and slipped it inside one of the men's pockets.

I bit my lip and held my breath nervously, certain that at any moment, one of the guards would grab me by the hair and yank me roughly back inside the hellish confines of the stagnant stadium, where my final memories of the earth would be of poor Magda, and her harrowing pleas for mercy.

One of the men grunted, and they both moved aside. I lowered my head again and let Elliot lead me out through the doors into another long hallway. We walked in silence, my lungs like lead inside my chest from trying not to break down.

"Just need to get in the lift," Elliot muttered to himself as we reached a pair of metal doors. He tapped in the numbers on the control pad, and then we waited. It felt like an entire eternity as we stood there in deafening quiet, me shifting nervously from foot to foot, the stench of puke violently attacking my nostrils. I daren't look over my shoulder, but a peculiar prickling on my back made me paranoid that we were being followed.

A loud ding signalled the elevator's arrival at long last, and Elliot ushered me inside. I kept my head lowered. He never let go of me. I didn't know whether or not to be glad of it.

After a short ride in the elevator, another ding sounded, and then the metal doors slid open with a clang. Clenching my lips together, I allowed Elliot to guide me down yet another hallway.

Another man sat on a stool at a final set of doors, apparently engrossed in whatever he was doing on his phone. He barely even looked up as we passed, much to my relief.

And then we were out in the open again. A cold, pleasant rush of air washed over me, and the damp, squishy ground beneath my feet reminded me that I had no shoes on. I expected Elliot to break away from me and give me some space, but instead, he seemed to cling even tighter, like a vice clamping down harder around my body.

"Where are we going?" I whispered.

Elliot fished a set of keys out of his trouser pocket. "My car is over here somewhere…" he clicked the button with his thumb, and a pair of headlights suddenly illuminated the pitch black of the night. "Here we are…"

He led me up to the passenger seat, opened the door, and pretty much hoisted me up into the seat. My teeth began to chatter then, the air suddenly not quite so refreshing. I flinched as he slammed the car door shut, and the locks came on with a jolt, startling me.

It's like the cold night has sobered me, not from the measly pint of cheap beer, but from the trauma. As I sit here on the leather passenger seat, listening to the silence, the horrific images of the night flash through my brain like bolts of lightning.

Adrenaline feels like it is rapidly leaking out of me as I exhale, seeping through my pores as nervous sweat drenches every inch of my clammy skin.

I flinch again as the driver's door is wrenched open, and I let out an involuntary yelp as I mistake Elliot for one of the scary-looking men holding guns at the doors. When his face comes back into view, I giggle manically, my heart pounding at a million beats a minute in my chest.

"I- I- I thought you were someone else…" I manage, as he frowns at me.

Elliot slides into his seat and shuts the car door, once again activating all of the locks. He starts up the engine without speaking.

His sudden reluctance to speak chills me.

The car reverses slowly, then turns, the golden light of the headlamps revealing the vast green fields that stretch out all around us. I hug my upper arms tightly, my teeth beginning to chatter.

"You'd be better off, you know," Elliot says suddenly, just as he turns off out of an inconspicuous gap in some hedges, out onto a deserted country road.

I turn to look at him, confused. "S-s-sorry?"

"You said you thought I was someone else," Elliot replies casually. "So, I said that you'd be better off if I was."

It takes a moment for the words to sink in. The familiar fingernails of dread begin scraping incessantly at my insides again.

"Pardon?" I ask again, determined that I must have misheard. I'm desperate that I must have misheard. Because if I understand what he is saying…

Elliot suddenly leans in, diverting his big, dark eyes away from the road for a second to meet mine. He grins, exposing a set of pearly white teeth. "You'd be better off if I was someone else, sweetheart," he tells me, "because I am your worst fucking nightmare."

Abdul

I now realise why Faith was feeling so generous yesterday, letting me go to the house for a proper wash, a bed, and a decent meal.

Obviously not as some kind of compensation for fucking up my entire life, murdering my friends, my girlfriend, and permanently traumatising me… oh no.

Of course not!

Faith knew that I would need strength for a long, gruelling shift, working all through the night, first off managing the control panel, only then to be immediately ushered into the stadium itself to clean up the foul remnants of the grim performance.

And as if that wasn't shit enough, I have Fern sprinting in and out of the place, wailing at the top of his lungs that Faith is going to chop his bollocks off for letting some girl escape.

Better him than me.

They still haven't found her.

I don't want to get my hopes up, but I'm praying she somehow managed to escape after I let her out into the stadium, and sometime soon, the police will bust this shit hole open.

Maybe I can write a book about the experience and get a movie deal while I'm at it. Forgive me for being cold, but fuck it, why not cash in on the trauma? May as well.

I begin cleaning the ring first, as that is where the bulk of the mess is. I have learned over time that blood is easier to clean sooner rather than later, and there is a fucking lot of it drenching the stage area. I have already had to change the water in the mop bucket about ten times already, and still, it's nowhere near done.

I'll be lucky if I get the entire place cleaned even just an hour before my next shift managing the control panel.

"Pig!"

I stop what I'm doing and look up. My back aches in protest as I stretch upwards and glance up from the ring to the staircase, where Faith is nimbly descending the steps. She's dressed in a long flowing skirt and a figure-hugging top that reveals a sliver of her flat stomach. Since Kevin somehow managed to get into the family, it's like those hideous matching tracksuits they used to wear have been abandoned. In a way, it makes them scarier because they appear somewhat normal on the surface, a standard exterior concealing sinister, evil secrets. Behind Faith trails, another woman with a bowed head, and Arlo marches behind her with the barrel of his gun pressed into her back.

Frowning, I rub the base of my spine and wince.

"Hurry up!" Faith turns to snap at the unfamiliar blonde behind her and briskly crosses the stage towards me as if she is in a hurry. "Pig! This is your new charge."

I stare as she gestures behind her, and the blonde woman comes forward.

She has a pretty face, which is somehow familiar, although I am unsure how. Her cheeks are stained with tears, her eyes big and puffy, her head lolling to the side, no doubt where she has been beaten, or something equally as awful.

"Pardon?" I ask, unsure if I understand what Faith is getting at.

"She's going to be your assistant, help you out with your jobs," Faith replies impatiently. "She is your responsibility. In fact, you are each other's responsibility. If either one of you gives us any shit, I will blow both your brains out. We clear?"

Grimly, I nod. "Crystal."

Faith grunts, "and if you see the woman that escaped, you sound the alarm straight away. Alright?"

I'm surprised when Faith and Arlo saunter off together almost immediately, apparently deep in conversation as they leave the new girl and me alone in the blood-soaked, underground stadium. It seems like they are really, genuinely beginning to trust me, a fact which shines a small glimmer of hope on my otherwise dismal situation.

Unlike when I first came to this place, the blonde woman is clothed, which I appreciate. It would have been a lot more awkward if she was naked.

Every silver lining and all that…

"It's your first day, so you can pick up plastic cups and rubbish," I say, nodding vaguely towards a roll of rubbish bags that sit on top of my modest cleaning trolley. "You got a name?"

She doesn't say anything, just stands, rigid, rooted to the spot, her lower lip trembling, and her hands clasped together. There's a small wound on the side of her neck, the size of a papercut, surrounded by a purple halo of bruising. Her eyes are wide as she glances around the place, her pupils flitting nervously, frantically.

I don't blame her for being scared.

Sighing heavily, I put down the handle of my mop and walk slowly towards her. I sense her tense up even more then, no doubt suspicious of me.

"Look," I say softly, "I know you're frightened. But if you don't do the work and play ball, you'll meet a worse fate…"

Her eyes widen, and reluctantly she reaches for the roll of rubbish bags. Still, she doesn't speak.

"I guess you must already know the kind of thing that goes on here…" I nod grimly at the grisly streaks and the shallow pools of blood that decorate the ground.

Silence.

I pick up the handle of the mop and busy myself cleaning. The poor woman is probably in shock. I contemplate telling her how I woke up in a cramped van full of shit, sweat, puke, and naked bodies and then had to sleep in an outdoor cage and slice up human corpses.

Unsurprisingly, I decide against it.

"My name is Nancy," she randomly announces, maybe after a few minutes of quiet. "What's your name... your real name?" she adds.

The name triggers a flicker of recognition in my head. "Nancy? I remember you. Your Kevin's wife... you used to come to the office with the little boy and the little girl..." I trail off, suddenly feeling completely ridiculous. I sound like I'm chatting to an old acquaintance that I bumped into in the pasta aisle at Sainsbury's, for fuck's sake. "I'm Abdul," I finish quickly.

Nancy nods, anxiously nibbling at her lower lip. I watch her shuffle around, cautiously picking up the discarded plastic cups, crisp packets, and fag butts, as if anyone of them could be a bomb about to detonate.

"Why are you here?" I ask her, forcing myself to get back on with the mopping.

She shakes her head, her lips curling downwards as she sighs and picks up three more cups off of the ground. "Because I'm a fucking idiot," she mutters, her voice sour with misery. "Came here looking for Kevin when he disappeared. There was a group of us looking for you all... we stopped at this pub..."

I stop then, "looking for *us*?"

Mirroring my movements, she also stops for a moment and stands upright, looking me up and down. "Five of us. The police thought you'd all run off of your own accord... there were texts...."

My stomach curdles. "Texts?"

Nancy nods, "saying you'd all decided to leave. But we knew something wasn't right. So we've been bombarding the police, putting out posters and a load of stuff online... we were getting nowhere, so we decided to come and look for you ourselves."

"All for Kevin?" I ask faintly.

She pauses uneasily, and her pupils flit to the floor. I sense that she is holding something back.

"Did someone come for me?" I ask hoarsely. I imagine my brother... my parents... my best friends...

When Nancy nods, I feel my heart plummet into the pit of my stomach.

"Who?" I croak.

"Priya, your cousin, right?" Nancy asks. "I have no idea where she is. I only know that Magda…" she trails off, and her face crumples at the memory as if she is about to break down.

But I'm too mystified, too busy absorbing her words to respond to her grief.

Priya?

The name causes my lungs to restrict, as if they are shrivelling to half their size, rapidly deflating balloons in my chest.

"Priya is not my cousin…" I say slowly, returning back to my mopping in a feeble attempt to distract myself.

Out of everyone in my life, Priya was the only one to come looking for me?

I don't know whether to be hurt or relieved.

Nancy frowns, "yes, she is. She told us she was."

"Priya is a girl I dated years ago…" I say vaguely, hoping that Nancy doesn't pry any further. Before she can, I decide to give her the low down.

"There are a few different jobs we are expected to do," I say quietly, still reeling from the news that Priya came looking for me. "At the farm, and also here, at the circus."

"And you've been here… all this time?" Nancy asks.

I nod, suddenly not in the mood to talk. "Faith… that's the woman who brought you down here… she's the head honcho. She has a family… they think that God wants them to kill people who aren't vegans."

Nancy's laughter catches me off guard. I flinch.

"Don't laugh!" I hiss, widening my eyes.

"You cannot be serious?" Nancy asks incredulously. "So, they're planning on murdering the vast majority of the world?"

"It's not murdering apparently," I explain, nervously scanning all around us, as if any moment now Faith is going to leap out of the shadows and shun us for our blasphemy. "They use the bodies for… *other* purposes… apparently to make the earth a better place…"

"Are you actually fucking kidding me?" Nancy raises her voice, her mouth falling open. "How the fuck is torturing people in a weird, sick circus for money in the name of making the world a better place?"

Brow furrowed, I take a step forward and lower my voice, "you need to stop," I warn. "If they hear you, you're screwed."

"I already am!" Nancy shouts, tossing the rubbish bag to the ground. "Abdul, what are we going to do?!"

Groaning, I shake my head and shrug hopelessly. I don't speak because I don't think Nancy wants to hear the answer to that question. I'm not a fan of it myself.

We work mostly in silence then, only occasionally one of us speaks to provide instruction or ask a question.

Normally, I might have made more of an effort to talk. I'd have appreciated another person to speak to who didn't constantly refer to me as a pig.

However, Nancy's words chill me, every syllable still scorching into the top of my spine, causing a sheen of goosebumps to erupt out all over my skin.

Priya came looking for me.

My stalker followed me here.

Sundance

Yawning, I stride down the passage, gripping the cool, metal can in my right hand. It's ridiculously early in the morning, and I didn't sleep well. Between the two of them, the babies kept me awake intermittently all night, and by the time I finally nodded off, my sister was banging on everyone's door, getting us all up for Operation: Find escaped girl, or we're all totally and utterly fucked.

Everyone is out in pairs, searching the surrounding woodland and fields, all of the closest buildings, and Ziggy and Star are even going to town to talk to the police. That's just how dangerously powerful my sister is- she's even got the local police force on her side.

It's unlikely that the escaped woman has gotten very far, given that the circus is so desolate… even if she had gotten out of the building, she would easily get lost, and there wouldn't be anywhere for her to hide.

But, of course, nothing is impossible. And my sister will leave no stone unturned until the girl is found. She will never let anything jeopardize the family and the businesses that she has spent so long building, least of all a rogue victim who managed to alert the authorities.

Personally, I find myself indifferent.

Clearing my throat, I delve into my trouser pocket as I come to a stop in front of a wide, heavy door and fish out the metal key.

I figure that this can't go on forever. And so long as I'm too much of a pussy to put a stop to it myself, my life is just a passive, meaningless, drug-infused blur. At least if they put me in prison, I'll get some comfort from knowing we're being served justice.

I take a deep breath, unlock the door, then give it a firm shove with my shoulder to open it. It creaks open, and I pause for a moment, wrinkling my nose. As I suspected, it stinks.

Instead of being deployed to roam the surrounding fields with a gun, Faith asked me to come down here, the room with the cages.

She wants me to speak to the other women they've got locked up, see if I can get any helpful information out of them.

"What good will that do?" I'd asked grumpily when she gave me the instructions, rubbing the sleep from my tired eyes.

"You're gay, women seem to trust you easily," my sister had replied bluntly, "and besides, you can't shoot for shit."

Gingerly, I step around the door and slip into the room, the stagnant air pregnant with fear. Black dog cages line the front and back wall, all but three empty. I run my tongue along the front of my teeth and wrack my brain for what to say.

Because, honestly, what can you say?

How am I supposed to get them to trust me when we're looking at each other through the bars of a cage?

First, I see a naked, long-haired girl, curled up in fetal position, apparently asleep in one of the cages facing the door. Quietly, I move closer into the room and notice upon closer inspection the oddly coloured puddle surrounding her body. Even more disturbing, I see that there's a random bald patch at the side of her head, which I assume is from where Fern yanked her hair.

My eyes close, and I exhale, gulping back the bile that crawls up into my throat.

It's disgusting.

And this was supposed to be the least upsetting job.

Creeping into the cold silence of the room, a low, sniffling noise disturbs the eerie silence. I open my eyes and turn around to face the cage opposite, where a dark-skinned Asian woman is sitting in one of the far corners. She hugs her bare legs to her chest and leans up against the bars, her big, intense brown eyes staring up at me from the shadowy nest she makes with her knees.

"Hi," I greet her quietly, giving her what I hope is a friendly smile. Slowly, I move closer and sink to my knees so that we are just a metre apart, with only the metal bars dividing us. When I see the fear reflected in her irises, a stab of guilt impales my chest. I bite my tongue. "I'm so sorry about this…" I whisper, my face falling.

She lifts her head so that I can see her face, her eyes fixed firmly onto me, filled with rightful suspicion.

"What is this place?" she asks me so quietly that I can barely hear.

Before I came, Faith drummed what felt like hundreds of things to say to get the women on side and to get them to divulge any useful information about the one who escaped. Now I'm here; my mind is completely blank.

"It's not good," I admit feebly, bowing my head with shame.

"Why am I here?" I hear her squeak. "Am… am I going to die?"

I pause, then run my fingers through my hair, tension forming in tight knots inside my skull like tumours. "Bad luck," I tell her, finally. "Really bad luck."

"You can help me, right? You remember me from the pub, don't you?" she whispers. I sense her crawl forwards and feel the warmth of her breath radiating through the gaps in her prison.

Swallowing, I force myself to nod. "Maybe," I lie, unable to look at her. "Maybe I can if you can help me."

"I'll do anything," she whimpers, shuffling closer still towards me. "Please, I beg you. I won't tell anybody about any of this. I promise…"

My chest tightens. I clear my throat again and eventually coerce myself to meet her eye. A twinkle of hope in her pupil breaks my heart.

At that moment, I find myself wishing more than anything that I could be more like Faith. For her, empathy and other emotions are all optional.

She can be empathetic, but only if it suits her. She is capable of being emotional, but only when she has something to gain from it.

She has this magical ability to switch even the strongest feelings on and off like a tap.

It's what makes her so dangerous.

Then there's me, sitting here on the brink of tears because this woman I barely even know is begging me for mercy, which I know I cannot give her.

And yet, I'm too much of a pathetic, weak coward to do anything about it.

"Where did your friend go?" I ask, forcing an uncharacteristic roughness into my voice. "The one that escaped."

"I have no idea, I swear. I was passed out when it happened," she replies, "I only even know about it because Violet told me…" she pauses then and sticks a finger through the bars, gesturing to the long-haired girl in the cage opposite. "But please... will you still let me go?" she whines.

Before I can reply, another voice interjects, making us both glance towards the other end of the dingy room.

"I can't believe you lost her... fucking pathetic."

Frowning, I stand up and walk towards the source of the noise. Immediately, when I clasp eyes on the inhabitant of the far cage, I gasp in horror. The can of air freshener in my hand falls to the floor, clattering so loudly in the quiet of the cell that it makes me flinch.

"Oh, don't act like you're surprised," she spits irritably. Her dirty, clammy hands are threaded through the bars of the cage, her naked body grimy and smeared with faeces and blood. I smack a hand to my lips, completely repulsed. Her hair is matted and shiny with grease, but most horrifying of all is her blackened, bottomless eye sockets and the bloody tear stains that streak her cheeks. "You people did this to me," she grumbles.

Instinctively, I grit my teeth. I notice green and yellow trickles of puss also trickling from her gaping wounds, her eyelids clearly rife with infection.

"Don't tell him anything, Priya," she calls, "they have no intention of letting us go."

"What?" whimpers the Indian girl, "but I..."

"Do you know where the other girl went?" I ask, vainly attempting to sound firm. "I can make it worth your while."

The woman in front of me lets out a loud, high-pitched cackle that seeps right under my skin and chills me to the bone.

"That's got to be a joke, right? I can't fucking see dumb arse. You and your cronies ripped my fucking eyeballs out," she retorts angrily.

Groaning, I rub the side of my neck.

What a disaster.

"I might have an idea."

I spin around to see that the long-haired girl, Violet, is awake. With bleary eyes, she blinks at me, her features pinched, clearly pissed off.

"You have some information?" I ask, moving towards her, frankly relieved to get away from the girl with no eyes.

Violet nods, sucking in air as she gazes up at me intently. "But if you want to know, you need to get us water and food…" she coughs, a dry rasp escaping her lips.

"And underwear, and a fucking potty or something at least," chimes in the eyeless woman.

"And some baby wipes?" Priya adds weakly.

Violet's pupils bore into me as I take a brief moment to think it over. She's smart, I realise. I doubt she knows anything at all; how could she? None of them know the building or even the surrounding area. She knows I can't let them go, but she also knows that if there is even a shred of hope for them left, they need to eat and drink.

I nod. "Fair enough. I'll be right back."

I turn on my heel and make for the door.

"Some weed would be nice as well," I hear her add. "You stink of it."

Nancy

Every inch of me aches when the circus ring and the surrounding benches are finally clean. Every movement, no matter how slight, sends a sharp, searing pain shooting into my joints. I've lost my concept of time, but we've been working for hours.

"What now?" I moan, to nobody in particular, allowing myself to slump down on the bench.

I have never been so mentally and physically exhausted in my entire life.

Hours of hard labour and being trapped inside my own head, taunted by memories of last night, has drained me of any grain of energy I had left inside my weakened body. Now, I'm too depleted to even cry any more tears. Every time there is a flicker of anxiety in my bones, it dissolves just as quickly as it appears, as though my mind is already dead to the world.

"We should be able to rest for a little while," Abdul says grimly, wiping a layer of glistening sweat from his brow.

Right on cue, one of the side doors in the stadium opens, and Faith appears, followed closely by the tall thug that threatened me with a gun earlier on. It's unnerving how they just happen to float in at that moment, as if they have been hiding in the wings somewhere, always watching.

I swallow uneasily, instinctively balling my hands into agitated fists just at the sight of that smug, self-assured look that appears to permanently inhabit Faith's face.

She looks like the kind of woman who has never been told 'no.'

"Pig, Arlo is going to take you back to the house as a reward for your hard work, yet again," she barks across the room. "Get a night of good sleep."

Abdul and I exchange worried glances. He cocks his head in confusion, apparently troubled that she has only addressed him and not me.

"Not you," Faith says silkily, nodding towards me.

She stops her descent down the stairs as she reaches the aisle where I sit. Placing her hands on her hips, she narrows her eyes at me.

"If you're going to be Pig's assistant, I think it's best I give you a little taster of your duties."

I gulp and watch hopelessly as Abdul hesitantly trails up the stairs with Arlo. I can tell by the way his stare dithers and how he drags his feet that he feels terrible for leaving me. Maybe if I wasn't so fucking terrified, I'd appreciate his kindness.

Just as Abdul disappears into another of the doors, he flashes me a small, sympathetic smile. I attempt to return the gesture, with meagre results.

Once we're alone, I grit my teeth and finally succumb to meet Faith's unpleasant stare. A mischievous smile suddenly tugs at the corner of her lips, and I swear I can feel my soul leave my body...

...obviously too frightened to stick around for much longer.

Faith takes me out of the building.

She isn't visibly armed, but neither am I, and I don't fancy my chances up against her if I tried to fight. I'm weak from fatigue and hunger, and besides, I've never had to throw a punch in my life. In her line of work, I'd assume Faith has the opposite problem. So, like a little lap dog, I follow her obediently, through a narrow, clammy labyrinth of passages and elevators, until we are finally out in the open again.

Outside, it's cold, and the air has that crisp, smoky scent clinging to it. I shiver, my bare arms prickling in the icy breeze. The sky is a watery blue, slowly melting away into morning.

"Get in," Faith commands as we approach a rusty old vehicle, the kind that looks like a paedophile would use to lure in children off of the street.

I do as she says and slide into the passenger seat. She locks the door, then hastily strides around to the other side of the car, getting behind the wheel, and then starting up the questionable-sounding engine.

For the entire journey, Faith doesn't speak.

Needless to say, I don't attempt to strike up a conversation.

I debate hitting her whilst she is driving or scrabbling around for an impromptu weapon. However, the winter gloom still engulfs the desolate British countryside, and the car is hurtling so quickly down the empty road, I fear that a crash would be fatal for both of us.

So, instead, I just sit there, shifting uncomfortably in my seat.

With every second, my head throbs painfully as I simultaneously fight exhaustion and combat the ever-increasing dread that quickly spreads through each of my internal organs.

By the time we reach our destination, outside is still dark and gloomy, and the distant calls of birds are the only indication of dawn.

Faith swerves onto a driveway concealed behind hedges, parks up, and then switches off the engine. The car is immediately flooded by the interior light, the yellow glow illuminating that nasty grin of hers. I look away quickly, the mere sight of the evil glint in her iris sending crippling shivers down my spine.

"So, welcome to the farm!" Faith says cheerily, unclipping her seat belt. "This will be your new home."

I don't respond; just chew away at my bottom lip until I can taste blood. My stomach churns as I remember what Abdul told me about this place earlier on.

A human farm.

"Can I see Kevin?" I ask.

Instantly, I realise I have made an error, as my words fade quickly into the razor-sharp silence that towers like a brick wall between us. I chance a sideways glance at her.

She looks as though I have slapped her hard across the face.

"No, you cannot see Kevin," she replies sharply, after a few tense moments. "Kevin is with me now. He has repented for his previous life, and now he has joined with me and the family to carry out our important work."

I barely have any time to absorb what she has said as she swiftly opens up the car door and snaps at me to get out.

Back out in the open, the cold air cascades over me like a shower of icicles, bitterly stinging my cheeks. I follow Faith's orders, especially when I strain my eyes and realise that the farmhouse that stands in front of us appears to be completely isolated.

I'd have no hope if I tried to run.

There really is nowhere to hide.

Faith leads me up the driveway, up the front steps, and opens the front door. Inside, the house smells strongly of must, as if the place hasn't been lived in for a long time; however, a bright light exposes the hallway, a staircase, and some doors lining the passage walls.

Blinking, I look around me, disturbed by how perfectly normal and domestic the place looks.

"Come on," Faith says gruffly, weaving her skinny arm through mine and tugging me through the house like a dog on a leash, out into a tiled kitchen, then out of a back door into a miserable back garden.

It's like entering a graveyard.

A haunted one at that.

The troubling stench of decomposition relentlessly attacks my nostrils the moment I step out of the house, and over the wind, I hear the pitiful cries of a woman in the distance. I squint my eyes as the panic gnaws at my bones in a vain attempt to find the source of the noise and the smell.

Rattling cages and moans of pain also join the symphony of suffering.

"What is that?" I wonder out loud before I have the chance to stop myself.

"Cattle," Faith replies bluntly as if it were perfectly reasonable for cows to cry and moan in protest about being locked up. "It's a farm, remember?"

My breaths become sharp and painful, like shards of glass pumping in my lungs.

With my heart thumping so hard and so fast, I feel as though I am about to keel over and go into cardiac arrest.

Maybe that would be less painful than whatever this crazy bitch has in store for me.

She takes me into the wide, gaping mouth of another building, of which I can just about distinguish the outline of against the inky blue sky. It looms above us like a vicious monster, glowering down at me in cruel mockery.

Once inside, Faith turns on the lights and firmly closes the door behind us. I realise then that we're in some sort of high-ceilinged barn, made entirely of wooden planks which are, judging by the horrific odour, mostly damp and rotting.

I glance around, blinking silently at old, discarded hooks, lumps of rope, random pieces of furniture, and mechanical parts that are dotted around the dismal place.

My teeth chatter, the icy fingers of winter seeping in through the cracks of the decrepit structure.

Only then does Faith let go of me. Instinctively, I hug my upper arms in a feeble attempt to retain some warmth.

We stare at each other suspiciously for a moment, sizing one another up.

"Just know, you're only here because of Kevin," Faith tells me. "Apparently, he sees something good in you. He believes you are capable of repenting for your sins."

A vile taste teases the tip of my tongue. Pretty rich of my cheating fuck of a husband to make a comment about me repenting for *my* sins.

"My sins?" I repeat.

Faith nods solemnly. She pushes her jet black ringlets behind her ears and starts to pace, her long, flowing skirt swishing around her feet. "Humanity treats animals with unspeakable cruelty," she says.

Slowly, I shake my head. "But Faith… don't you see that what you're doing to humans *is* unspeakable cruelty?"

She scoffs and rolls her eyes. She reaches a rusted metal hook that is dangling from a wire on a pole. The thin line looks as though it will break at any moment. "No, it's not," she replies firmly, gently fingering the sharp edge of the hook. "Through our businesses, we generate cash, which is used to contribute to a world where *all* species are treated as equals. Our farming process provides nutritious, balanced meals to poor, malnourished animals who have been bred purely to be slaughtered and devoured."

I don't speak because the woman has rendered me speechless.

It occurs to me then that this girl isn't evil.

Somehow, in spite of my hatred and my fear, I can see it in the glassy, distant glaze of her eyes that she genuinely, truly believes that what she is saying is true.

She's apparently this well-spoken, intelligent woman who has somehow managed to form a cult, literally gotten away with mass murder, and made a business out of torturing humans.

But yet, she is blinded to her own painfully blatant hypocrisy.

"What do you have to do to get out of here?" I ask softly, although I am not sure I am emotionally stable enough to receive the answer.

Faith's eyes snap back towards me. "You don't," she replies simply. "You're with us, or you're against us."

With a sharp intake of breath, I tense my legs to stop my knees from knocking unsteadily beneath my torso.

I realise then that escape is a chance I'm just going to have to take.

Maybe just a bit too quickly, I glance around the barn.

I curse myself as Faith's expression hardens, and she suddenly withdraws a knife from the waistband of her skirt. Lunging forward, she poises it near my middle, as if she is about to shove the thing into my stomach.

"Come on, enough talk," she hisses, jerking her head to a doorway further into the barn, which is partially concealed by more junk. "I cancelled a scheduled show tonight for this," she adds, an evil smirk creeping up onto her deceivingly beautiful face.

Addison

Pain.

It infiltrates every cell inside my body, like a million jagged razor blades impaling my flesh, roughly tearing skin and muscle to shreds.

I blink.

Even my eyelids sting like salt on an open wound.

Woozily, I blink again and attempt to focus my pupils.

Above me is a slanted roof, held up by wooden beams, the kind you only find in an attic. Wincing, I slide my eyeballs about in their sockets, my head pounding incessantly as I try and fail to make sense of my bleak, unfamiliar surroundings.

"Hello?" I croak weakly, barely even loud enough to hear myself.

With an exhausted groan, I attempt to haul myself up but find that my shoulders, neck, and elbows are pinned tightly down by something.

The realisation settles, and my memories of the previous night suddenly come flooding back at an alarming rate that makes my head spin.

I scream.

I fucked up.

I don't know what I expected.

Maybe it was my desperation that led me to be so naïve.

I was all messed up inside, my brain a chaotic mash, frantic just to survive.

So much so that I wound up entrusting a person who had paid thousands of pounds to watch innocent people be brutally tortured and killed, live on stage.

Then I even had the audacity to be shocked and horrified when the sick fuck turned out to be nothing but a deadly opportunist, all too pleased to bundle me up in his car, whisk me back to his lair, ply me with drugs, then tie me up in some sort of torture chamber.

Tears sting my eyes and leave a burning trail as they streak down the sides of my face. I scream again, the taste of blood congealing at the back of my throat. I make another attempt to move, but it's no use. All of my limbs are tied.

Like a red-faced newborn, I scream and scream until my lungs give out, and I almost pass out again from the exhaustion. Defeated, I sob miserably, weeping in the lonely, hopeless gloom.

Sometime later, I hear noises.

The merry chatter of men who have perhaps shared a few beers. Exchanges of boisterous banter and heavy-footed steps are clunking upstairs.

A distant round of amused chuckles, and then a meaty hand is turning a key in a lock.

My blood runs cold.

My body freezes rigid as if I am already nothing but a corpse.

I hear the door burst open.

A light switch is flicked, flooding the room with bright orange light that pierces my eyes, like needles in my irises.

Lower lip wobbling, I clamp down on the inside of my mouth with my teeth and childishly squeeze my eyes shut, as if this will somehow make me disappear. Like a heavy fog of poison gas, I sense them entering the room, swarming around me, their bloodshot eyes bulging greedily, leering at me in my vulnerable state. The pungent odour of stale beer mixed with smoke and perspiration snakes up into my nostrils, and grim, sleazy whispers tease my eardrums.

"Oh wow… not exactly a looker now, is she?" comments one man.

"She's an ugly one, alright, but what does that matter?" retorts another.

"Come on, wake up, darling…"

"We want to play!"

"Let's get her kit off…"

My eyes flash open in alarm, my body recoiling, writhing madly about on the table like a helpless fish out of water. I open my mouth, a hideous, animal-sounding scream erupting from my burning lungs.

They're laughing. Through my tears, they are nothing but long, blurry shapes swarming me, but I can see their bodies quiver and wane, and I hear the delighted titters that ensue.

"Please," I beg, "please don't do this…"

Of course, I know it's no good. They're not about to just release me. They brought me here for a purpose, and I'm not going anywhere until I've served it.

With a glint in his eye, I finally notice Elliot standing at my feet. There are about six others, all with the same evil, repulsive expression plastered over their reddened faces. Elliot holds up a knife and deliberately shows it to me, savouring the fear that must haunt my features as I catch sight of it.

"No!" I moan miserably, shaking my head. "Please…"

The closer the blades comes to my trouser leg, the more hysterical I become. An animal caught in some unsavoury trap, I bleat wildly, thrashing my head just to block out their jibes.

"Let's see what you got hiding under there girly…"

"Go on, Elliot, just get on with it!"

I feel the cold flat of the blade on my ankle, and then a deafening tearing noise rips through the air.

Suddenly, I become cold as the fresh oxygen bathes my now bare, clammy leg.

There's a brief pause, where they all fall silent.

Then their hands are suddenly all over me, apparently satisfying an insatiable, uncontrollable urge to tear off the rest of my clothes. With their bare hands, they rip the material, roughly pulling it apart and shredding it to pieces until I am fully exposed, and my cheeks burn red with shame. I can practically feel them drooling over me, like a pack of vicious, starving dogs salivating over the scent of my flesh.

"No…" I cry hopelessly, although I'm now too exhausted to fight. My limbs are like boulders, dead with fatigue. "Don't rape me, please… I'll do anything…" I snivel.

I've read books and seen films about the horror of sex rings. It's the sort of thing that makes you feel sick to your stomach, and yet somehow, you can't stop reading. Because, as awful as it is, it'll never happen to you. Right?

More laughter.

I stare up at them with wide, frightened eyes, painfully aware of the soiled mess between my legs, from where I've been left up here for hours.

"We're not going to fuck you, poppet," a fat, stout, balding man says, feigning a soothing voice. I wince beneath his touch as he strokes my hair and pokes his disgusting tongue out of moist, puckered lips.

I continue to sob because, of course, I don't believe them. Why else would I be stripped naked like this against my own will?

A sudden clatter of what sounds like metal against ceramic makes me jerk my head, and I strain my neck to see another figure, tall, lanky, and greasy, carrying a pile of plates, a mixture of metal cutlery balanced on the top.

"We just want to have a dinner party with you, that's all my sweet," another of them grins, revealing glistening rows of yellow teeth.

"Buyer's rights," Elliot announces, "form a queue you lot, I'm going first…" he snatches a plate and balances it on the table between my feet. "Rich, where's the carving knife?"

The reality of my situation is suddenly rammed painfully hard into my stomach, leaving me breathless, nothing but a terrified squeal trapped in my throat. Vigorously, I shake my head as the other men grumble and tut but obediently make a line behind Elliot.

Rich, the bald man, hands Elliot the cutlery, a long, particularly sharp fork with just two prongs, and a knife that looks bigger than my arm.

"Cheers, mate," Elliot says, candidly flipping the instruments in his hands as if he's manning a barbecue. He turns then, a vile smirk dancing across his lips as he cocks his head. "Now, Addie," he addresses me, "you'll be pleased to know that we will be eating from the bottom upwards, which means it's unlikely you'll die tonight."

My face crumples. "NO!" I scream, "NO! SOMEBODY HELP ME! PLEASE!" I scream as loud as I can, but I know it's nowhere near loud enough. In my mind, I pray, I beg, I plead.

Please no. Please.

Elliot rolls his eyes, "God, you could at least be a bit grateful, Addie…"

In one swift movement, he raises the fork and then slams it down into the bone in my ankle. The metal prongs rip effortlessly through my skin and flesh, sending splatters of blood exploding from the punctures.

An earth-shattering crack seems to stop time and suck up all the sound in the atmosphere as the metal hits bone, and an unbearable surge of pain shoots up through my leg.

Before I can even scream, another agonising strike rips into my calf as, in terror, I watch him slash the flesh with the blade of the knife.

The wound instantly gapes like a mouth, and a crimson river immediately gushes from inside it. My face frozen, eyes fixed tightly on the horrifying act of butchery, Elliot roughly slides the knife the other way, sawing back and forth, back and forth. A river of tears stream down my cheeks, but no sound comes from my mouth. The pain winds me, knocks every shred of energy from my body. Elliot continues to cut, sticking out his tongue in concentration as he slices with the knife, at first long drags through muscle, but then shorter, quicker movements. Eventually, he drops the knife, long gloves of bright red now staining his forearms and hands.

"That's how ya do it, lads!" Elliot chuckles, clearly proud of himself. With his hand, he takes hold of the clump of cut flesh, lost in a generous sea of blood, and pulls at the raw meat.

"FUCK!" I shriek, "STOP!"

Still stuck to the bone, Elliot has to yank the gory handful hard, and a horrific snapping noise slices through the air, sending an almost crippling shiver of pain down my spine.

Quickly, I descend into shock. My skin sweats profusely, my pulse slows to the forbidding rhythm of a death drum. The man who I thought was my saviour rips the chunk of flesh away from my mutilated calf, ripping the final shreds of muscle still attached. He dumps it on the plate and licks his lips, leaving me stewing in an ever-growing puddle of thick, scarlet suffering.

Unable to talk, I gaze hopelessly at the bloody tangle that has been made of my body and feel my heart sink as the next man in line steps forward, the same greedy sparkle in his eye as his hands reach excitedly for the carving tools.

My vision blurs, and I taste blood flooding my mouth. I realise I've been biting down on my tongue, and now the crimson juices trickle down my chin.

Nancy

A ferocious storm relentlessly rages on in the pit of my stomach, churning a sickly cocktail of nerves and dread there. Sensing the sharp point of Faith's knife, just inches away from the flesh on my back, I reluctantly continue to drag my feet, every step growing heavier and heavier. Instinctively, as I walk, I strain my ears for any signs or sounds that indicate life. However, all I can hear is the rapid thrum of my own heart and Faith's slow, drawn-out breaths teasing the back of my neck.

Pursing my lips tightly together, my eyes flit nervously around the barn, searching for a clue.

Where is she taking me? What will she do?

"Ugh…" before I can stop myself, an involuntary grimace of disgust spills from my lips. I smack a hand to my mouth and find myself retching as a despicable odour suddenly assaults my senses. I wrinkle my nose and come to a halt, just a few metres before the darkened door frame, the contents of its room concealed by a dirty, foggy curtain of plastic.

Faith prods me in the back, and I yelp in pain as the tip of her knife penetrates my clothes and skin.

"Keep moving," she says calmly, ignoring the leaking wound that begins to spill onto the fabric of my clothes.

Trepidation tightens it's vice on me, squeezing and squeezing until I feel like I'll combust.

The foul stench just gets worse, congealing in a sickly knot at the back of my throat.

"Go through, I'll get the light," whispers Faith as we approach the curtain.

Unable to breathe, I'm teetering dangerously on the edge of a cliff, feet dangerously slipping and sliding, my life hanging on by a thread, just waiting for a sudden, blood-curdling, vertical drop to the death.

Hesitantly, I hold out my hands and grope the cool, clammy plastic, then blindly stumble over the threshold and into a room that somehow feels ten degrees colder than outside.

A shiver of electricity surges through me, leaving my limbs hardened and stiff, gooseflesh breaking out over every inch of my skin.

"You ready?" I hear her ask, in that terrifyingly silky voice that seems to slice through the air like a kitchen knife.

I stop in the darkness and fold my arms, clutching at myself in a vain attempt to self-soothe.

Somewhere behind me, I hear a shrill click that resembles a crack in a frozen lake- just a tiny, unsuspecting indicator that at any moment now deadly, icy jaws will open, and all hell will break loose.

A second passes before the light flashes through the room like a lightning bolt, and the room is finally unmasked.

It's a large warehouse-type place with lots of surfaces, boxes, metal trays, metal tables, and more of those horrible hanging hooks. In the far corner is a few box rooms, each with another narrow doorway leading into it.

I gasp and instinctively take a step backwards as I notice that one of the hooks is covered by a stained sheet, and there is something hanging from it like a bad ghost costume. Nausea slaps me across the face again when my eyes travel downwards towards the grim metal bucket beneath the hanging lump, and it is filled with something that looks thick and black like oil.

"What is this?" I mutter almost inaudibly.

"This is where you'll be staying," Faith grins. She strides towards me and places a hand on my shoulder, pressing the knife into my side so that it teases my skin. "And I am going to show you the kind of work you will be doing whilst you are with us."

Her skinny fingers pinch my skin, and forcefully she guides me toward the grim-looking sheet that hangs from the hook.

"What is that?" I ask uneasily.

We stop in front of it, and she lifts the knife, tracing the blade along my throat. "Well, why don't you find out?" she asks.

Quiet.

Half-heartedly, I raise a hand, poising it near the grimy sheet. Bile streams into my mouth, the bitter taste of it simmering on my tongue. Shuddering, I slowly flex my fingers…

"Get on with it!" barks Faith, raising her voice so that I startle.

With a sorrowful deep breath, I grasp the sheet and pull it, grimacing as the cold, damp patches make contact with the pads of my fingers.

The moment the material shrugs off of the hunk of flesh that hangs from the hook, I scream.

I drop the sheet and scramble backwards, tripping over my feet in the process and landing hard on my backside.

"NO!" I scream, squeezing my eyes shut and holding my head in my hands, my palms scrabbling at my eyelids as though I can rip away the image now ingrained in my mind.

Faith chuckles, a smug expression on her face as she puts her hands on her hips. "What's the matter, eh? Kevin said you'd be up for the job. Having second thoughts?"

When I open my eyes, I think I might faint. A chaotic mixture of sadness, shock, and pure, unadulterated terror swirl like a tornado in my head.

Because there, the hook rammed through the bottom of her mouth, and holding her up by her mutilated jaw hangs Magda. Sweet, funny, outspoken Magda. The girl who just wanted to find her best friend.

"You're fucking sick!" I scream, sobbing uncontrollably as I take in my poor friend's white, waxy flesh and the disturbing way her eyes are almost popping out of their sockets. I scrabble forwards onto my knees, conflicted by a desire to go to her and take my hands in hers, but also simultaneously repulsed by her brutalised state.

Dripping into the bucket leaks, two jagged stumps where her knees used to be before they were slowly and painfully hacked off. Poor Magda must have gradually bled out until she was just a blood-soaked shell.

Burying my face in my hands, I cry uncontrollably.

My heart throbs, the ache radiating through my entire body like a contraction as I grieve the poor, darling girl and the life that was taken so cruelly away from her.

However, as I sit there, knees tucked under my chin, rocking back and forth as if I am losing my mind, it isn't long before my pain evolves into something else.

Something much stronger.

Boiling hot anger bubbles beneath my skin, steam rising from my bones, my skin burning with fury.

"Get up now," Faith commands.

When I look up, she is still smiling.

"I'll show you to your quarters," she chuckles patronizingly, apparently satisfied with her malicious actions.

My head down, I trail behind her, clenching and unclenching my fists. "I'll be keeping an eye on you until the night shift comes- so don't you be getting any funny ideas," she adds as if she can sense the rage that soars through my veins.

I can't wait to scratch that smug little smirk right off of her sadistic, deluded face.

And I will.

If it is the last thing I do.

Abdul

I wake up, according to the clock mounted on the wall, just after midday, to beady, troubled eyes boring into me.

Before I open my eyes, I feel the hairs on my neck stand up and a twinge in my bones- the unsettling feeling of being watched sinking heavily inside my chest.

Slowly, I force my eyelids open and roll over in the soft sheets. I'm relieved to wake up to the scent of fresh linen, as opposed to the odour of rotten flesh and dried blood that I have unfortunately grown accustomed to from many a sleepless night at the slaughterhouse.

As I suspected, across the room, by the bedroom door sits a familiar face. His skin is washed out, and grey and ugly, prominent scarring marks his scalp.

Kevin.

Exhaling, I slide my tongue across my lips and meet his gaze.

It's the first time we have spoken since before the work retreat, back when things were normal. Back when I was just a normal Indian guy, working in human resources, and he was my dickhead boss who seemed to have taken an odd shine to me.

I squint when I notice a bundle of blankets clutched in his arms, pressed up to his chest.

"Hello Abdul," he greets me, finally, a hint of apprehension about him, as if he is actually nervous about speaking to me.

"I thought you were dead," I admit, bluntly, because I don't know what else to say. "I thought they'd killed you like they killed Bobby, and they killed Prue." The words, when spoken out loud, sting my tongue like a venomous snake bite.

Kevin sighs and lifts a hand to rub his temples. His features are contorted, the lines in his face deepening with conflict. "I managed to get out. Otherwise, I'd be dead too…"

My mouth falls open, and I feel my eyebrows knit together.

"Sorry? So why are you still here?" I lower my voice, pushing myself up in the bed so that I am leaning up against the pillows. Horrific images of the circus flash in the back of my mind, and I have to remind myself that the man in front of me is the same man that tortured those innocent women. "Why didn't you get help?"

Kevin's eyes go glassy, and I can't help but feel alarmed as a solitary tear drips down his cheek. He shakes his head in shame, "I don't know…" he whispers.

Impatiently, I chew my lip. "Did you want to talk to me about something Kevin?" I ask. There are plenty more things I'd like to say to him, most of them blasphemous, but I hold my tongue.

He can't be trusted, after all.

Wordlessly, Kevin gets up from the chair and floats silently over to the bed. He glances around the room as if someone is about to crop up out of nowhere. My body instinctively tenses as he comes closer to me.

"How is Nancy?" he asks softly, regrets deeply etching every crevice of his face.

I arch an eyebrow.

"Okay, that's a fucking stupid question…" groans Kevin. He sinks down onto the bed, lowering the bundle. A horrified gasp escapes me as I catch sight of the deformed mash of flesh that forms the infant's face.

Kevin follows my gaze and smiles grimly down at the sleeping baby. "This is my baby," he says weakly.

"Congratulations," I respond drily. "If I'd have known, I'd have brought balloons."

"Hollie was the mother…" Kevin continues, his voice hazy. "We made her before… well, all of this…"

I don't bother to act surprised or even interested.

"And I suppose she's going to be raised to be just like… one of *you*?" I question him, raising my eyebrows searchingly.

"I'm not one of them," he snaps, furrowing his brows.

"Sure."

"I do what I have to do to survive," he hisses, lowering his voice. "And I'd rather kill than be killed. Wouldn't you?"

Honestly, I shake my head. Because I don't think I would.

"If I knew I was responsible for putting someone through all that pain and suffering, I could never live with myself anyway," I tell him truthfully.

Kevin recoils as if I have just slapped him hard across the face. For a moment, I think that he might punch me, but he doesn't. Instead, he lets out a long exhale of breath and frowns unhappily.

"Well then... you're a better man than me," he says sullenly.

Yeah, no shit.

Sundance

"Where are you going?"

I stop in my tracks and feel my cheeks flush red, like a naughty child being caught out stealing biscuits from the kitchen cupboard. Quickly, I turn on my heel and offer a pleasant smile to my sister, who eyes me suspiciously from up the gloomy, grey corridor.

"I'm getting information, like you asked," I tell her.

Faith tuts and puts her hands on her hips, "you've been at it all morning. What's going on in there?"

Swallowing, I clasp my hands together behind my back, not so subtly hiding the plastic carrier bag behind me. "I'm sweetening them up… I think they know something."

Faith arches an eyebrow and cocks her head. To my dismay, she begins to take a few slow, calculated steps forward. Instinctively, I back away, unable to stand the piercing green of her irises cutting right through me as always.

"Ok…" she says finally, although I can tell that she is doubtful. "Shit, this is all so stressful…" she groans, stopping to rub her forehead. "Normally, we'd have found her by now. Where the fuck could she be?"

I shrug and mumble something useless.

"Well," Faith sighs, giving me a grim smile, "you keep at it. I'm going to re-search the stage area…" she pauses and bites her lip, "I'm going to give it another hour, and if we still can't find her, I guess it's game over…"

A look of genuine sorrow clouds my sister's pixie-like face.

If I didn't have any sort of moral compass, I might feel sorry for her.

But secretly, as we part ways and I speed up my brisk walk back down to the dog cages, a hopeful smile tugs at the corner of my lips. When Faith says *game over*, of course, she means that she'll be hitting the self-destruct button. That means the short stint of the circus will finally be over. Who knows? Maybe even Faith will cut her losses and quit the farm too. Maybe we can have a normal life. Well, as normal as it ever could be. I could get some strong anti-depressants off of the black market for the traumatic stress, maybe actually put some effort into turning the pub into a business.

With an optimistic spring in my step, I hurry down the last stretch of the underground passage and unlock the large door with one hand.

Is it sick of me to be looking forward to this?

Yes. Yes, it is.

My smile droops, and I hesitate. I sigh heavily and listen to the slow grating of metal scraping against the inside of the lock. Purposefully, I press on, nudging the door open with my side, and slip gingerly inside the room.

As I enter, Violet flinches and springs up from the bottom of her cage, like a skittish animal. She looks distressed for a moment, but her expression soon softens as she realises it's me.

"Hi. I got you your things," I announce, raising the carrier bag for them to see.

Fifteen minutes or so later, I'm sparking a joint, using an old coffee mug as an ashtray. Aside from the flicker of the flame and the burn of the rizla, the only sounds within the dismal basement prison are the hungry gulps of the girls, each one guzzling from a large plastic bottle of water.

Inhaling the first toke, I lean up against the outer wall of the cage beside Violet's. Curiously, I look between the bars of the metal enclosure opposite, studying Priya, the Indian girl. Ungracefully, she wipes her moistened lips with the back of her wrist, then gasps for breath, her body quivering as she takes in deep, thick sucks of air.

A few more moments pass before she looks up and catches my eye, her intense brown irises boring searchingly into mine.

"So what happens now?" she asks glumly.

I stifle a groan.

Selfishly, I don't want to talk about anything heavy. There's this childish part of me that wants to put on a charade and pretend I'm just an ordinary guy smoking an ordinary joint with ordinary friends. If we talk about the shitty reality of their inevitable fates, no doubt, it'll break the illusion. They'll become hysterical. I'll transform from Sundance, the nice guy who brought them water and weed, to Sundance, the cowardly arsehole who is essentially trying to groom them.

"So, you're Abdul's cousin?" I change the subject, lowering my gaze. I hold up the joint, and Violet takes a puff through one of the squares in her cage.

Priya nods, pursing her lips together. "Do I want to know what happened to him?" she asks in a small voice.

"He's alive."

Her lower lip falls open, and her eyes widen. "Really? So… where is he?"

"You're lying," Jade chimes in from the corner of the room. My nose wrinkles as I am forced to glance across at her, even for the briefest of moments. "I bet he's dead. Can't you two see? He's just trying to sweeten us up, so we give them advice on how to catch Addie. That's all."

In spite of the circumstances, the resentment she aims towards me stings, so I choose to ignore her.

"He's at the farm," I lie. "He works there."

Priya's brow furrows into a confused frown. "A farm?" she repeats. "What do you mean? Like with cows and sheep and shit?"

I realise at that moment that this situation is a minefield. No matter what I say or do, no topic of conversation is safe. Everything in my life… everything I know is tainted.

Before I realise it, I feel my eyes watering.

"What's going to happen to us?" Violet asks me, her voice a low, frightened whisper in my head.

Hastily, I blink away my tears and swallow back the guilt that forms a hard, tight knot in my throat. "I've got to go…" I mumble, stubbing out the joint in the mug and scrambling to my feet.

"Why? What's going on?" Violet calls after me. "Please? Just tell us. I can tell you're a good person…"

I freeze within a metre of the door. My fists clench, and I squeeze my eyes tightly shut to stop myself from breaking down. "I'm not a good person…" I mutter, "I…"

"You're helping us to survive…" coaxes Violet softly. "You want to help us, I can tell…"

Priya doesn't speak, but her intense stare bores into my back.

I sense it prickling against my skin, burrowing into my flesh.

Jade scoffs, and the bars of her cage jangle and clatter as she throws her frail body weight into it. "I don't know why they can't just get it over with already. Put us out of our misery. That's the kindest thing to do."

"Shut up, Jade!" Violet shouts, "for fuck's sake, you're just making everything worse!"

"I'm being realistic," snaps Jade, "there's no fucking way they're letting us out alive."

"But… Sundance might…"

"Then where was Sundance when they took my friends?" Jade screams, the high-pitched rasp of it bouncing off the walls. "Wake up and smell the shit, Violet. This is it. This is our lot."

A low, sorrowful sigh escapes me.

"Priya…" I just about hear Violet whisper. "Priya… there's still hope, right?"

Silence.

"Sundance is one of the good guys…" mutters Violet, almost manically, apparently to herself. "He's going to help us… he's going to…"

"If he didn't help Hollie, why would he help us, Violet?" Priya interjects, her voice sharper, colder than I've heard before. It slices swiftly through the air like a knife.

Painful, fractured flashes of memory streak across my mind like lightning bolts as I recall that time, all of those months ago. The time that I finally worked up the balls, after spending my entire life being nothing but a weak, powerless doormat. I drugged my own sister. I stole a key. I helped Prue to escape. And everything was going to be alright. Prue was going to get help; the farm, and the family, and all of the other sick, twisted shit that was going down would have been destroyed.

I'd be behind bars, but at least I'd be free from the tight, unrelenting shackles of guilt that keep me mentally chained. Life in prison would be worth it if I knew that I'd saved Prue, Hollie, and even Kevin and Abdul… I wince as Bobby's face crosses my mind.

It was too late for him.

Overcome with a sudden flurry of emotion, I turn around and look from Violet to Priya.

"You're wrong," I tell them solemnly.

"Wrong about what?" Priya asks, arching an eyebrow.

Swallowing, I take a few steps forwards and then sink to the ground so that I am kneeling on the hard, dirty floor. "I did help Hollie…" I exhale and shake my head in disbelief. "And all the others… Prue, Abdul, Kevin, Bobby…*she's* the one who exposed the plan to the family… had the entire thing shut down."

Violet frowns. "What?"

"She was pregnant, so she was allowed to stay in the house," I explain. "I gave a key to Prue… I drugged my sister, Faith, and I told Hollie to distract the guy who is basically her deputy. Hollie snitched. The family came looking, and they found Prue and killed her." I sniff and rub away more tears. "I *did* help them. At least, I tried to…"

Priya and Violet stare at me open-mouthed, their eyes almost popping out of their sockets.

"W-w-what do you mean she was allowed to stay in the house?" Violet asks incredulously. "Where else would she stay? What were they doing to her… oh my god…" she gasps. "Did they… rape her? Is that how she got pregnant?"

I groan and rub my forehead. "There's too much to explain."

"But you can help us, right?" Priya whispers hopefully. "You could give one of us a key to get out of here…"

Violet nods encouragingly, "and we won't say anything to anyone else, will we?"

"No, course not."

Sighing, I chew my lower lip and anxiously tap my foot against the ground. "If only it were that simple… this place is an underground maze. Even with the entire set of keys and a map, it would be a job finding your way out."

"Couldn't you help us?" Violet asks, "you could get us out at night time or something?"

"Or," Jade interjects again, "do the smart thing. Get the fuck out of here now and get the cops. Bring them back here. Get helicopters and flashing lights and sirens and all that shit."

I lower my eyes and fiddle guiltily with the hem of my trousers.

"I can't," I whisper bitterly. "I can't turn my sister in."

A loud, violet clang suddenly rips through the air, startling me. I scramble backwards in an army crawl, alarmed by the disturbance.

"JUST GET US OUT OF HERE!" Violet shrieks, pounding at the sides of her cage with her fists. "FUCKING JUST LET US OUT!"

Tears spill down her cheeks, her face crumpled as she sobs uncontrollably, her whole body wracked with pain.

When my own eyes start to simmer, I force myself to get up and head to the door.

"SUNDANCE! COME BACK!"

Furiously blinking away the liquid weakness pooling in my vision, I hastily exit the room and shut the door firmly behind me. I try to sprint down the corridor as quickly as I can. Desperately I want to escape the harrowing echoes of Violet's spine-tingling screams, but they only resound louder in my head, echoing like shattering glasses against my skull.

I run, and run, feet pounding heavily against the floor until WHACK! Like a raging bull, I slam heavily into something, the force of it causing me to fall backwards so that my head collides painfully with the hard floor beneath me.

"Sundance, are you okay?"

Groaning, I look upwards through squinted eyes, my eyelids as heavy and solid as bowling balls. Karma towers above me, concern etched on her pretty, pixie-like features. She cocks her head to the side, her long, glossy red curls swishing over her shoulder, her pale skin almost luminous in the underground lights.

"I'm fine," I lie hastily before scrambling to my feet, much to my pained skull's sore protests. "What are you doing down here?"

Karma often takes on the role of being the 'lovely assistant' at the circus. It's sickening to see how much she adores doing it. However, other than that, it's not often she can be found down here, in these claustrophobic, man-made catacombs.

"Faith's got us all working overtime trying to find that fucking girl," groans Karma, rolling her eyes, her long eyelashes fluttering. She places a pale hand on a slender hip, the bottom of her flat stomach exposed beneath a tiny, tight-fitting top. It's hard to believe that, just over six months ago, Faith was militant that we all needed to wear those hideous tracksuits. Since Kevin somehow managed to lull her under his spell, the rules have slackened. Apparently, dressing normally will make people more trusting of us.

"Any luck?" I wonder, still blinking away the tears that pooled in my eyes.

"Yeah- thank fuck," she says with a grim smile. "Ziggy and India were working on the door that night… they finally admitted that they let some bloke and a woman out without seeing the woman's ID. All for a bag of MDMA," she shakes her head, an amused smirk tugging on her lips. "The idiots can't remember who the guy was, though."

My mouth involuntarily contorts into a grimace. "Shit. I bet Faith's furious."

"That's an understatement," replies Karma, her expression darkening, "but she's so busy hunting this woman down, she's like a fucking bloodhound. A bunch of them have gone off doing home visits…"

As part of the service, Faith insists on taking addresses and personal information so that people cannot snitch without incriminating themselves.

"How would whoever it is have got the girl, though? Could they have snuck backstage?" I wonder.

Karma shrugs and yawns, "honestly, I've no idea. I'm not worried about it though, why should we be? Everything always turns out okay in the end. God's on our side, remember?"

I resist the urge to roll my eyes. Sometimes I forget that most of the members of our family have fucked up their brain cells so badly from years of drug abuse and dysfunctional backgrounds that they actually believe Faith's bullshit about how we're doing the 'Lord's work.'

"How did you get on with them?" Karma asks, nodding behind me, towards the door down the corridor where I just came from.

Swallowing, I start to walk onwards. She trots casually beside me, unaware of the chaotic turmoil that continues to rage on inside my head like a hurricane. "They don't know anything," I say quietly with a shrug.

"Fair enough," Karma sighs. We both stop in front of the bookcase. I activate the concealed door with a button beneath one of the books. "Faith wants them in the show tonight."

I freeze, and my stomach churns with dread.

Karma steps past the now shifted bookcase into a small passage in which the metal doors of an elevator gleam. When she senses I am no longer at her side, she turns and cocks her head. "You look like you've seen a ghost, Sun," she frowns. "Believe me; we're all thinking the same thing. Is it really a good idea to put on another performance when Faith is wound up tighter than a cheap watch? Even if she finds the girl, Ziggy and India are definitely going to get the kettle…"

My cheeks are drained of blood, and I can feel the distress that manipulates my features, although it's not due to my sister. The faces of Priya, Violet, and even Jade snake up into my mind like wisps of smoke. I'm almost winded by a knock of guilt.

They're just three innocent girls.

None of them deserve to die.

Addison

I'm dying.

I can feel the life gradually leaking out of me- it oozes slowly from my pores and drains from my wounds.

It hurts so fucking much.

For the first time in my life, I truly know what it feels like to *want* to be dead.

Whimpering, I blink up at the tiny window, where a stream of white light now filters through. My head spins, starved of oxygen from where my body has been working overtime, just to keep the air in my lungs.

Like a limp, mauled rag doll, I lay beside the table that I was previously shackled to, on dusty floorboards that smell strongly of bleach.

My memory is so fractured that I can't pinpoint the exact moment that they took off the restraints. All I can remember is how my body jerked roughly to one side, and then a deafening roar of laughter bounced off of the walls as I fell and collided with the hard surface of the ground. I must have passed out because, after the almighty smack of my cheek against the floor, everything went dark, and I was plunged into blackness.

Now, I'm alone, wishing it could all be over.

Clamping down tightly on my lower lip, I force myself to turn over onto my back, putting all of my energy into my elbows.

A sharp gasp of pain gets trapped inside my throat, and my eyes water as I twist my torso, and fresh, blood-curdling agony harpoons itself from my knees and swiftly embeds itself into my core.

"Fuck…" I wince, holding my breath for a few moments, riding out the vicious wave of pain that surges through me.

But when I catch sight of the lower half of my body, the pain, along with every other shred of my soul, temporarily escapes me.

The white sky from outside is like a spotlight, flooding through the tiny attic window, illuminating the horrific image that burns my pupils in front of me.

I open my mouth to scream, but it freezes like a sharp blade of ice in my esophagus.

My knee caps are exposed, yellow and brown stained bone, partially shattered, protruding through torn and bloodied flaps of dead skin. My left shin bone is fully intact, glaring up at me, naked of flesh, lying in a bed of glistening, punctured muscle which quivers with every breath, sending shockwaves of pain through my veins. Beneath the horrendous, bloody tangle of tissue, my foot, although stained, appears to be intact, hanging on by just a few bloody shreds, like a loose button clinging for dear life to a shirt.

"Oh my god…" I cry quietly to myself. Involuntarily, my eyes slowly crawl to the right, and I let out another shocked yelp. "No…" I shake my head in disbelief, jamming my eyes shut.

It's not real. It's not real. It's all just a fucking nightmare.

Except it is.

Through squinted eyelids, I stare watery-eyed at the gory mass of angry red, ground meat where my leg should be. The skin at the top of my right foot has been completely ripped off, exposing all of the tiny, partially fractured bones.

Before I can register what is happening, a hot surge of vomit erupts from the pit of my stomach and gushes in a thick, projectile wave from my lips, splattering all over my naked, blood-soaked torso. A shower of yellow and green gut acid lands on my raw, gaping wounds- each deadly fleck like a razor burying into the stinking flesh.

"HELP!" I scream so loudly that my lungs feel like overinflated balloons. "PLEASE, SOMEONE HELP ME!"

Nancy

"Oh my god- what happened?"

The sudden human noise startles me, and I sit bolt upright on the bed of rancid sheets. As I jerk up from the mattress, a sharp gust of air stings my raw cheeks so that they feel as though they've been skinned to the bone with a potato peeler. I guess they look as terrible as they feel, from where hours of bitter, salty tears have relentlessly corroded away at the flesh.

Abdul stands in the doorway, his dark eyes wide with worry.

"Magda…" I choke, snivelling weakly.

He doesn't appear shocked, just turns his head, glancing back out into the workshop with all of the dirty metal hooks and tables. "Oh, Nancy… I'm so sorry. Is… that… your friend?"

"She fucking hacked off her legs, Abdul," I cry. "And then, instead of burying her nicely, she fucking brought her here, shoved a hook through her mouth, and…" my voice breaks, and I shake my head in disbelief. "Is that… is that what's going to happen to us?" I stare at him searchingly, scanning his expression for answers that are not there.

He sighs and moves slowly forwards, running a hand through his dark, overgrown hair. "We're safe at the moment," he says gently, in a way that tells me he knows that this is no sort of consolation.

I exhale, closing my eyes in desperation. I immediately regret it, as the grotesque image of Magda's grey, waxy face, eyes bulging lifelessly from her head, instantly scorches my mind.

"Are you alone?" I ask him suspiciously.

"We are now," says Abdul. He moves towards me and perches on the edge of the bed, grimacing dismally at the wretched, blackened sheets. "Your babysitter just left."

"Are they watching us?" I whisper, glancing around the room.

"I don't think so. Why- what's up?"

A shrill, manic hoot of laughter escapes me.

What's up?

"Sorry," Abdul apologises quickly, "I guess that's a stupid question."

On my knees, I crawl over to his side so that our skin is almost touching. "Abdul… we have to get out of here…" I whisper, enunciating each word slowly and carefully, "I can't die here. I have kids."

He looks back at me pitifully. "There's a small glimmer of hope. One of your friends got out. They still haven't found her."

My heart skips a beat. I take a sharp intake of breath, "who?"

"The tall ginger one."

Addie.

I could almost cry with happiness. Abdul must sense my optimism because he hastily reminds me, "I said, a *small* glimmer of hope. Remember, there are miles and miles of woodland around, and the nearest village is corrupt. These people have got away with all sorts for years…"

"Right, so we need to do something too," I say firmly, springing up from the bed, ignoring the searing pain in my cheeks. "It seems like they are pretty trusting of you- there must be a way…"

Abdul sighs and shakes his head, "they're trusting of me, but I'm one man, and there are dozens of them. Without a car, I've no hope, and I'd need to get far away before any of them noticed."

Chewing my lip, I force my brain into action. If I ever want to see my children again, I have to focus.

"What about one of the babysitters? If we could somehow get a knife or even one of those guns, we could force them into letting us take the car, I…"

"It's too much of a risk," interjects Abdul, "because if there's more of them inside the house, they'll come running. One of them will sound the alarm, and even more, will come. We'll be dead before we even get out the door."

Pacing the tiny, grimy box room, I search my brain for the answer. There's got to be a solution. There just *has* to be.

But, as the minutes drag on and my feet grow heavier, I find that even I am starting to gradually lose hope. We're trapped. Helpless animals, locked in some evil contraption by the big, scary predators. Eventually, mad with emotion, I fling myself onto the soiled ground and let out a loud, angry roar of frustration. "FOR FUCK'S SAKE!" I hold my head in my hands and start to sob uncontrollably again.

"My little girl is just a baby," I whimper. "She won't even remember me. My mum is fit at the moment, but she's getting older- who is going to look after them when she's..." I stop abruptly, as a cold shiver of electricity shoots down my spine. My eyes widen with horror. "Oh my god... what if my mum comes looking for me?" It's a thought that doesn't bear thinking about. My mum would bring the children with her as well.

I'd rather be ripped slowly to shreds than have my children fall into the hands of these monsters.

Abdul kneels in front of me and tightly grips my shoulders, "Nancy... Nancy, come on, breathe... try to calm down..."

"Don't fucking tell me to calm down!" I wail.

"Okay... okay... look, I have an idea, but you have to stop crying..." he hissed, tightening his vice on me.

"What? What is it?"

"Ugh..." he groans, "it's a long shot. And it could backfire, which is why I was hesitant to mention it to you. It could end up doing more harm than good."

Frantically, I sink my nails into the sleeves of his coat, pushing my face closer to his, "what is it, Abdul?" I hiss impatiently. "Spit it out!"

Abdul glances around the room before lowering his voice. Still clutching each other, he leans in so that his mouth is just centimeters from my earlobe. "When I was at the house... Kevin came to see me," he whispers.

Just the sound of my husband's name makes my blood boil. I clamp down on the inside of my mouth, stifling another angry outburst.

"He was asking about you... and, he said that... he is only doing what he has to... to survive." I sense a hint of doubt in Abdul's voice.

"So, he wants to get out?" I whisper.

Abdul nods, "apparently so. But, it's just that... well..."

"What?"

"I don't trust him."

You and me both, kid.

I sit back, taking this information in.

"If only *I* could talk to him," I say wistfully, slowly. "I think I could convince him. Maybe he could find a way to distract the others and get us a car..."

Nodding slowly, Abdul thoughtfully picks at a shred of dead skin on his thumb. "He *is* in the best position… he's apparently made a huge, unexpected impression on Faith…" he stops himself and looks away from me, awkwardly. "Sorry…"

With a roll of the eyes, I half scoff, half laugh. "I'm so far beyond giving a fuck about him and his affairs. If anything, it sounds more promising. Kevin isn't capable of truly loving someone. Whatever there is between them, it's only lust on his end, I guarantee it."

"So, you think he would help us?"

Pursing my lips, I meet Abdul's eyes. It's a shame; perhaps if he was ten years older, and under different circumstances, I wouldn't mind him taking me out for dinner.

"It's worth a shot," I say firmly.

I don't share with Abdul that, as well as escaping, I also have to plans to tear Faith apart.

Limb from limb, skin from bone, I will rip that bitch into nothing.

She's fucking with the wrong woman.

Sundance

We're not supposed to have heroin in the house.
Many of the family members are ex-junkies.
Well, so they say.
Faith has a strict rule on the substances that are allowed in the house and those that are not. However, as in any prison, people always find a way.
Alone, I lay stretched out on one of the sun loungers in the pool house, high as a kite, mesmerised by the gentle, aqua blue ripple that shimmers in the lights.
Most people that get addicted to crack are homeless. Abused, damaged souls who never had anyone to bail them out when shit hit the fan. Maybe they'd call me ungrateful, but I'd switch places in a heartbeat. I'd rather be self-destructing on smack to get away from bitterly cold nights on the street, the humiliation of begging and having everyone look at you as though you're lower than shit on the bottom of their shoe. It seems like a more bearable fate than self-destructing on smack to get away from the constant, burning hole of guilt in your soul and the horrendous, blood-soaked images of the worst kind of suffering, branded forever onto your brain.

I want to save them. Just like I wanted to save Prue, Hollie, Bobby, and Abdul. Just like I wanted to save every man, woman, and child that ever made the fatal mistake of coming here.
But I'm locked. I'm stuck inside a tight box, with barely even enough oxygen to breathe, let alone try to get out.
How can I betray my sister? The person who raised me and has always loved me no matter what. For as long as I can remember, it's been Faith and me, just us against the world.
And she's the one who saved me when her mother tried to sell me for her next fix. She wanted me to do things to disgusting,

older men, things that even just the thought of made my skin crawl.

Faith slaughtered her for that.

How can you betray someone who loves you that much?

Too detached from anything to think anymore, I let my eyes shut, and I will the rest of the world to just blur into oblivion.

And, with what's left of my consciousness, I pray that my eyes will never open again.

Addison

"Hey, girly… how you feeling?"

Stiffened all over from the pain, my eyelids slowly flutter open. I blink and feel my heart sink as Elliot's awful, monstrous face fades into view.

Maybe I'd cry if I wasn't just so damn exhausted.

I'm lying on the floorboards, and he's hovering over me, a nasty grin dancing on his lips, his eyes scarily wide.

I whimper.

"What's wrong, darling? Got a bit legless last night, did we?" Roughly, he grabs the back of my head and hoists me up so that my body is bent upwards, and I am sitting upright. "Come on, sweetheart got to sit up, have something to eat and drink…" a loud, blunt scraping noise pierces my ears as he drags something from behind me for me to lean against. Once he's satisfied with my position, he pats my shoulder and then backs away. He scoops something up off of the table.

"The boys had a fantastic time last night," Elliot says with a smile as if it's intended as a compliment. "Food was delish!" He smacks his lips. Carelessly, he picks up what's left of my left leg, and hastily pushes it outwards, then dumps a ceramic plate with what looks like steak on top of it.

"FUCK!" I scream, the pain tearing through my body. "FUCK!" my head falls back, and I tighten my fists.

"Whoops. Sorry!" Elliot lifts a plastic cup of water to my lips. "Drink up!"

I wolf down the liquid, which tastes musty and rotten. In spite of everything, my mouth is parched so that it feels like my tongue is cracking with every breath.

"Atta girl! Now, I've got a real treat for you…" he gestures down at the plate in front of him. The slab of meat swims in a shallow pool of red juice. "I didn't want you to have to miss out on all the fun… this here is just a taster of what we had at the dinner party last night…"

Shaking my head vigorously, I feel my stomach swell again, threatening to shoot more disgusting stomach acid up my esophagus. "No,…" I groan, biting back hot bile.

"Oh, yes!" Elliot exclaims delightedly, "you've got to eat. I can't have you dying on me, not yet, at least! We've got…"

A loud, shrill ring echoes through the house. A flicker of alarm crosses Elliot's face. He furrows his brow and grabs my chin, digging his nails into my skin. "Don't you even think about making a noise," he warns darkly. Before I can protest, he delves into his pocket and produces a ball gag, which he hastily fastens around my head.

"I mean it!" he snaps, bringing his face so close to mine that our foreheads collide. "Seriously, you make any noise, I will come back up here, and I will dissect your cunt one bit at a time. You hear me?"

Vigorously I nod his words like daggers in my chest.

I watch him stand up and quickly leave the attic. He slams the door shut and locks it behind him.

I know I've got to make a snap decision, here and now.

Stay quiet, or take my chances on freedom.

I choose freedom.

As loud as I can, I project my voice. I scream so loudly that my ears hurt. Fuelled by the will to survive, I even pound my fists into the floorboards. "HELP ME! SOMEBODY HELP ME! PLEASE!" I shriek my throat and lungs on fire. I grab the plate and fling it across the room so that it smashes against the opposite wall.

"HELP! HELP ME!" I scream.

I'm only momentarily silenced when another cry rips through the air. Except this one is fainter and more distant. It's gone almost as soon as it enters the air, and it only spurs me on more to make noise.

"HELLO? SOMEONE HELP ME! I'M IN THE LOFT!"

A coughing fit interrupts my cries for help, and I double over as my entire chest feels as though it is about to collapse. My head foggy from the blood loss and the pain; I almost pass out again as I try to regain the wind knocked from my body.

Then… the sound of footsteps creaking up the steps. The gust of hope that enters my heart forces my head up as if I am a puppet on a string.

"Hello?" I call out excitedly.

In my delirious state, it hadn't occurred to me that it might well be Elliot coming back up the stairs. My blood runs cold as I remember his earlier threat. A warm sensation tingles between my legs, and the fear causes my bladder to empty. Acidic liquid trickles down my bare thighs, and I scream again as the hot gush of piss stings my raw wounds.

As if on cue, a loud, forceful bang scares the shit out of me, followed by the heavy wooden door swinging wide open, slamming into the wall. I hold my breath, lower lip wobbling uncontrollably as I wait.

"Hello?"

Tears of relief stream down my cheeks. It's a woman's voice.

"Help!" I squeak, bursting into ungraceful sobs again.

In the doorway appears a short, petite woman, her face contorted by her concern. Piercing green eyes flit across the room, scouring every inch of the gloom, naturally apprehensive about taking another step.

"Please help me!"

When her dark pupils find me, instantly, she lunges forwards and sweeps across the floorboards, sinking down onto her knees in front of me. "Oh my god…" she gasps, her face draining of all colour. She pushes her long, black curls behind her ears, revealing dainty ears studded with jewellery. "What the hell happened?"

"Please… call… an… ambulance…" I feel myself drifting out of consciousness, as though my body will finally allow me to sleep now that help has found me.

The woman bites down on her lip, "okay honey, but can you tell me what happened? The emergency services will want to know…"

I'm sure it can wait, but I'm too weak to argue.

"My friends and I… we were kidnapped… locked up… by these people… they tortured my friend… it was a show… I got out… this guy took me here…" I splutter, my chest tightening.

When the woman does not immediately leap up and find a phone, unease begins to gnaw at me again. I look up at her and try to decipher the unfathomable expression on her face. Her features are pinched and angry. But not surprised, or frenzied, or even shocked at my mutilated lower limbs. Instead, she slowly gets up to her feet and strides back across the room to the door.

"Arlo!" she yells; the shrillness in her voice makes my skin crawl. "Arlo, get up here now, and bring that lying piece of shit with you."

Shaking my head in disbelief, I stare searchingly up at the woman as she walks back over to me. She folds her slender arms over the front of her skimpy vest top and seems to assess me grimly.

"What… what is this?" I pant, panic returning to the pit of my stomach. "Call an ambulance… please…"

The woman clicks her tongue as if she is considering me for something. As though I'm a turkey in a supermarket that she is comparing to an entire fridge full.

She doesn't have time to answer me because, within minutes, a tall, muscular man who must be double the woman's size in both length and width appears. Behind him, by the scruff of the neck, he drags Elliot, whose face is red and wrinkled, his cheeks glistening with saliva and blood. A purple lump swells at the side of his head.

"What the fuck is this?" the woman demands sharply, pointing in my direction. Arlo roughly shoves Elliot forward so that he is standing weakly in front of her, his knees knocking nervously together beneath his weight.

"I… I… I just found her…"

"You found her? Where exactly?"

Elliot swallows. He glances desperately at me, then back at the black-haired woman. "I can't remember… I was drunk."

I hear the almighty whack that follows before I see it. She swiftly slaps Elliot across the face with surprising force, almost making him topple over sideways. Afterwards, she grimaces at her hand and wipes it on the front of her jeans. Her eyes linger back towards me and then fix on the wooden table.

"Had some fun with her, did you?" she snarls, her irises glittering furiously. "Arlo, get this lying piece of shit on the table."

"No… please…" Elliot pleads, the pitch of his voice heightening as Arlo effortlessly drags him over to the table, lifting him and slamming him down onto the top, causing a deafening crack to rattle the skeleton of the attic.

"Tie him up," the woman instructs.

"Faith, no…. please…I beg you…" Elliot squeals like a pig about to be slaughtered, his body shaking madly, just as mine had the previous evening.

The woman, Faith's expression, remains motionless and stern. Cold and unfeeling.

"Come on… look, I'll pay you for her. Name your price…"

Faith reaches into her back pocket and slides a short but sharp-looking blade. Before Arlo has even adjusted all of the restraints, she steps over me and rams the knife, hard, into the outstretched palm of Elliot's hand.

"FUCK!" he screams, the noise ripping painfully through the air.

"Do you realise what you could have done?" Faith screams right back at him, twisting the knife so that the sound of cracking bones and ripping flesh becomes the background noise to her anger. "All of my work… all of my imperative work… my family…my empire…" she trails off, shaking her head furiously. "If you got caught… if *she* got out… it'd all be gone. Years of faith, years of tireless labour…" finally, she wretches the knife out of his hand. A thick, stinking waterfall of blood erupts from the puncture and begins to spill down the side of the table, landing in splatters a few centimetres next to me.

I'm blinded by the multi-coloured blur of tears and frozen with the harrowing realisation that, once again, I've been saved by just another evil monster.

As if she can sense my thoughts, Faith squats down beside me. She smells strongly of incense of some kind, which is overpowering, and nor pleasant, or unpleasant.

"What's your name?" she asks me.

"A-a-addie…" I mumble pathetically, too frightened to be defiant.

Elliot howls on the table so loudly that I can barely hear myself think.

"Shut the fuck up!" snaps Faith, kicking the leg of the table. "Or I'll give you something to scream about!"

Although her words are not aimed at me, I flinch, all the same, more tears pooling in my eyes.

"Addie," she addresses me, "I guess now you must sympathise more with poor, innocent animals around the world who are bred purely to be brutalised and salvaged. You've lived it yourself…"

her voice is soft and silky, a far-cry from her vicious shouts just a few moments ago.

I don't say anything but force myself to nod with what little energy I have left.

"I'm going to give you two options," Faith says. "Because you're strong, and I can see you've learned an important lesson."

My heart thuds rapidly inside my chest, and I feel my fists seize up. I dare myself to look up and meet her gaze.

"My friend here, Arlo, is a retired doctor. He is very skilled. If you would like another chance at life and would like the opportunity to give back to the earth, he can heal you."

"Heal me?" I repeat, my voice barely even a croak.

Faith purses her lips and examines my wounds. "Well, to be frank, your legs are screwed. They'll have to be amputated above the knee. But he can kill any infection and make sure they heal correctly. Eventually, maybe we can even get you some prosthetic limbs, but this is only if you agree to join our family…"

I frown, stunned by this bewildering offer.

"If I don't agree?"

She sighs heavily, "well, we can't let you go, so we'd just have to put you out of your misery. I'll make it quick. Then we'll use your remains for our animal feed mission."

It's too great a decision to make when my entire body is wracked with crippling agony, and I'm too exhausted to even string together a coherent sentence.

"Addie?"

"Fine…" I gasp. "Fine…"

Without another word to me, Faith stands up. "Put her under. I'll take care of this…" I faintly hear her murmur to Arlo, who obediently stalks out of the room.

"Faith… please…" Elliot whimpers.

"People like you…" scowls Faith, flipping her knife from hand to hand, "people like you are scum. You're not like all the others- ignorant, passive in your sins… no, you actively, *willingly*, put the work of God in jeopardy. The only hope this damned world has left."

Elliot sobs.

"People like you…" she repeats, slowly, as if she is savouring every word, "*cannot* be allowed to breed. It's a crime against nature.

I cannot have you populating the earth with more greedy, sick, twisted individuals."

"W-w-w-what do you mean?" Elliot whimpers.

Faith lifts the knife to her mouth and chomps down on the handle, the steel handle clinking against the metal stud shoved through her tongue. I hear the groan of a zipper, followed by the fabric being pulled down roughly.

"NO!" Elliot shrieks, "NO! YOU CRAZY BITCH! STOP!"

Ignoring him, she touches his small, limp penis and stretches it upwards, looking it up and down.

"PLEASE!" he cries, writhing frantically on the wooden table. "PLEASE DON'T DO THIS!"

Faith teases the shaft with the point of the knife. Her eyes flicker over towards me. "What do you think, Addie? Do I chop his dick off or give him another chance to fuck with me?"

"NOOOOO!" Elliot howls.

Barely able to differentiate what is real and what is just my exhaustion playing tricks on me, a small smile tugs in the corner of my mouth. "Chop it."

Immediately, a deafening rip echoes around the room as Faith stabs the man's genitals with the knife. She twists it around, the swish of blood and the shredding of his muscle surprisingly satisfying to my dying ears.

"Split it in half; that should do the trick," says Faith casually. She rips the knife upwards until Elliot's dick is severed by a bloody, jagged line down the middle. "And, just for good measure…" in one swift movement, she slices off his testicles, a vile, disgusting mixture of blood and bodily fluid now sloshing off the sides of the table.

"YOU FUCKING CUNT!" Elliot groans. His voice is growing weaker, quieter, more defeated.

"Now, I'm not going to kill you, as we have a contract," Faith continues matter-of-factly, "however, if you don't want to incriminate yourself and become one of our performers at the circus, I strongly suggest you keep your mouth shut. Understand?"

Footsteps thunder towards me. Through half-closed eyes, I see that Arlo has returned, a syringe and needle in his hand.

Abdul

It's night time again.

Time for yet another show.

I cannot explain the strange sensation that overcomes me when I hear the news about Addison.

I'm sitting in front of the control panel, ready to begin another grisly, stomach-churning shift with Rowan, when he casually drops the revelation into conversation as he nonchalantly chews on homemade chips.

"They found the girl," he tells me, tiny flecks of spit erupting from his lips as he talks and eats at the same time. "Somehow, the little bitch got out! One of the punters kidnapped her."

I have to purse my lips together so tightly that they ache, just to stop myself from letting out an instinctive groan.

It would have been disappointing news at any rate, given the tiny glimmer of hope I'd harboured, that maybe the escapee would get help. A childish, unlikely fantasy, but one I couldn't help but subconsciously cling on to.

Now, knowing that the girl... Addison... is a friend of Nancy's; Rowan's announcement punches just that little bit harder.

Like an iron fist plunging into my guts.

"What did they do?" I force myself to ask, although I dread to hear the answer. Whatever it is- whatever unspeakable thing they've done to her- I'll have to be the one to tell Nancy. And it seems unfair, after all the bad news I have already had to impart on the poor woman.

Rowan sits back in his chair and licks his lips. His eyes are trained carefully on the monitor screens. Absent-mindedly he replies, "Faith has taken her in."

My mouth falls open, and I have to quickly shut it before he realises my shock. "Taken her in?" I repeat.

"Don't get jealous," Rowan teases, laughing as he swivels his chair so that he is looking directly at me. "Faith gets vibes about people. About whether they can change. Whether they can be a part of the family."

I arch an eyebrow, "so, because she escaped, she gets to live at the house?"

He shrugs and yawns, clearly bored of the conversation. "The bloke that took her… nasty cunt…" Rowan shakes his head, his face contorting with clear repulsion. "Ate her."

"Ate her?" I gasp.

"Exactly," Rowan nods, just as he picks up another chip and tosses it carelessly into his mouth. "Fucking ate all of her legs. Arlo's had to amputate."

Worryingly enough, I understand.

In Faith's eyes, it's a case of predator becomes prey. She thinks that Addison is just another clueless piglet that needs saving and avenging.

"Good evening, ladies and gentlemen!"

The sound of Kevin's voice over the microphone rips through the air, interrupting our conversation. As always, he's dressed in the ridiculous ring leader outfit; a jaunty grin splashed across his face. In no way do I detect any sign of the remorseful, concerned husband that I briefly saw earlier. It's as though he's been split in two. One half sadistic, deranged killer, other half trapped, manipulated victim.

The audience cheers; it's resounding chorus sending sharp, icy chills shooting up and down my spine.

I flinch.

"I still think it's mad that Faith still wanted the show to go on tonight," Rowan comments, stuffing another fistful of potato into his mouth. "She's so dedicated…"

I give him a brief, sideways glance and watch the look of pure, unmistakable awe cross his face. When he talks about her, his voice is full of admiration, as if he's talking about some great pioneer or war veteran. They all do.

She's got them all, well and truly, hooked.

I cannot even begin to imagine what that kind of effortless power feels like.

"First up tonight!" Kevin announces, gesturing his white-gloved hands to the centre of the ring, where I've positioned the white, circular glow of a spotlight. At the corner of the stage, I see

Karma, in a tight, sparkly leotard, cheerily wheeling another victim out into the open.

"A very beautiful addition to our show!"

My heart skips a beat when I see her.

The victim.

I was, honestly, expecting it.

After all, I knew that Priya was here. I knew that, even in the worst of times, she'd still find a way to come back and haunt me.

But still, to see her face, and her figure, huddled up, terrified and vulnerable in the wheelchair, causes me to freeze solid. She looks so tiny and so helpless from afar. Just a little dainty doll, too far away, and too fragile to be helped or saved.

"Like what you see, eh?" Rowan chuckles, elbowing me as if we are old friends. His touch burns my skin, and I have to resist the urge to retch with disgust. "Good job, you've got that assistant now. At least you can get some relief."

Maybe if I was paying him more attention, I'd have to swallow back bile to stop myself from projectile vomiting all over the place. Sex is the very last thing on my mind and has been for the last half a year. If anything is a mood killer, it's the stench of rotting, human flesh right outside your bedroom.

However, I find myself strangely transfixed anyway by the raised ring, beadily watching the girl who made my life a living hell. She is being wheeled slowly onto and across the stage so that the audience can savour the anticipation that hovers thickly in the air. With every step, she is being led closer and closer to her brutal, painful fate.

Priya is crying. Her brown face is screwed up, and the trails of tears glisten dazzlingly on her cheeks, as though slugs have slid down from her eyes to her jawline. Even from such a distance, I can see that her entire body is rigid with fear.

She's sobbing so loudly that she is reminiscent of a child throwing a tantrum in the midst of a supermarket, red-faced and shameless as they furiously stomp their feet and demand sweets.

Kevin continues to talk, and Priya continues to scream and wail.

Unable to tear my eyes from her, I stare, taking in every inch of her terror, lost in a daze.

"Love at first sight, is it?" Rowan chortles to himself, mistaking my stare for some kind of infatuation.

For some strange, baffling reason, I feel the urge to enlighten him.

"I know her," I tell Rowan, although my voice is hazy and distant, and my pupils are still fixed tightly on the illuminated stage.

Despite how vulnerable and how terrified she appears, I'm unable to feel… anything. Whereas I'd normally feel distraught, heartbroken for the poor, defenceless victims forced to play a part in this sick show; I find myself painfully indifferent.

Unmoved.

Uncaring.

"Oh shit. That's deep," coughs Rowan awkwardly. "Though, I guess you can't have cared for her that much, or else why would you have been fucking that other woman… what was her name…"

"Don't." I blurt out, my face snapping towards him, brows furrowing and expression hardening. I shock myself with the sharpness in my voice and immediately hold my breath as I gauge his reaction. I need to learn to control my emotions, but when I think of Prue, it becomes hard.

To my surprise, Rowan holds his hands up. "Sorry."

I frown then, temporarily stunned by the fact that he hasn't smacked me around the face for that smart comment. Still, I don't want to push my luck, and so I swiftly change the subject.

"She wasn't my girlfriend," I tell him, looking back at the stage. Kevin is chatting, performing elaborate gestures, and strolling back and forth across the stage. I zone out from his tedious showman bullshit. From the corner of the stage, I see a large, filled water tank on wheels being pushed in by Karma and a few of the other cronies. I wait for my heart to sink as I notice the surface of clear liquid at the top of the glass container. Its ripples shimmer in the spotlights.

"Arranged marriage?" Rowan speculates, with a knowing nod.

I resist the urge to tut at his stereotypical assumption.

"No, she stalked me," I reply. "We went on maybe two or three dates. It was nothing. We were much younger then, as well."

"She stalked you?" repeats Rowan, apparently flabbergasted. "As in…"

I sigh as all the memories come flooding back to me.

At first, it was pitiful. Pathetic.

I felt sorry for her.

But it wasn't long until it took a dark turn, and all of a sudden, I saw Priya everywhere. If I went out for dinner, she'd just *happen* to be at the same restaurant. Suddenly, we went to the same doctor's surgery and the same dentist. I'd catch her staring at me through the clothes rails in shops. She applied for the same jobs that I did. She added all of my family on Facebook and even tried befriending my mother, of all things.

"She made my life hell," I confess.

It all came to a head about a year after our first meeting.

When I woke up, and she was there.

Next to me.

In my bed.

That's when I snapped and finally lost my shit with her. I guess my newfound loss of patience for her crap just made her even more persistent because she started camping out outside the flat where I lived at the time. She'd bombard my roommate. Call up my work and my family. She even reported me missing to the police when I stayed out one night.

In the end, I'd had to move away.

I left my job, my flat, my home town, all of my longest friends, and my closest family, just to be free of her.

Whether the move was a good idea depends on how you look at it.

I mean, I got to meet Prue. I had a blissful amount of time being in love with her and getting to see her five days a week.

But then, on the other hand, if I hadn't had to move, I'd never have gone on that fateful work trip.

I wouldn't have ended up here.

And after all that, Priya- the crazy fucking bitch- *still* managed to hunt me down.

Madness.

After he's heard the story, Rowan laughs as if I have just told him a hysterical joke.

"You're complaining about a woman being in your bed?"

I decide to ignore him and instead focus my attention on what's going on in the circus ring. Involuntarily, my hands cramp with anticipation as I watch them lift Priya from her chair. Her slender, naked limbs writhe and twist; her eyes appear to burst from her skull.

Rowan says something to me, but I don't hear him.

I'm too busy, too invested, in watching the show. And besides, the noise is drowned out by the violent roars and cheers protruding from the crowd.

They hoist her up onto the side of the tank so that the back of her buttocks is leaning solely on the hard edge of the glass tank. Her face cracks and winces. She is begging, pleading. Excited giggles and cheers of anticipation leak from the throng of psychopaths in the audience. On stage, the… *family* circle the tank, taunting, poking at her naked body, kicking and rattling the glass tank so that the entire thing shivers and vibrates. A sheen of sweat shimmers on the surface of her clammy skin.

Overall, it's only a matter of minutes before Priya plunges into the water, the sharp ridge scraping her back on the way down, spraying the back of the tank in her blood.

Despite the noise, her final scream rips through the air and penetrates my ears like the sharp edge of a blade being thrust through cartilage. The shrill cry is severed by the splash of the water, and instantly an intrigued hush descends over the audience.

My face remains still, unmoving. Inside my head, I'm willing myself- *begging-* to feel something. I'm desperate to feel even the tiniest scrap of sympathy or remorse for not giving her more chances. I urge bile to crawl up my throat or my stomach to churn in pure repulsion as the scarlet blots of blood congeal in the water like a giant lava lamp.

"I do not envy her," Rowan comments grimly.

My stalker thrashes wildly inside the tank, her limbs smacking against the glass, her mouth falling open and her pupils dilating as the water beings to flood her lungs.

Around the glass, Kevin marches proudly, a cruel grin creeping up onto his face.

In a brief second of insanity, I feel my own lip curl upwards.

Immediately, I smack a hand to my mouth, horrified. My cheeks burn red.

"What's up, Pig?" Rowan asks, frowning curiously at me.

Wordlessly, I shake my head.

"Oh my," laughs Rowan, folding his arms, a smug, satisfied smile stretching his features. "Enjoying it, are we?"

"N-n-no," I muster, clenching my hands so tight to the seat of my chair that my knuckles turn white.

He chuckles to himself and slaps me on the back.

"Don't be so hard on yourself; you're only human," he says. "I'm almost proud of you right now."

I feel sick.

I swallow back clumps of vomit that rise to the back of my throat and then bite down hard on my tongue. I train my eyes again on Priya's rapidly flailing body and feel hot, salty tears simmer there.

But not because I feel sorry for her.

Not because I'm terrified, or heartbroken, or repulsed, or traumatised by watching a girl I used to date drown to death on a stage, whilst sickos laugh and watch the show.

My tears are because of the undeniable fact that Rowan is right.

I enjoy watching Priya die.

Sundance

When I am finally released from a deep, drug-induced sleep, I'm shaking all over, and my skin is coated from head to toe in a suffocating sheen of sweat.

Darkness shrouds me in the pool room, and the only way I know where I am is the sound of the water lapping the stone edges and the strong stench of chlorine attacking my nostrils.

Despite the painful thrumming in my skull, I scramble to my feet and blindly rush across the tiles, then crash through the door and into the main house.

The hallway is brightly lit in its usual orange glow, and the air is warm.

Heart pounding, head spinning on a rapid axis, I thunder down the passage, my knees wobbling like jelly beneath me, and make a beeline straight for the front door.

"Sun?"

Behind me, Dawn is poking her head out of the kitchen door and is cocking her head; a confused frown spread out across her face. On her hip, she balances baby Daddy, whose wide eyes are blinking blankly across the reception area at me.

"I-I've got to get to the circus…" I explain in rasping pants. Swallowing, I shove a hand into the pocket of my hoody and sigh a breath of relief when I hear the familiar clink of my car keys, the cool metal smooth under my fingertips.

"Why?" Dawn asks curiously, arching an eyebrow.

"Yes,- why?"

My heart sinks as Faith steps out from behind her, also carrying a baby. Except, despite being the same age, Beau is roughly about three times the size of Daddy. Against Faith's skinny, petite frame, Beau looks even more monstrous. In fact, it's an almost comical sight. Faith looks like she will collapse beneath the weight of the deformed child and fold up like a deck chair at any moment.

However, apparently, Faith is oblivious to the abnormal size of her adopted daughter. She looks at me expectantly, her shiny emerald eyes glinting suspiciously in the glow of the lampshade above. Like a miniature clone, Beau trains the same sort of expectant look, her tiny pupils penetrating me.

"I…" I squeak, trying to force the words out. "Faith… I love you, but… this is wrong. All of this is wrong," I say finally. "We've got to stop it. All of it, the farm… the circus…"

Faith's jaw drops in horror, and Dawn becomes as pasty and white as a sheet. As a kind of silent, subtle warning, she widens her eyes.

I ignore her.

"There are other ways we can get people to stop eating animals," I blurt out, "and… we can raise money for animals other ways…" I desperately raid my brain for more facts, more figures, more excuses… but my mind has gone blank.

The more she stares at me, the faster all of my bravery drains me.

In two seconds flat, I'm reduced from a fully grown man, with morals and a mind of his own, to just a skinny little boy again, in a constant state of panic, always quaking in his boots behind his big sister.

Without thinking, I turn on my heel and bolt out of the house, tearing open the front door and ignoring the painful scorch of my sister's eyes on my back.

Immediately, a cold blast of air washes over me, like diving into a frozen lake. With numb, trembling fingertips, I scramble to unlock the door to the car and hurry inside, never once glancing up to see if I am being followed.

I know that I don't have much time.

The entire car journey, I fear I could pass out at any minute because I feel so faint. My pulse punches my eardrums, like a heavy, brass pendulum swinging back and forth, back and forth inside my skull. I'm afraid that, in just the blink of an eye, my body will switch off, I'll lose control of the wheel, and the car will spin violently off of the road.

I'll be dead.

I can't die.

Not yet.

I make the journey in about half the normal time, speeding erratically through the cruel, dark night. As I make the abrupt turn in the road, my car tyres screech loudly in protest until I come to a rough halt just outside the huge building.

Out of the corner of my eye, I see that Rain, a sturdily built recruit of the family, is on the front door, sitting like a brick wall on the stool. I clamber hurriedly out of the car and slam the door shut behind me. Rain looks briefly in my direction but barely even acknowledges my presence.

It only serves to remind me that I'm not like any of these people.

I'm not a lost, damaged soul who lost their way and did whatever Faith told them to, for another chance at life.

Ignoring Rain, I dart across the courtyard towards the small, inconspicuous front door.

"Oi, you can't leave the car here!" he grunts at me, narrowing his piggy eyes.

I don't reply. Blood rapidly pounds through my veins at the speed of light as I hastily unlock the front door with my own set of keys and press through into the suffocatingly stuffy passageway inside.

The stench of weed clings to the steamy atmosphere beyond the door, and the strange, tinted lights and the lack of windows gives the place an eerie, dangerous feel.

I suppose it's fitting.

As fast as my quivering legs will carry me, I continue on through the centre of the house, through the secret door in the bookcase, and down the elevator, to the bottom floor beneath the control panel. Soon, I arrive in the midst of the grimy network of underground passages and am immediately struck by the sound of a roaring crowd and thunderous applause. My stomach flips.

I panic that I might be too late.

Tears well up in my eyes. My feet pound the stone floors as I run towards the source of the ruckus. On the way, I bump into various people, all of whom barely even give me a second glance.

People don't like me here because I'm not like them.

"Our second act of the evening…"

Kevin's booming voice stops me in my tracks. That means that somebody has already died. But it also means that I have a chance to at least save one or two lives. I drag my feet along, forcing myself to continue up the corridor, where the sound of the crowd is getting louder and louder.

When I finally get to the doorway that leads into the small back room, I can already see right through the next set of fire doors. Kevin is at the front of the ring, gesturing to something. In front of him, I see a semi-circle of hyperactive, maddened faces, their eyes, and mouths open with excitement.

"… it's that time of the night where you can bid for a chance to be a part of the show…"

My skin crawls. I trail through the busy room full of props and other eerie, unsettling pieces of paraphernalia.

A sharp gasp escapes me when I reach the side of the stage and catch sight of a huge, multi-coloured wheel stationed in the centre of the ring. Violet is attached to it by her wrists and her ankles, blood weeping in tiny drabs from her shackles. Her face is pasty and grey; beads of sweat ooze down her forehead and trickle into her trembling lips.

"… to be a part of the knife-throwing act tonight…"

My pupils rest on Karma, who is wearing another stupid, tarty outfit. This time, she's waving about a set of dirty, rusty-looking knives, fanning them out as though she's trying to sell them on a telemarketing channel.

Purposefully, I march forwards, lungs heavy and feeling as though they are brimming with hard, dried concrete.

The insufferable heat from the stadium clings to me like leeches sucking relentlessly on my pores, and the horrendous stench of pain and suffering wafts like a nightmare into my nostrils, making me retch and gag.

Nobody notices me as I press on, not even when I get to the corner of the ring, and the sadistic atmosphere almost becomes too much to bear. It swirls around me in a chaotic spiral, like a real-life hallucination dancing in front of my eyes. My vision blurs, and poor Violet's dangling, naked body, becomes a sickly grey blur in front of the painted wooden circle.

"Bids start now!" announces Kevin, just as I step over the threshold and gingerly place a foot into the circular arena. At that moment, he spins around and finally catches sight of me, one of his eyebrows arching into a confused frown. The audience becomes doused in a loud, heavy hum of excitable conversation, temporarily distracted from their ring leader.

"Sundance?" Kevin asks, cocking his head. He walks towards me, confusion saturating his features. "What are you doing here?"

"SUNDANCE! HELP ME!" Violet screams, her voice frantic and high-pitched as she begins to writhe and struggle inside her restraints.

I swallow and purse my lips together. Suddenly, I feel incredibly foolish. I don't even have a weapon. Nothing to threaten with or to defend myself. I just took off in a blind, emotional fit, probably because of all of the shit I've been injecting into my veins.

"Faith wants you to release her," I say dumbly.

Kevin's mouth opens slightly, "oh... really?"

I nod vigorously.

I am a terrible liar.

And yet, he buys it. Because as much as the others don't like me and think I'm nothing but a weak, frail little pussy who is only good for rolling joints and shooting up, no-one has a reason not to trust me.

They all know that I'm the most important thing to Faith.

They know that she trusts me with her life and her entire legacy.

So why would I lie?

"We've got to let her go," Kevin turns and calls out to Karma uncertainly. Immediately, her heavily made-up face crumples into a disappointed frown, but she shrugs and drops the knives onto the ground beside her.

They glint in the elaborate array of stage lights.

I wait a few seconds.

Carefully, I watch her roll her eyes and toss a sheen of red, glossy hair over a slender shoulder, thoroughly miffed that there will be no brutal bloodshed.

Everything seems to grind to a painfully slow, almost halt.

We are not quite frozen in time, but the minutes ooze by at a snail's pace. The sound of the crowd seems to fade out to white noise, and my gaze drops from Karma's slim, sparkly figure to the knives that remain discarded on the floor.

I take my chance.

I lunge forwards and grasp the handle of one of the knives, everything moving in slow-motion as I turn my body and plunge the blade through the air at Karma.

"LET HER GO. NOW!" I screech, my bloodshot eyes filling with tears. "*NOW!*" I scream, darting forwards, nicking one of Karma's skinny, bare arms with the point of the weapon.

Karma and Kevin's faces simultaneously fall, dumfounded.

Their confusion spurs me on.

"NOW! I AM NOT FUCKING JOKING!" I scream, the release of sound a kind of therapeutic relief to my lungs.

Wordlessly, Karma, and Kevin exchange glances. Kevin nods at her. Karma delves into her pale, plunging cleavage and removes a small, metal key.

I resist the urge to puke.

With my body turned, the array of spotlights dancing on the ring burn my eyes like acid being thrown at my face. My vision blurs and dances, leaving me stunned and confused.

Still, I watch Karma hastily scrabble with the key to unlock Violet's restraints, and I feel a sigh of relief escape my lungs as I watch the naked, battered woman fall from the board into a broken heap on the ground.

At this, the audience hush.

The sudden quiet smashes over my daze like glass, and suddenly everything is painfully crisp and sharp.

Real.

For a moment, I stand there, the knife still poised outwards, painfully aware of the many pairs of beady, confused eyes that bore into me from the vast crowd of spectators.

I piss myself.

Literally.

A hot feeling shrouds my crotch and dribbles in pungent spatters onto the ground.

No-one moves.

No-one says a word.

"Sundance!"

At first, it's like a blurry, hazy, barely even audible call, like the vibrations are just mere, distant ripples in water.

"Sundance!"

… or the sounds of reality, blasting through a deep, heavy dream, demanding to be heard…

"Sundance!"

… quiet, and unimportant to begin with, but becoming louder and more incessant with every call…

"SUNDANCE!"

My head snaps, and I am released from my trance of fear.

The knife falls from my sweating palm and lands on the stage.

I feel my eyeballs bulge from my skull and the weight of what feels like a million expectant gazes staring me out across the moderate stadium.

Faith.

She'd stood there, just a few feet in front of me.

I expect her to be angry. Fuck, I expect her to be furious.

I've jeapordized the business. Jeapordized our work.

But, when I look into her familiar face, I don't see any ill-thought embedded in the creases of her expression. Instead, I see comfort. Warmth. Light.

Home.

I burst into tears, like a pathetic little kid.

Immediately, my sister rushes forwards and engulfs me in her arms, her familiar scent instantly warming my nostrils, sending comforting endorphins rushing through my head.

"It's okay… it's okay…" she whispers, stroking the back of my head, holding me close to her, as though I am just a child again. "Let's get you home…" she soothes, entwining her hand in mine.

I'm not me anymore.

For a brief, passing moment, I was Charles.

I was the kid that Faith kidnapped, the kid whose father she tortured and killed. I was the kid who had been held prisoner for all of these years, at the hands of a fucked up cult who robbed me of any kind of chance at a normal life.

That was me- the *real* me- for a second.

But Charles is gone, and Sundance is back.

The strong, loving, perfectly well-rounded young man has fucked off into oblivion, probably forever now. And in his place stands the cowardly little bastard I really am.

I let my sister take my hand and pull me back across the stage.

Her comforting scent, the familiar sound of her breaths, and the soothing tones of her voice calm me. They numb me.

So much so that I ignore the distant screams of Violet, who I leave behind me in the ring.

Nancy

It's been hours since Abdul left.

I predict that it is the early hours of the morning.

I drift in and out of sleep. The fug of unconsciousness laps over me in a disorientated wave, consuming me all at once, then seconds later leaving me feeling cold, damp, and uncomfortably awake.

In the disgusting, filthy bed, I lay on my side, body hunched up as though I am an insect curling up inside its shell.

The place stinks so bad that my nostrils sting with every intake of oxygen, and my eyes burn from the hot, salty tears that flow constantly.

All over, I ache. Stiff, rigid, unable to relax, I shiver slightly in the cold draught, icy fingers pinching cruelly at my skin.

The room is lit with a single bulb dangling from the low ceiling. It flickers and buzzes, omitting a mirky glow that bathes the dismal room in a pasty light, and illuminates the grim, ripped photos that stain the four walls.

A sudden sound of movement- heavy footsteps beyond my grim box of a prison- force me to sit bolt upright on the mattress.

Abdul.

Swallowing, despite the dry, sandpapery interior of my throat, I leap up from the bed and shuffle across the room, a tiny flicker of relief igniting in my chest.

As awful as this place is, it becomes instantly more bearable with Abdul around.

He's got this calming persona that seems to soothe me.

Without him around… when I am all by myself in this hell hole… there isn't a single shred of hope left inside me. At least when he is here, he reassures me.

They trust him.

As long as they trust him, there's… *something*. A chance to escape. A chance to somehow trick these sick fucks and make a run for it.

Before Abdul even enters the room, a crazed, manic grin stretches out across my face. I imagine my babies running into my arms when I finally arrive home. Breathing in their familiar scents, feeling the weight of their tiny bodies inside my arms.

"Nancy…"

My mouth falls open.

It isn't Abdul.

Body freezing, I blink, stunned as I register the presence of my husband appearing in the doorway.

His face is pale and washed out, deep creases lining his face, making him look as though he has aged about a decade in the short amount of time that we have been apart.

"… Kevin…" I force myself to say, finally.

My fists involuntarily clench, so tightly, it makes the bones in my wrist ache. The urge to lunge forwards and pummel the piece of shit into a pulp makes my head spin, but I know that I need to think this through carefully.

Nothing can be left to chance.

Everything, from now on, must be carefully thought out and calculated. Every move I make, and every word that escapes my lips.s

I've got to get out of here.

"Kevin…" I repeat, forcing his name out in an exasperated gasp of relief. With gritted teeth, I force my feet to move and shove myself into him, planting the side of my head against his chest. "I'm so glad you're here."

His arms entwine around me, embracing me tightly to him. It feels different from how I remember. He smells different too, as though he is a stranger off of the street, rather than the man I married and had two children and a home with.

"Oh baby…" he whispers, so quietly that it's merely more than a whisper on my shoulder. "Oh, baby…" he repeats himself.

I want to vomit.

"Have you come to get me out of here?" I ask, the words prickling my throat because I am so thirsty and hoarse.

He holds me at arm's length, his lips pursed together, his eyes wide and serious. Quickly, he glances over his shoulder. Letting go of me, he reverses a few steps and quickly looks around the slaughterhouse beyond the wall of my box.

"What's going on?" I probe, clearing my throat as I take a step towards him. "Kevin?"

"I can't do anything now," he hisses at me, nervously chewing a thumbnail. "But don't worry, I'm going to get us out."

"Why can't you just take me now?" I whisper, fresh panic flooding me. "Kevin... I've got to get out of here... the kids... I..."

"I know," he interjects, cutting me off.

He grabs me by the shoulders again, the rough pads of his fingers digging into my flesh. "I know, but... I can't tonight. I've got a plan."

His touch is like a hot iron on my skin. Or the slimy tentacles of some underwater beast. I resist the urge to shrug him off and slap him around the face.

"When then?" I ask, my face crumpling.

Kevin glances around again, the fear of being caught clear as day, the anxiety etched deeply into his features.

"I... I don't know..." he admits, with a hopeless sigh.

Fresh tears roll down my cheeks. Instantly, he grabs me, snatches me up, squashing my torso in his vice-like grip.

"Someday soon... someday soon..." he soothes, rubbing my back up and down as though I am a newborn with colic. "I promise. I... I just wanted to come and tell you... just... be prepared..."

Blood, from where I've clamped down so hard on the insides of my mouth, congeals in the corners of my lips, rusty and gross. I swallow it down.

"Right..." I whisper back. "Right..."

He pushes me away, although he doesn't let go of my upper arms. His eyes are huge, his pupils scarily dilated.

"They caught me..." he tells me, his face moving closer to mine as he breathes the words. "They got me first. They... mutilated me."

"But, you escaped..." I say, in a tiny, heartbroken voice. "You escaped. Why didn't you come home? Why didn't you tell the police? You could have come home. You could have saved our family..."

Hopelessly, my husband shakes his head, his eyes closed.

"The abuse… was so bad… I wasn't in my right mind. When I escaped, I was deranged. I wasn't thinking straight."

Bullshit.

"And what about *her*?" I hiss at him. "That woman you love."

At the mention of Faith, Kevin bows his head with shame. "I don't know what's wrong with me, Nance. I don't know if it's a phobia of commitment… or a sex addiction… either way, I know that I need help."

I want to laugh in his face.

He needs help.

He needs help?

How about me? How about the poor, stupid bitch of a wife that went looking for her cheating scumbag of a husband, only to be captured by his newfound cult of murderous sadists?

"But, you *do* love her?" I ask him bitterly.

It doesn't matter. Not even a tiny bit.

So why am I wasting my breath asking?

He's saved by the sound of scuffling echoing on the cold flooring of the slaughterhouse. Every footstep echoes obnoxiously loudly, alerting anyone in the vicinity to even the mildest of disturbances.

My husband lets go of me and hastily rubs his reddened eyes. A gruff, indifferent expression appears on his face, and he folds his arms tightly across his chest.

Seconds later, one of the armed guards appears in the doorway.

"All done?" he asks Kevin, in a way that indicates that Kevin is somehow a figure of authority around here.

In response, he nods stiffly, then turns and leaves the room. He leaves me standing there, coated in my own filth… broken, bruised, and beaten down inside.

PART TWO

Arlo

The human body.
It's a weird thing, isn't it?
Almost perfectly crafted, each and every organ, each and every fibre holding its own unique purpose.
On the outside, you could think we are these intricately engineered robots, programmed to be intelligent beings who could achieve all manner of greatness, such as discovering electricity or building a contraption that allows space travel.
Although, in reality, we are nothing of the kind.
In reality, we are nothing but oversized, walking bags, stuffed with blood, muscle, fat, and bone.
Nothing programmed or genius about it.
We just *are*.

Gently, I peel back the sodden, rotten-smelling gauze.
I've seen many wounds in my time.
Fuck, I've cut up hundreds of dead bodies. Operated on even more. Even since joining the family, every week, there's been some sort of grotesque experience just waiting around the corner for me.
Needless to say, I'm undeterred by the charred, mutilated appearance of the stump.
The smell is not a good sign, though.
Not for the girl anyway.
Nor is the green and yellow puss oozing from the edge, the disgusting fluid leaking in between the blackened crust.
I put the bandage back against what is left of the amputated leg and let my eyes travel slowly upwards to the face of my latest patient.
"I'm dying, aren't I?" she says coldly.

She was pale before, but now she is positively ghostly. Almost transparent. Through her clammy skin, I can see the spidery legs of bright blue veins.

Sighing, I get up from my crouched position beside the bed and sit down on the mattress. "I can save you, no problem," I tell her confidently.

It's not one hundred percent true. There's always the small chance she will die of sepsis. I mean, it's not like we are in an actual hospital. The conditions are not as sanitary as they should be, and I've had to perform extreme surgery with minimal instruments and with just me and one other (medically untrained) person.

But still, people survived amputations back in the Victorian era.

Even before that.

Addie groans.

I watch her carefully.

"It hurts so much…" she whimpers.

"I'll get you more pain killer."

"You mean heroin?"

"It's not full heroin," I protest, although truthfully, I'm not altogether sure. It's not as though the medications Faith has supplied me with are from legit medical suppliers. For all, I know the alleged morphine could be vinegar.

The girl's eyes close, and she raises her head slightly to the light, her thin lips squeezing tightly together as another wave of pure agony ripples through her body.

"I've changed my mind," she says, keeping her eyes squinted shut. "I don't want to be saved. Just kill me."

I don't respond and, instead, slowly get up from my position on the bed. It's not that the grim state of her moves me in any way. Whilst I'm just a walking bag of blood, flesh, and bone, I might as well be made of titanium. I've watched countless men and women cry, and scream at me. I've listened to them beg for their lives, beg for their husband, their wife.

I once ripped a tiny baby from its mother's arms and ignored her tearful pleas to return him.

No… Addie's miserable disposition doesn't phase me in the slightest.

However, the smell is rancid and churns in the pit of my stomach.

And besides, I can't kill her.

Not now.

She made her choice, and Faith won't accept this last-minute change of heart.

"Don't go…" she moans as I turn and begin to walk away. "Please. Just end it all. Please."

I open my mouth to tell her she's wasting her breath. Turning on my heel, I meet her watery, bloodshot gaze.

"You're lucky, you know," I inform her, narrowing my eyes at her pitiful expression, "you might not see it now. But you are."

The girl expels a shrill grunt of disbelief followed by a humourless blast of laughter.

"You could've died a slow and painful death being eaten," I remind her, placing my hands on my hips. "And now- yes, it's painful at the moment- but now you're about to start a new life. A life with endless, limitless possibility…"

She blinks at me.

I blink back before walking back over to the end of the bed and sinking down again onto the covers.

"What was your life like? Your old life?" I probe her.

Her lower lip opens, quivers for a second, and then closes again.

Just as I suspected.

Her story is splayed out all over her face, a damning confirmation that Faith had gotten her story totally right. Like always, she'd pieced it together with different shreds of fabric, like an imperfectly woven patchwork quilt. A sliver of information from Facebook, a chunk from Google, a few titbits from her work website…

Addison's old life is miserable.

Worse than my old life… which is really saying something, considering that the man I used to be was a doctor on the run from the police for inadvertently killing a patient whilst in a drunken stupor at work.

My life was cold and dark and empty. It was bad.

But at least I had… something.

I had a job. I had booze. I was always handsome and fit. I could impress people, simply on account of my occupation.

Addison has nothing.

An ugly, awkward-looking woman who is likely still a virgin, has no friends, still lives at home, and works a shitty dead-end job. Only ever shares photos of her cats.

"It was... good..." she sighs, letting her head fall further back into the pillows.

I tut and roll my eyes. "Your old life was a disaster," I counter, "I know it. You had nothing. Why else would you come all this way looking for a brother who buggered off and left you?"

Tears fill her eyes, and the whites of them shimmer with the hot, bitter liquid. Still, she doesn't speak.

"You've got this amazing opportunity," I continue, "Faith makes sure all of us live a good life. Better than beyond your wildest dreams... what's your biggest dream, Addie?"

She sighs miserably, her face scrunching up as though she is in a lot of pain.

"What was it? A husband? Children? Lots of money?"

Addison swallows and shakes her head.

"You're deluded..." she whispers.

Her words sting, like the vicious slap of a whip cracking against my skin. "How am I?" my cheeks burn hot and red with anger.

"What happens when you get caught?" she croaks. "You'll all go to prison. Would that be worth it? Just for a couple of years of living in this place? And besides, at what cost is it? Having to torture people- who would do that, just in exchange to live here? How can you live with yourself?"

The answer to her questions immediately pops into my head.

Yes. It's all worth it. Every single last bit of it.

Not for the money, though. Or the mansion. Not for the power, or the effortless life of parties, drugs, and sex, with none of the typical adult problems that burden most people.

But it is, for Faith.

I'd kill a million more men; I'd rob a bank, I'd blow up a fucking school for her smile.

"Why else would we all be doing it?" I reply.

She pauses and then breathlessly admits: "I have no idea."

"Let me enlighten you," I move closer to her and lower myself at her bedside so that our eyes are level, even though hers sag lazily, probably delirious with the pain. "Do you believe in God?"

"Not now I don't..." she groans.

I take her wrist in my hand. It's so skinny and brittle; I can imagine myself snapping it with just a small flick of the fingers. Her skin feels clammy and hot to touch. Probably from the start of an infection coursing through her veins.

"Nothing bad can happen to Faith…" I whisper under my breath, my lip curling upwards. "She *is* God."

More tears trickle down her cheeks.

"If you're faithful to her, and you help her cause, you'll be repaid. Anything you want."

"What about my freedom?" Addison's eyes suddenly snap open, and she asks me through gritted teeth.

"That's not an option."

"So I can't get anything I want then… some God," she hisses, wrenching her arm away from me. "What about death? Can I at least get that? Put me out of my fucking misery."

Her shitty attitude is bewildering to me. I gape at her, blinking in disbelief at the disgust that saturates her expression.

"You act like what we do is wrong… so immoral…" I accuse her, sitting back on my heels.

"You torture people for money," she mutters.

"But it's okay for people to do it to animals? Why are humans worth more than poor elephants, and camels, and all the other species which are used and abused for the advantage of human beings? Have you been to a real-life circus?" I demand raising my voice.

"Yes, I fucking have, and there are no animals anymore!" she snaps, "welcome to the 21st century."

"What about the farms?" I ask her icily, "where baby animals are killed for meat, ripped from their mothers? Kept in filthy cages, murdered for their meat, raped for their milk, and for more babies. What about the sick fucks who hunt foxes and deer? Just for fun?"

Addison stops talking. Her eyes tighten shut, and she allows her head to slump to the side, as if her batteries have depleted, and she had been drained of her final shreds of energy.

Anger and frustration niggle away at the back of my head, irritating me. I clench my fists and pull myself to my feet before storming out of the bedroom.

This time, she doesn't protest. She doesn't ask me to stay. She doesn't argue back. Surely that means I'm right.

I knew I was, anyway.

But, then…
… why do I feel so defeated?

Faith

Before I even open my eyes, I sense that something isn't right.

The side of my head is pressed up against Kevin's chest, and I can hear the familiar pounding of his heart. I inhale his usual scent, which instantly, but only briefly, soothes me.

As I glance up, I blink and can tell that he is awake, even in the darkness. He is sitting slightly up against the headboard, cold eyes staring blankly into space. He doesn't frown or scowl, but I can feel his unhappiness. It's unbearable.

"What's wrong?" I ask him softly, pushing myself up so that our eyes are level.

At first, it's as though he doesn't hear me. He doesn't even blink.

A cold chill rushes in through the open window at the end of the bedroom, causing the voile curtains to flutter softly. I wrap my own arms around myself and tuck my knees up under my chin. I stare at him intently, absorbing every inch and shadow of the face that I have so quickly grown to adore.

I didn't intend to fall in love.

In fact, since I was just a child, I've always made a point of doing quite the opposite. I never longed for a partner- male or female. All I cared about was a family. A life where I always came out on top, where I always had the final word, and I never wanted for anything. Exactly the sort of life that I have created.

And, it never felt empty.

I never felt empty.

Not for a long time, anyway.

I certainly never considered that there was something missing. It was me, Sundance, our work, and our people. That's all I ever needed and wanted.

But then I met him.

Kevin.

Obviously, we got off on the wrong foot. When I first met him, all I could think was that he was just another piece of shit man that cared more about his stupid prick than he did about his wife or children. It was easy to just dismiss him as another bit of livestock for the farm.

But then, when it came to it, there was something about him that spoke to me. It wasn't love at first sight, but there was something in his eyes, as cold and frightened as they were, that made me hesitate.

I didn't have him taken to the farm, where I knew he would definitely be killed.

Instead, I made him my pet.

My bunny.

I felt the evil and the sin leak from his pores as I pierced his flesh, and I watched that smug, arrogant demeanor rapidly fade as I stripped him of all of his dignity.

There's something very special about being faced with a person you made. Really, *made*.

He's different from how he used to be.

An involuntary smile creeps across my lips. I reach out and stroke the top of his hand, enjoying the feel of the tufty little hairs that stick out from the top of his wrist.

"Hey," I repeat myself, "what's wrong?"

Suddenly, he snaps his head towards me, his eyes wide and afraid.

My lips fall downwards into a frown at the underwhelming reaction.

His expression immediately softens, and he grabs hold of one of my hands, squeezing it tightly in his. "I'm sorry," he whispers into the darkness, "I'm fine. Just cold."

I arch an eyebrow. "I'm not stupid," I tell him. "Tell me what's on your mind."

It's a command, and he knows it.

He shifts uncomfortably in his seat, suddenly unable to meet my eye. A wave of unease drifts over me then crashes down hard on top of my head. The ugly little monster niggling in the pit of my stomach suddenly lets out a loud, aggressive roar, rearing its full ugliness.

Why didn't I ever fall in love before?

Because, as I said, I'm not fucking stupid. At least, I wasn't.

In just a few short months, it's as though I am quickly unravelling from the inside. Nothing could hurt me before, and now here I am- fucking jealous

Jealous. How fucking absurd. How can God be jealous? How can I be jealous of anyone? Of her?

When he doesn't speak, I shrug off his hand and slope off out of bed, embracing the icy cold pinch of the wind on my skin.

"Faith…" he whispers out to me.

I turn my back and bite back hot, bitter tears. I ignore him, purely because I don't want him to know I'm sad. He can think I'm angry all he likes. In fact, I hope he's pissing himself with fright, worrying himself silly about what I'll do to him for this. For humiliating me.

I won't kill him. I love him too much for that.

But he's got to learn a lesson.

Everything was so perfect. Me, Kevin, and Beau. The perfect little family. Our future was filled with so much hope, so much promise. We had it made.

Then *she* came looking for him and broke the spell.

Now, every time I look at him, I see it in his eyes.

He's thinking of her every chance he gets. Plotting against me.

I feel it in my bones.

Pushing my way out of the bedroom door, I frantically scrub tears from my cheeks with the back of my wrist.

Over my dead, rotting corpse will I let anyone see me cry.

Ever.

Shivering, I stand there alone, in the deserted upstairs corridor for a moment, listening to the whistling of the wind outside.

My eyes flit across the tasteful oil paintings of animals, proudly showcased in their extravagant frames. The collection is worth thousands. I had it imported from an artist in Japan. It was one of the first very expensive things I bought.

But I'm starting to realise that nothing as mundane as a painting seems to matter when you're suffering from a broken heart.

Uncertain, I glance around the familiar passage, staring at each door along the hallway in turn. Behind each one lies a family member. A person who loves me.

Fuck- a person who'd kill for me, even.

But, at a time like this, when it matters, there's only one that I really want.

As I hurry down the carpeted corridor towards my brother's bedroom, I think of what I could say to him.
We argued earlier.
After we got back from the circus, I was angry with him.
It was like he'd temporarily gone mad. I know he's always had moments where he hasn't been thinking straight, and he's questioned our work. But he always came around. He'd never let me down, not really. We're family.
And there was a time, not so long ago when we were all the other had.
But then, earlier on, I caught a glimpse of something in him that I'd not seen before. It was a look that matched Daddy's the first time I poured scalding hot water over his head. It was a look that matched Mother's when I killed that weak, pathetic excuse of a woman.
It was a look that said, *I'm against you.*
And I couldn't stand that. Not from Sundance.
So we argued, and I said things to him that I regret. Things that I know I can probably never truly take back.

In my mind, I piece together an apology, which lets him know how much he means to me but also makes him see that his erratic behaviour could have cost us our lives. I know that I've always been far too soft on him; Arlo had always said so.
But then again, perhaps I've taken it too far this time.
He was threatening to go to the police. He was about to set free our livestock. I had to keep him secure, at least until he had calmed down.

Gingerly, my pace slows as I reach the bolted door that leads into Sundance's quarters. The sight of the metal padlock secured to the latch makes my cheeks redden and burn with guilt.
On the wooden stool just beside the door, the single key sits on it's back, glinting slightly in the well-lit hallway. I hurry to pick it up, suddenly desperate to set my little brother free.
I hope he's not still angry or upset.

As I'm fiddling about putting the metal into the keyhole, I tell myself that I'll suggest we go up to the loft. We can smoke a joint or two together and watch the Spongebob movie like old times.

Sundance loves old cartoons, always has done.

Secretly, so do I.

Finally, I hear a definitive scrape of metal, and the key clicks as I turn it. I release the padlock from the latch and place a hand on the door handle, pushing it downwards and tapping lightly on the wooden panels.

"Sun?" I whisper into the gloom of his bedroom. I pause, waiting for his response. I hardly think walking in on him having a wank will do our relationship any favours.

For a few seconds, I wait, frozen in the little angle of the ajar door, half in the hallway, and half in his bedroom.

"Sundance?" I hiss, slightly louder this time. I press forwards, causing a loud creak to expel into the otherwise silent air.

Still, there's no response.

I guess he's asleep.

Probably stoned.

Clearing my throat, I nudge the door open even further and inch my way into the shadowy depths of his room. It's colder in here, even though I can see that the window is not open. Gooseflesh erupts up my arms. I clutch at the skin, rubbing frantically as I blink into my mirky surroundings, feebly attempting to make my eyes adjust to the gloom.

"Sundance!" I whisper again, peering further into the room.

I can just about make out my brother's sleeping figure, a deathly still lump slumped across the bed beneath the sheet. I pause for a moment and prick my ears, listening for the soft, subtle rhythm of his breaths.

For what feels like hours, I just stand there, still as a stone statue, listening.

Listening to silence.

Silence as sharp as razor blades penetrating my eardrums.

With every slow, passing moment, a vice constricts tightly around my chest, only lightly at first… but the pressure quickly builds.

Hesitantly, I force my foot forwards, moving painfully slowly. Beneath my skin, the carpet feels rough.

"Sundance?" I call out again, louder this time.

Feeling about a centimetre tall, I force myself to pad forwards.

I'm taken back a few decades.

No longer am I the big, brave, powerful Faith.

I'm Olivia again.

Little, pathetic, poor little girl.

Poor little girl. No mummy, no daddy.

No fucking hope.

"Sundance?" the panic in my voice quickly becomes more evident. It scratches my throat on its way out, like a skinny cat trying to claw its way out of a ditch.

In my head, I envision him suddenly sitting bolt-upright, jolted awake by the irrational alarm that vibrates in every syllable of my speech.

But he remains still.

Hysteria builds inside my chest. I lunge forwards and grip onto the unmoving shape beneath the bedsheet.

Arlo

I'm going under, slowly drifting beneath a murky surface, when all of a sudden, a shrill screech erupts through the air and roughly pulls me from my pool of unconsciousness.

Instantly, I recognise the voice.

Faith.

As though I wasn't almost asleep just a second ago, I spring up from my bed and sprint from my room, grabbing my gun from the bedside table as I go.

Kevin

Trembling, I'm perched on the edge of the bed, blinking nervously into the darkness that consumes the room. Despite the icy chill that clings to the air, I'm sweating from head to toe.

Faith is gone.

She's pissed off.

Is now the time to run? Maybe my only chance?

I'm just about to force myself to stand up when I hear a blood-curdling scream that makes every hair on my body stand to attention.

I freeze.

Faith

I know, as soon as I touch him.

Although it's too dark to make out anything but foggy shapes, and although my eyes are quickly blurred with a thick smudge of tears, I know.

I know that my brother is gone.

I know that I must be screaming because, within minutes, someone flicks the light switch, and Sundance's bedroom is flooded with a warm, orange glow. It exposes him. His familiar, pale face is almost translucent, his eyes dark with black, cloudy smudges. He's gaunter than usual, so that he already resembles a skeleton, even though I know that just a few hours ago, his heart was still beating.

His cold eyes are fixed to the ceiling, wide and unmoving, as if he's stargazing.

The shock of red hair on his head is the only part of him that makes him appear remotely human. My gaze is drawn to it; the fiery orange tufts sprouting from his hairline. It takes me back to the old days when he was only small, and I was pretty much his mum, even though I was just a kid myself.

The memories snowball and explode like bright fireworks crackling inside my skull. They take me back to cold, crisp snow days when we'd play in the untouched snow blanketed across the fields around the farm. Blissfully warm, sunny days having picnics in the woods, rescuing injured birds, and petting wild rabbits. Pointless, wasted weekends of sitting on our arses watching dumb, mind-numbing cartoons. Crazy, silly inside jokes that no-one else would get. All the times I won. When everything started to go right, and he was the only one, I couldn't wait to tell. The way he'd look up at me every day, those bright, innocent eyes blinking up at me with pure, unadulterated admiration.

He was my fucking heart.

"Faith… Faith…"

A distant voice calls my name, as if I'm underwater, and someone above the surface is trying to get my attention. I ignore it.

Blinking away the tears that cloud my vision, I watch my brother's still, lifeless figure.

Maybe if I stare enough, he'll reanimate.

Nothing is impossible, not for me.

I'm fucking God.

Swallowing, I bite back my shock and re-emerge from my daze. I lunge forward and grab my brother's slightly rigid shoulders, almost recoiling at the icy, clammy touch of his skin.

"Faith…" I hear Arlo's calm, soft voice and the touch of his hand on my back.

"Get off me," I snap, grimly gritting my teeth. Vigorously, I shake Sundance's body roughly. "Get up, Sundance," I demand. "Now!"

Behind me, I sense more activity. Gasps of horror.

"It's fine," I tell them airily, without glancing around. "It's fucking fine, alright. He's going to be fine," I become rougher with him. I dig my nails into the flesh on his arms, drawing blood. I scratch him as I move him backwards and forwards. I jump on top of him and smack him hard around the face. I grab thick handfuls of his hair and yank them hard until they are ripped from his scalp.

"All because you're pissed off about this circus!" I shout at him, furious. "Fucking ridiculous. Come on, get up. Get up, for fuck's sake." I punch him hard and pummel his face with my fists. I scream and screech, spit erupting from my mouth and spraying his skin.

Exhaustion aches in my bones, but still, I keep going. I ignore the pain because I've got to wake him up.

I have never been so mad.

Suddenly, a firm arm snakes around my waist and pulls me off of him, off of the bed, so that I tumble to the ground. Like a tantruming kid, I kick out my feet in a blind rage.

"GET OFF ME!" I scream, baring my teeth like a wild animal, knitting my brows together in a furious glare. I spin around on my knees to see about ten of the others all squished into the room, their faces ghostly pale, eyes wide with terror.

Arlo stands above me, a grim expression on his face.

"SUNDANCE," I try again, turning back to my dead brother. I grab his arm and pull his skinny body towards me, although his limbs feel so tense and rigid that it feels like he might snap apart. But I don't give a fuck. That'll teach him. It'll serve him right for pulling a cheap stunt like this.

As his body slides slightly across the sheet, ten or so empty blister packs are exposed beneath his torso, and some of them skitter to the floor.

Something about the sight of them- the ripped, metallic foil, and the crumpled plastic, makes me stop, all of a sudden.

My body freezes, but inside I feel acid convulse in my muscles, a chaotic, internal whirlwind aching inside my bones and flesh.

I look at my brother.

I look at him long and hard, and it's just then that it hits me.

It hits me like a huge, fuck-off-sized brick being flung off the top of a building, directly on top of my skull.

A loud, shrill laugh escapes my lips before I can stop it.
After that, dead, eerie silence fills the atmosphere.
Not even a breath or a quiet, muffled word.
It's deafening.

More laughter tumbles from my mouth, and I jerk my head to the right to face the crowd of sullen-faced people congregated there at the end of my brother's bed. Seeing their moody expressions just makes me laugh even more.

"Madness," I splutter, shaking my head in exaggerated disbelief. "Just when you think you know someone…" more manic, hysterical giggles interrupt my sentence, "… they go and leave you!"

No-one else laughs.

It's been a long while since I was the only one to laugh at my jokes. That just makes me laugh even more.

"And I thought I knew life," I admit through tears of manic amusement, "I thought… I thought I'd done my time; I thought I had it all!"

"Faith…" Kevin takes a step forward. I hadn't noticed him standing there. He offers a hand. I spit at it.

"But I don't!" I continue, turning back to look at my brother. He looks even worse now, thanks to the beating I gave him.

Oh well.
He fucking deserved it.
No, he didn't.
I regret it now.
I stop laughing and start sobbing uncontrollably.

Slowly, my heart splinters inside my rib cage, piercing my internal organs like pins in a cushion.

There's a sharp prick in my arm when I'm not looking.

In that last flash of consciousness, I turn round and see that Arlo had stuck me with one of his injections.

A smile spreads out across my tear-stained cheeks.

No.
I don't know about life.
Not one bit.

Arlo

Faith's been out of it for almost six whole hours by the time she finally starts to rouse from her drug-induced coma.

I know that she'd probably prefer to wake up next to Kevin, but the spineless prick has made a prompt, stage-right exit at the first sign of trouble.

Just like I thought.

From the moment I laid eyes on that fucker, I could smell the rat on him. He was never one of us.

And he never will be, either.

I glance to my left, at her still, sleeping figure on the bed beside me. She's on her side, her dark eyelashes dainty and perfect against the smoothness of her cheeks. Her hair surrounds her face like a black, twirling veil, a stark contrast to the snowy white of her skin.

She really is perfect.

When I sense the familiar rhythm of her breathing change pace, I quickly look away. I return my focus to the television screen blaring at the foot of my bed, and I pretend to read the flash of subtitles at the bottom of the picture.

It was only six months or so ago that we'd sleep together most nights.

Not sex, of course, but she'd sleep beside me.

But that was back then, and this is now. The way she went on about it, I don't think I could ever compete with Kevin. I don't want her to be freaked out that I'm still over here, secretly deeply in love with her, watching her sleep for hour upon miserable hour.

My body stiffens as she stirs, and gradually her eyes flutter open.

"Arlo?" she croaks.

"Hi…" I whisper softly, looking down at her at my side.

She doesn't move, but her stunning, emerald irises blink up at me, wide and afraid.

I shift around so that I am also laying on my shoulder, and our bodies are faced inwards, directly at each other. She doesn't flinch or recoil, just gazes at me searchingly.

"Was it a dream?" she asks me, in a voice that suggests that she already knows that it wasn't.

Shaking my head, I slowly reach out a hand and gently stroke the exposed skin of her elbow.

The whites of her eyes glisten.

Earlier on, I suspected she was suffering from a type of psychosis. Grief can do that to people. Fortunately, the sedative I administered to her earlier will make certain that she remains fuzzy for the rest of the day. Otherwise, she'd be plunged into a black, neverending hole of madness once again, plummeting further and further out of my reach.

At least she's calm now.

"I'm sorry," I tell her, feebly.

What do you say to a person who's lost someone they loved? Nothing seems good enough. Nothing seems appropriate. Fuck, I had to do it hundreds of times before in my old life, and I still felt like a useless cunt each and every single time. At least, back then, I didn't care.

Too drunk. Too selfish.

"Why?" she moans.

I let out a deep sigh, turn over, and lean down to retrieve a glass bottle waiting down the side of the bed. I turn back and place the homemade booze onto the mattress between us.

It's so potent that even with the cap screwed on, the stench clings to the back of my throat and overwhelms my senses.

Faith wordlessly snatches it up, wriggles her head upright, and begins gulping down generous mouthfuls straight from the bottle. I watch her enviously, although I know that this is no time for me to have one of my gnarly relapses.

So instead, I just sit there beside her, her faithful companion.

Twenty minutes pass, and she suddenly lets out a loud, painful-sounding sob, breaking the silence. For a second, I worry she's going to have another manic episode.

Unease chews on my intestines.

"You want to talk?" I ask, my voice barely audible because I'm speaking so quietly as if too much noise will break her.

She takes another swig of the drink, not even flinching as the bitter fluid scorches the back of her throat. When she resurfaces, her head lolls as she flashes me a look that indicates that she is already plastered. Her pupils are impossibly wide, consuming her eyeballs.

I'm jealous of the partial numbness she must feel.

"You know what the last thing I said to him was?" she slurs.

I shake my head because I don't know, and also because I don't think I want to find out.

"I told him that…" her voice breaks, her eyes scrunch up tight, the agony is strewn across her face, "I told him that he never failed to disappoint me…"

"That's not the worst thing…" I soothe her.

"It is to him," she goes on, massaging the sides of the bottle top with her thumbs, licking the bitter residue of alcohol off of her lips. "All he ever wanted to do was do me proud. And he always did, and I always told him. But then, I had to go and say that. The most stupid fucking lie in the whole world…" she performs a wide-armed gesture as if to demonstrate.

"Why would he do this? Just because… just because of me?" she gasps as if her oxygen supply is being cut off.

I swallow and shake my head, pausing to consider my next move.

"He obviously just got invested," I tell her.

"Invested?"

"You know, with those girls. That's why he wanted to save her." I don't add that this was an inevitable outcome. Without fail, Sundance always used to get attached to the livestock. He couldn't help himself. He could never dissociate them and see them for what they actually were. No-one in the family liked him, so he ended up kissing up to the enemy. From the very start, he was one big, fat flight risk.

"The devil…" she whispers, staring hard into space. She lefts the bottle slip slightly so that a splash of the booze drips onto the bedsheet.

My skin prickles uncomfortably, "what?"

Her head snaps towards me so abruptly that I flinch, her eyes wide and frantic as her pupils clasp onto mine. "He got possessed," she says, in an even quieter voice than before. Her words are so throaty that each syllable scratches at my eardrum.

"Those girls… they got into his head… they were sent by the devil. Trying to get Sundance to bring us down…" she continues, muttering now, so quickly that it becomes hard to understand her.

I don't know what the fuck to say, so I keep my mouth shut.

At that moment, she springs up to her feet, sending the glass bottle flying, strong-smelling liquid splashing everywhere, and saturating the carpet. Sunlight from the window streams in onto her animated, maddened face, making her irises shine wickedly.

"Take me to the circus," she instructs.

"Are you sure you're up for work?" I ask doubtfully. "Maybe you should rest. Take a day or two off."

"I'm not working," she snaps, spit erupting from her lips. Her hair, now she stands up, is frizzing in chaotic spirals all around her face. "I've got to get rid of the evil spirits- before anyone else gets possessed."

I stifle a chuckle by biting down hard on the flesh inside my cheek.

"But, Faith, the ones we're holding down there are for the next few shows. If you finish them off…"

"ARLO!" she roars, her voice so loud and rasping that I almost shit my pants. "Don't fucking argue with me."

She has that look in her eye, which has grown all too familiar. The look of rage that flashes out from her face when she is about to throw one of her tantrums and seriously hurt someone.

In spite of her size, she's terrifying.

So, quickly I get to my feet and stand across the unmade bed from her. Her fists are clenched so tightly by her sides that her knuckles have turned a bright, alien-like white.

I wonder whether I should give her some more sedatives. But then, she's already had a lot and, mixed with booze; it could kill her.

Instead, with a feeling of deep-seated unease embedded into the pit of my stomach, I give a defeated nod of compliance and start to trail out of the bedroom, holding the door open as she marches around towards me.

Faith doesn't usually get her hands dirty.

But when she does, twisted, fucked-up carnage always ensues.

Jade

I'm losing my fucking mind.

I didn't think I could descend any further into madness; to be honest, I thought that I'd already hit rock bottom on my arse.

You lose your concept of time when you're boxed in in a place like this, with no clocks or windows. More so when you can't see a thing, you're feeling half-dead from blood loss and hunger and are just waiting around for your own inevitable demise.

It's just me, trapped inside the hellish prison of nothingness.

Nothing but my own thoughts, and excruciating pain, and the deafening silence that lingers like a thick smog in the air- slowly suffocating me. Just enough to make me feel as though my lungs are being crushed tightly in an unforgiving metal vice, but not enough to put me out of my misery.

And I never thought I'd say it, but since I've been alone, it's been even worse.

They took the last girl some time ago. I know it's probably only been a matter of hours, but it feels like an eternity.

I didn't like her, but there was something almost soothing about having the rhythmic background noise of another human breathing.

For a moment, there was a group of us, but now I'm alone again.

Which begs the question- why?

Why haven't I been taken yet? Why are they keeping me alive?

When will my suffering come to an end?

At first, I think that my mind is playing tricks on me, as the sound of approaching footsteps starts to echo inside my head. But when it continues and gets louder and louder, I flinch and instinctively scramble to sit up straight against the side of my prison.

I hold my breath, too afraid to even make a sound.

It was easy to pretend I didn't give a shit or that I wasn't scared when the other girls were in here. On my own, I'm left to face the true fact that I'm actually fucking terrified.

Entire body tensing up, my muscles and limbs ache- impossibly rigid as blood pounds inside my ears, and my rapidly beating heart threatens to burst through my chest at any moment.

A scrape of metal followed by the loud, pained screech of the door being pushed open penetrates the air, instantly chilling my blood as it drifts through my arteries.

"I want you to stay outside…" a female voice that I don't recognise. Whoever it sounds menacing, authoritative.

"You don't want me to stay as back up?" a male voice responds. "To help put it out?" he adds. This one I *do* recognise. My skin crawls as the image of his rough, hardened face appears in my mind, sharp and striking.

Flashes of memory haunt me now- of his rough hands grabbing me, slamming me onto the floor so hard that I thought my bones would snap into pieces. I struggled, but he was like a tight, iron vice holding me in place. Paralysed. I remember the glint of the knife's edge, and the terror that got caught in my throat, and the feeling of the blade being jammed hard into my eye socket. Most of all, I remember the agony.

The last thing I ever saw- my last moment of vision- was that face. That cruel, wicked face staring down at me, tight-lipped and mostly expressionless. It wasn't even a crime of passion- he wasn't upset, or angry, or manic with sick, sadistic pleasure. To him, it was just another job. Just another standard action. That's what my life meant.

"I'll be fine," the woman says firmly.

Finally, I let myself breathe out. The door is promptly slammed shut, and five seconds of tense silence commences. I hang there in limbo, my brain racing with thoughts of my fast-approaching fate.

Painstakingly slowly, I hear her move towards me, each step like a gunshot in the icy atmosphere.

"Please… just kill me…" I muster, hugging my knees tightly to my chest. My voice trembles and wavers. "I've suffered enough…"

Suddenly, the metal bars around me vibrate violently, and an earsplitting clang resounds in my ears. I scream.

"Is that right?" a whisper tickles my skin through a gap in the bars.

Instinctively, I scramble backwards, shuddering through my sobs as they ripple like thrashing waves through my skeleton. "Please..." I croak, "please..." I'm whimpering now, pleading desperately for some kind of mercy.

She doesn't reply. I hear the sound of a chain clicking and a key scraping the inside of a padlock, eerily close to my face.

"I'm afraid I don't agree with you," the voice informs me sharply, "I don't think you have suffered enough. In fact, I think it would be impossible for you to suffer enough in order to have repented for all of your sins."

"What the fuck?" I cry out in disbelief, "what sins? I've done nothing wrong to you. I don't even know you."

"You've got the devil inside you," she hisses.

All of a sudden, a sharp pain sears at the top of my head, and I'm pulled upwards by my hair until I'm forced to stand up. Another scream escapes me and rips through the air.

A foul, bitter stench overwhelms me, and I feel a splatter of hot spit land on my face. She's still holding onto my hair like I'm her puppet.

"You're my enemy. You came here, and you got my brother. You took him. You took him from me. Took him to hell..."

My brain whirs, I shake my head vigorously. "No..."

My body is pulled roughly forwards, and I feel myself being dragged out of the iron confines of the cage. I land in a broken, battered heap on the floor, unable to speak through my grievous sobs of pain.

A sharp kick is rammed into the side of my rib cage, knocking the wind out of me. I double over, unable to breathe.

"Open your fucking mouth," she growls. The weight of her body crushes me. It feels as though she is straddling me, tucking me tightly between her thighs. She's on me, breathing hard and fast like she's been running a marathon.

A slap across the face burns my cheek. Snivelling, I obediently open my mouth, lips quivering and teeth chattering as I wonder what horrors she has in store for me.

"It's the end for you now, demon," I hear her whisper, "you thought you could come here, destroy everything. Destroy my work…" her voice cracks, "…you destroyed my brother…" her voice falters. She sounds child-like, heartbroken.

"I DIDN'T DESTROY YOUR FUCKING BROTHER!" I scream manically back at her. "YOU AND YOUR FUCKING PEOPLE ARE THE ONES WHO ARE DEMONS. YOU ARE PURE FUCKING EVIL. YOU FUCKING GOUGED MY EYES OUT; YOU KILLED MY FUCKING FRIENDS…" another face flashes up in my mind. Lots of them, actually. Friends, parents, siblings, co-workers… neighbours that I didn't even like, the man that works at the local corner shop. All people I'll never see again. All the people that might never find out what happened to me.

My painful thoughts are interrupted, and my beloved memories are shattered like glass, as I feel something hard and plastic be shoved into my mouth. Instantly, a foul, strong-smelling stench overwhelms and attacks my senses, and a disgusting, bitter liquid floods the inside of my mouth.

Spluttering and choking, the thick concoction rushes down my esophagus, and stings the skin around my mouth.

It burns. Unbearably so.

I feel the inside of my throat, and my windpipe blister and scorch, right down into the pit of my stomach, where it feels as though a fire has been ignited.

I writhe and struggle in vain beneath the evil woman, and over my broken gasps, I hear her chuckling to herself.

When she's done, the bottle is ripped from my blistered lips. Blood fills my mouth, and my tongue feels like it has been ripped to shreds, making it painful to even cry out anymore. She douses me in whatever is left in the container so that my entire body stings from the harsh, acidic chemicals.

"That'll cleanse you, good and proper," she tells me.

Blind and unable to talk, a series of rasping noises spill from my lips in quick succession. The pain is unbearable. .It's agony. It's starting to feel like the devil really *is* inside me.

"Open your mouth again," she says. "Now."

Vigorously, I shake my head and make one last, final attempt to wriggle away, even though I know it's absolutely no use.

"FUCKING OPEN IT, DEMON!" she screams in my face. She jams her fingers into my mouth and pulls open my lips. Thick, warm blood gushes from the disintegrated insides of my cheeks.

It's choking me now, congealing in my throat, blocking up my airways.

The click of a lighter.

I freeze, and for a split second, my agony is paused by an almighty wave of terror.

I smell gas.

"You're going to burn in hell. Just like Sundance," she whispers.

I feel the burn of a flame on my lip.

It spreads like a plague, hard and fast. Before I know it, I'm involuntarily convulsing in flames, the heat clinging to my skin, smoke clogging my lungs.

"Burn demon!" the woman sings, giggling hysterically, as the flames start to crackle and swarm every inch and oraphace of my body.

I lay there, burning to death, being suffocated by the blaze, my skin melting, and being torn and ravaged from the bone. I listen to her manic, high-pitched cackles of laughter and have my nostrils attacked by the pungent aroma of my own burning flesh.

"BURN!"

"BURN!"

Kevin

When Faith and Arlo take off, I take my chance.

Faith isn't thinking clearly; her usually cold, calculated mind is clouded by a thick fuzz of grief, which works to my advantage on this particular occasion.

I slip away, out of the house, and nobody bats an eyelid. Faith trusts me and therefore, so does everybody else. I know where she keeps the car keys and the weapons. I know the clearest, simplest route out of this place.

And, most importantly, I know how to get to Nancy.

If anyone asks, I tell myself that I will feign innocence and pretend like I'm following her to the circus. I'll play the concerned boyfriend, the poor, grieving brother-in-law, devastated by Sundance's death…

But, to my surprise, no-one even asks. No-one even looks up at me as I casually traipse through the house, pocket jangling with the weight of a set of keys that don't belong to me.

Everyone has been moved by Sundance's death; it would appear. To me, this is odd because when he was alive, nobody seemed to have a kind word to say about him. I suppose it's more because everyone knows how totally fucking crazy this will make Faith. She's devastated. And everyone knows what happens when Faith gets angry or upset. In the short time, I've known her, I've come to realise that it isn't a pretty sight.

Hastily, I crunch across the gravel driveway and slip into the driver's seat of one of the cars. In the pocket of my hoody, my clammy, trembling fingers hold on tightly to a thick, heavy pistol that I only learned how to fire just recently. My pulse rings loudly in my ears as I struggle to put the keys into the engine, one eye permanently fixed on the front door through the windscreen. At any moment, I expect one of them to come crashing through the doorway, armed, face contorted with anger, screeching accusations.

I'd be really fucked.

But, no-one comes.

I escape.

I drive straight off of the property, feeling like a free bird only just released from its the cage. I even let out a loud, shrill laugh of relief as I feel the car speeding quickly away from the house, rapidly passing by the hedges that surround the road.

I don't know why I am feeling so chipper when the hardest part is still to come.

A grim frown stretches out across my face as I vainly try to piece together my so-called plan of action.

Chances are there will be someone there at the farm. Faith told me that one of the family members are supposed to be on guard there at all times- after all, they've got prisoners there.

But, I'd also noticed that, as the months went on, she was getting a little bit careless. More lax. The other women would tell me I'd thawed her icy heart and made her less stern and uptight. Needless to say, she'd started granting the other members of the family more time off of their shifts. She was giving Abdul (or Pig, as they refer to him) much more leniency.

Drumming the rough pads of my fingers against the steering wheel, I come to an uneasy conclusion. If I run into anyone at the farm, I'll tell them that they've been given the rest of the day off.

Any problems, the gun will have to come out.

The rest of the journey flashes past, seemingly at the speed of light, and, before long, I'm pulling up outside the old, traditional-style country house.

Just the sight of it makes my skin break out in gooseflesh.

Fucking ridiculous, really.

All of the awful, horrific things I've done over the course of the last half a year. I've watched people burn, drown, suffocate, and be stabbed and strangled to death. Yet, there I am, faltering just at this place. The place where my wife has been held, prisoner.

Of course, the whole thing becomes much, much scarier when you consider yourself on the other side.

As much as it sickens me to admit it to myself, there was something enjoyable about the power and the feeling of control that pulsed through my veins when I was up on that stage. There was something glorious about having such a thick, wide crowd laugh at my jokes, applaud my performance, and hang on to every single word that I said.

In their eyes, I could do no wrong.

It was nice to be in the company of people who didn't think I was a total cunt.

But it's over now.

Back to reality.

I force myself out of the car, swallowing back the fear that congeals like a thick, spidery web in my throat. Gripping both the gun and the car keys tightly inside my sweating palms, I march purposefully across the driveway towards the front of the house.

Faking it works. I should know.

Pretend I'm confident, fearless, and that's what everyone will think I am.

Fingers shaking madly, I let myself into the house and close it tightly shut behind me. Blinking in the gloom of the first corridor, I peer around and pause a second, straining my ears for any sign of life.

Apart from the distant bleating of a crow, it's silent. I proceed, starting off slow and hesitant before my steps increase in pace, and I find that my knees are like jelly with each movement.

When I reach the kitchen, my head is spinning. I grab the sides of the doorframe to steady myself and jam my eyes shut. Bile climbs my throat.

"Well, hello there."

The sudden voice breaks the quiet like a detonating bomb in the atmosphere. My heart skips a beat as I look in front of me and see the slender figure sitting casually on one of the kitchen countertops.

"Karma…" I croak, blurting out her name before I can even attempt to disguise the shock in my voice.

She flips a wave of fiery red hair over her shoulder and tilts her head, batting her thick, black eyelashes at me.

"I wasn't expecting to see you here," she purrs, a flirtatious smirk pulling at the corner of her mouth.

My face freezes into a troubled frown as I watch her open her legs, exposing the small black strip of her underwear beneath her skirt. She bites her lower lip and winks at me enticingly. "Follow me here, did you?"

Fuck.

Now really is *not* the time for this, but I feel a shameful twinge in my jeans. Flustered, I feel my cheeks burn bright red and shake my head.

"No," I tell her. "You can go home. I'm taking over your shift."

Instantly, her pretty face drops. Her mouth opens.

"What?"

"I said, I'm taking over," I repeat through gritted teeth. "So just go now, will you?"

Much to my dismay, she isn't playing ball. She narrows her eyes at me indignantly so that the shiny black pupils glitter with fury.

"Are you kidding?" she demands, folding her pale arms across her chest. "You're going to fuck me every chance you get for the last month, then just randomly start giving me the cold shoulder?"

I glance around, paranoid that there are spies in the walls or hidden cameras and microphones.

"I'll fuck you later, okay?" I hiss, lying through my teeth. "Just go home, Karma."

She pauses and sucks in her teeth, clearly irritated beyond belief.

I hold my breath.

"Why?" she presses me, arching an eyebrow suspiciously. "Why do you want to get rid of me? What are you up to?"

She slides off the kitchen side, her bare feet padding against the tiles. Every step she takes closer to me is like an iron vice tightening on my balls.

"Nothing, I just... I just needed to get away..." the confident demeanor I tried to pull off is rapidly unravelling. My heart drums hard, incessantly rattling my rib cage.

She isn't buying it. Her gaze hardens. I realise now that I've made a big mistake.

I should've just fucked her.

Because now, she's suspicious.

I tighten my grip on the gun, ready to pull it out. But somehow, she senses my plan, and before I can move, her hand snaps forward, faster than my mind can comprehend. I whip out the gun and hold it in front of me, jabbing the shaft of it into her chest so that she backs away, the colour instantly draining from her cheeks.

Just an ounce of control regained, I puff out my chest and start shouting aimlessly. I don't know what the fuck I am saying; I just want to scare her.

"BACK AWAY! BACK THE FUCK AWAY!" I scream at her, hitting her in the sternum with the barrel of the gun. She gasps and almost trips over backwards.

"STAY AWAY!" I continue to shout, "MOVE, MOVE OUT THE WAY!"

"What are you going to do, Kevin?" Karma asks me calmly, although there is no denying the nervous glint in her eye. "Kill me? What then? Faith will come after you. She'll kill you, and your wife, and even your kids."

At that, I slam the gun with full force into the side of her face, causing the skin to break and expel blood from it's newly bruised exterior.

"DON'T YOU FUCKING TALK ABOUT MY KIDS!" I screech.

She giggles, clutching the side of her face where my gun collided with her cheekbone. "I dare you to shoot me, Kevin," she jibes, "seriously, do it."

Desperately, I glance around the shadowy kitchen for some kind of inspiration. We're alone.

"See," she snickers, pulling back my attention, "see? Nothing but a pussy."

"Shut up!"

"Or, no. Sorry, I got that wrong, didn't I?" she grins at me delightedly, and takes another step closer, so that the gun is embedded between the mounds of her breasts. "Not a pussy… a *bunny*."

I pull the trigger, in just a split, brief moment of pure madness, squinting my eyes so tightly shut that they ache.

Silence follows.

No earth-shattering gunshot or explosive eruption of a bullet blasting through bone and flesh.

Just silence.

Cold, miserable, fate-sealing silence.

I open my eyes.

Karma stands there, a wicked grin dancing on her lips and an evil sparkle tinting her eyes. My wrist trembles and the gun falls to the floor.

"You shouldn't have done that," Karma winks.

In one swift movement, she withdraws a sleek, metal knife from the back of her skirt waistband, brandishing it expertly in front of my eyes so that the metallic shimmer of it dazzles me.

Rooted to the spot and too shocked to move, I become numb and useless as she grabs my shoulder and pulls me roughly around so that she is holding me from behind.

Before I can struggle or retaliate, she pierces the top of my spine with the knife, lunging it straight through the nerves, severing my spinal cord in an instant.

Paralysed, I collapse onto the floor, and my cheek smashes hard onto the kitchen tiles. I almost drown in fear as my brain desperately screams for my limbs and muscles to work, but I know that I'm now hopelessly trapped inside my own skeleton.

I can't move.

Seconds later, she lifts my head by what's left of my hair and plants an icy cold kiss on my cheek. A vile, disgusting paste of drool, tears, and mucus drip down my face, pooling on the cold tiles beneath me.

"You fucked with the wrong girl this time, hun," she informs me gleefully before letting my weak neck flop and my face slams back down onto the hard flooring.

Everything goes black.

Nancy

Blood splatters across my face. The feeling of the droplets on the surface of my skin causes me to shudder and my stomach to churn uncomfortably as I almost choke on a mouthful of my own acidic bile.

"You get used to it," Abdul tells me grimly.

"Really?" I ask.

Wordlessly, he shakes his head.

More unhappy than ever, I cringe as I rip the jagged knife's edge from the torn, fatty ligaments of raw human carcass that lays strewn across the metal block in front of me. The stench alone is enough to make me vomit. Already, I've puked about five or six times. Abdul is understanding, at least he was at first, but he's starting to look a little impatient.

"You know, if anyone catches you, you'll be fucked," he says with a heavy sigh. He slices his own knife through a bruised and bloodied calve, severed from the rest of its body.

I try not to wonder if it belongs to any of my friends.

"I already am," I reply underneath my breath.

Most of my hope has already diminished into nothingness, leaving me just a hollow, faithless shell. However, the promises of my cunt of a husband keep echoing around the corners of my mind. I know that I shouldn't count on him helping me. I couldn't even count on him to help me when we had it all. What are the chances now, when we're being held hostage by this godforsaken cult of sick, sadistic fucks?

At that moment, there is a clattering of footsteps behind us. We both turn to glance across the floor of the slaughterhouse, beyond the industrial-sized tubs of human remains and the glistening blood spatters that stain the concrete ground.

It's her.

Seeing her sends a bolt of electricity shooting down my spine, setting my innards on fire. I clench my hands, ignoring the squelch of rotting blood left on my fingers.

"Come with me, now," she barks across the room at me, her voice echoing, bouncing scratchily against the ceiling and floors.

I shudder before glancing over my shoulder at Abdul, eyes wide; horror rapidly flooding my senses. He frowns past me, fixing his eyes onto Faith.

"Me, or her?" he asks.

"Both," she replies simply.

Exchanging puzzled, nervous looks, we drop our tools and traipse with feet as heavy as lead back across the room. As we go, my brain buzzes. Will this be my final breath? What will she show us? What will she make me do? Will it hurt? Is there a heaven? And a hell?

For a brief, split second of madness, I consider turning back, picking up the saturated hilt of one of our jagged blades and then making a run for it.

I envision myself lunging into her, like a medieval knight jousting with a long, sharp spear that will instantly rip through her flesh and impale her.

Killing her.

Ending her.

And putting an end to all of this chaos at the same time.

But my senses prevent me from doing anything of the sort.

Of course, I know that, just behind her, lingering in her shadow, will be one of her henchmen, ready and armed with a gun. My brains will be blasted from my skull before I can even break out into a sprint. My body will hit the ground, and my blood will seep into the ground beneath me. She'll toss her head back and laugh.

I'd be saving her a job.

After all, it's no secret that she wants me gone.

How long until Kevin's hold over her fades?

Abdul and I walk slowly towards her. I long to reach out a hand and entwine his fingers in mine, purely for the minor comfort of feeling the warmth of another *living* person's skin.

But I don't.

Instead, we follow behind our captor, neither of us saying a word. Every so often, I sense his head turn just a tiny fraction, and I meet his eye for a short, passing moment. His solemn stare prompts me to remember all that he has told me over the last few days.

Do whatever they say.

Don't try to run.

Swallowing, I will my knees to stop knocking together. I feel small, weak, and pathetic, especially trailing along after her like a little lost stray.

She leads us back through the odd, eerie bleakness of the warehouse and the rusting hooks and machinery that remain hoarded inside its tinny walls. As we approach the main entrance, a chill creeps in and snakes up my arms, causing my teeth to start chattering.

I'm surprised when we reach the mouth of the warehouse, and I see that Faith is guiding us outside of the slaughterhouse. The light of day, although it hasn't been *that* long, somehow stings my eyes, as if I've been trapped underground for years. Blearily, I blink my swollen eyelids and glance around at the cold, groggy day that consumes the vast, wide courtyard of the farm. I scan the rows of high, wire fences that keep us in, like walls of an extended cage.

Abdul told me he managed to escape from here, once.

I've got no idea how.

As soon as we step outside, the harrowing soundtrack of weak, pitiful groans washes over me like a wave full of drowned corpses. The slight wind carries it like a bad smell. I flinch uncomfortably and try not to cast my eyes in the direction of the filthy cages that lay some metres away from the warehouse.

Wordlessly, Abdul, and I continue to walk. Faith leads us around a corner so that we are fast approaching the side of the house. For a moment I think that she's taking us somewhere in a car. Maybe I'll start being allowed that same privileges that Abdul is- being taken back to the main house for a shower and a decent night's sleep.

But it doesn't take long for it to dawn on me that Faith would do nothing of the sort for me.

She hates me.

Anything nice Faith ever offers me; I'll instantly approach with suspicion. It'll be a trap of some kind, to lull me in and then rip me apart when I least expect it.

It's a relief when the sounds of the caged prisoners die down. Ahead of us, down a damp, muddy alleyway which is mostly swamped in darkness, I see a tall, shadowy figure standing upright, and then a large lump laying on the ground.

I chew nervously on the inside of my mouth until I can taste the rusty drops of blood congealing on my teeth. I cross my arms tightly over my body in a vain attempt to protect my body from the cold weather and whatever it is that lies ahead of us.

"This is mainly for you," Faith turns casually, still walking, and nods in my direction. Her voice is dull… bored as if she can't really be bothered. "But you'll appreciate it too, Pig," she sticks her tongue out at Abdul, a glinting tongue ring scraping against her teeth as she does so.

My pace slows as I lower my gaze and focus tightly on the lump on the ground. It doesn't take long for me to identify that it is a body. Likely a corpse. It looks frozen solid, despite not being held down in place.

The tall figure turns. I recognise the man.

One of Faith's cronies.

Maybe if it was just Faith, Abdul and I could take her down, but we have no hope with this oversized thug around. He looks as though he could snap my neck with just one brief maneuver of the fingers.

"Oh fuck…" Abdul gasps, stopping in his tracks.

Startling, I find myself stopping too, freezing beside him. At first, I wonder what it is he's so shocked about. Over the last few days, the two of us have seen enough dead bodies around the place- what makes this one any different?

But then, I see it.

My jaws fall open.

I feel the hot, piercing eyes of Faith and her bodyguard boring into me, gauging my reaction, no doubt waiting expectantly for me to fall down to my knees and let out an animal-sounding moan of pain. They're listening for my devastated cry to echo all around the expansive acres of land that surround us; to further demonstrate how isolated and alone we are.

And how totally and utterly screwed *I* am.

But somehow, the scream doesn't come.

Maybe it's stuck somewhere in the back of my throat, an impossibly tight ball of emotion lost in a dusty corner of my voice box.

Either way, it doesn't come.

"Is he dead?" I blurt out, my voice escaping my dry, chapped lips in a throaty croak that scratches the back of my mouth.

He's stiff and rigid on the ground like a straight, wooden plank lying flat on his back. But his pupils move, frantically scrabbling about in their cold, inhuman irises like tadpoles in a pond. Although he's fully clothed, his waxy skin is stained with splashes of black-red blood and coated with the mud that blankets the floor in a sludgy mess.

He looks pitiful.

Pathetic.

"Kevin?" I add before I can stop myself. My left foot moves forward unsteadily, the cold recesses of wet mud squelching up to my ankle. "Kevin, are you… are you dead?" my voice fades to an inaudible murmur.

My husband's head moves slightly, in what could be construed as a sharp nod.

He's alive.

Faith appears irritated by my apparently underwhelming reaction. She folds her arms in front of her chest and narrows her eyes at me, now standing still in the mud, her wellington boots coated in a thick layer of brown muck.

"You've got a choice to make," she says simply.

I glance up at her, awaiting instruction. Faith and the tall man exchange an amused look- as if they are a pair of school bullies sharing a private joke at my expense.

But my own expression remains unmoved. Perhaps it's the shock, or perhaps I've gone mad- but, for whatever reason, I find myself hardened, numb even.

Faith stretches out an arm and points vaguely up the alleyway. Her emerald green eyes flicker mischievously as if she is daring me, challenging me.

"Either Kevin here comes to a rather…" she trails off, as if for dramatic effect, "unpleasant end…or, Arlo will blow both of your brains out." As she says it, she turns to Abdul.

I sense him flinch beside me. Again, I resist the urge to hold his hand.

At that moment, the wind picks up, and a gust brushes past us, omitting the faintest, quietest of howls as it goes.

"What kind of unpleasant end?" I find myself asking.

Faith and Arlo smirk at one another. My blood runs cold.

"Arlo- would you care to demonstrate?" she asks, looking up at her tall, despicable minion.

Without a word, Arlo bends over and scoops up Kevin's unmoving torso and limbs up from the mud, as easily as if he is nothing but a broken china doll. Faith gestures for us to follow, so Abdul and I continue to follow their lead, further down the alley until we reach a wide, gaping ditch that suddenly swallows up the ground.

Before I have time to process the scene in front of us, I watch helplessly as my husband is tossed carelessly into the pit, his body twirling gracefully through the air as he plummets.

That time, I do cry out, although some of it is torn away by the rapidly maddening wind. I lunge forwards and peer downwards into what is certainly a very shallow grave. Still motionless, Kevin lays slumped at the bottom, arms and legs bent at peculiar angles, whilst his eyes continue to stare up at me, as sharply as if they were centimetres away from mine.

A thick lump of mud falls on top of him, landing with a heavy clump on his chest. I glance back up to see that Arlo is now wielding a shovel.

"What are you going to do?" I ask. "What happened to him?"

"Karma," interjects Faith in a bitter snarl, "Karma happened to him. Thank God for that. That son of a bitch has had it coming his entire life." I watch the woman pull clumps of greasy black hair away from her face. She spits into the grave, a sickly, white trail of spittle dangling from her lips. My stomach turns. Something has happened to her. She's... changed. She's still a crazy bitch, but where's that perfectly polished out layer? Where's that effortless sass?

"Faith..." croaks Abdul. When I look at him, his face is drained of all colour. "Faith, is there no way around this? No other way?"

She shakes her head and gives a shrug of indifference in response as if it's all out of her hands.

"Our work is all about getting back what you put into this world," she replies sombrely, although there is no concealing the sick, gleeful way her lip creeps upwards in one corner.

She's enjoying every moment of this.

"After all, even Prue said it," she adds, her stare towards Abdul intensifying. His face crumples then. My heart aches for him.

"She thought your husband was a piece of shit," Faith tells me, "and it turns out she was right," a high pitched laugh comes from her lips, and she shakes her head as if in disbelief. "I'm a fucking mug for ever thinking otherwise. I'll *never* make the same mistake again."

I sigh and nod.

Abdul stares at me in horror for showing even a brief glimmer of understanding. Who can blame him?

But, regardless of how much I despise her, Faith and I have a common thread. Nothing connects women like a mutual heartbreak over the same man. Nothing brings us closer than being screwed over by the same selfish, messed-up dog.

Suddenly, Faith wrenches something out of Arlo's pocket. She holds up a gun and holds it to the side of Abdul's head. She stares at me with unblinking eyes and a pale, stony face.

"Choose," she demands coldly. "Choose now. You and him," she nods at Abdul, "or *that* useless piece of shit?"

I realise as I give my husband a second look, that he must be paralysed somehow. He remains laying down at the bottom of the pit, not even making any noise. But his eyes scream volumes. They scream out for mercy,... for forgiveness.

I think of our children. Our precious little boy, and our adorable baby girl. I think of the professional family portrait, framed and hung up above the state-of-the-art fireplace in our living room. I think of my wedding ring, stored safely in a jewellery box in my bedroom. I remember the huge party we had- the heartfelt speeches, the gorgeous food, and the emotional first dance we shared, whilst our family and friends watched and wept. I remember the nights we got drunk in front of a movie and ended each night having mind-bending sex in every room of the house. I remember all of the weekend trips and dinner dates where he made me feel as though I were the most flawless woman who ever lived. I remember the feeling of being asked out by the most popular boy in school and showing up to prom on his arm, all eyes on us as we drifted through the night just staring into each other's eyes.

A tear wells up in my eye.

But then, I hear the sound of the wind howling, and I remember where we are.

I remember the boyfriend in high school who would ignore me for weekends at a time, and all of the nights I cried myself to sleep thinking I wasn't good enough.

I remember starving myself for weeks before prom, worrying myself sick that he'd cheat on me again before I got the chance to go with him.

I remember all the nights he disappeared, and I was left at home in our house, frightened that he'd found someone else.

I remember how much I hated myself when I was pregnant, for being so fat and unglamorous.

I remember the agony of realising that the man I adored… the man I would die for, was in another woman's bed. The pure hurt that wracked every fibre of my being when it occurred to me that he never gave a fuck about me, or our children, or our home, or our life.

I remember how I threw up from disgust when it finally dawned on me that I'd wasted so many years on a piece of shit like Kevin, who would fuck anything with a pulse given a chance.

I remember the feeling of watching my husband torture and kill another woman for fun.

I remember finding out that he could have escaped, but he chose to stay with this bloodthirsty cult of deranged murderers.

A dry, humourless chuckle.

I imitate Faith, spitting down into the bottom of the bit, for once not caring what *he* might think.

"Goodnight, Kevin!" I pronounce, waving down at him.

His eyeballs almost bulge from his head. Instantly, Arlo begins to shovel more dirty down onto his still, paralysed body.

Abdul turns away.

But I stay rooted to the spot.

I wouldn't miss this for the world.

PART THREE:
1 week later

Addison

I feel like I'm sailing.

It's how I imagined death to feel like. At least, this is what I hope it feels like.

I don't want to be alive anymore.

Let's face it, my entire existence was pretty much a huge shit show from the start, and the only thing in my life that I truly cared about was my brother.

He's dead.

Not only that, but he died a painful death.

He suffered.

And how do you continue life, knowing that the person who meant the world to you ended their own in that way?

I suppose I understand what Faith is going through. That weird, short, hippy girl with the long, black hair and the bright green eyes. The girl that Arlo is in love with, and everyone else is infatuated with.

The girl who saved me.

Her brother died too. Sundance.

I know this because Arlo tells me. I suppose, since the pain that overwhelms my body has become so unbearable, he has started to view me as his own personal human journal. He comes into my room, and he tells me how worried he is about Faith.

Says she's changed.

I don't talk back because even breathing is exhausting.

But I understand how she feels.

You can be the strongest person in the world, but everyone has their weakness. Everyone has their downfall. The one sore spot that can make them crumble and fall in an instant. Everyone thinks Faith is invincible… fuck, at this place, they genuinely believe she *is* God. So none of them can piece it together. None of them can accept her grief without assuming she's sick or possessed.

Fucking mental.

And ridiculous.

"Faith wants to leave," Arlo tells me hopelessly, his face full of sadness and contorted with defeat.

No longer does he sit and tend to my wounds. I'm fairly certain I've got a form of gangrene, judging by the smell and the repulsed looks I get from him at regular intervals.

I shift slightly in my sheets, more from the impending threat of cramp than an actual desire to. As usual, I don't talk. I try to communicate with my eyes how much I disapprove of his emotional venting.

He ignores me.

"I… I just…" he slumps his head forwards into his hands- a poor, broken man.

Except, I find it quite difficult to feel sorry for him, given the circumstances.

I try to zone out, letting my eyes roll slowly into the back of my head. I give a low sigh of pure exhaustion and let my shoulders sag against the sweat-moistened pillows.

Sailing.

When I close my eyes, I feel like I'm rocking on a boat. Nausea teases my esophagus, and my blurry head tilts queasily. It's like the worst, most agonising form of seasickness.

But at least I hope it'll be over soon.

"Addison!"

The sudden sound startles me, and my eyelids flutter open. I groan as I realise I'm still laying on the same filthy bed, listening to the same torturous madman bitch to me about his unrequited love interest.

"How are you feeling?" Arlo asks me, his expression sharpening with concern. He cocks his head suspiciously, his eyes searching mine for any more traces of impending death. He stands up then and delves into his bag of pills. Fuck knows what they are. Pain relief, antibiotics… whatever it is in the medical cocktail he keeps feeding me- it's somehow keeping me alive.

At that moment, I choose to change tact.

I summon the very last of my energy supplies and say a silent prayer that I won't be needing them anymore.

"How do you think I'm feeling?" I rasp, bowing my head as my voice is dragged from my throat like a ball of sandpaper. "I'm alone, in this fucked-up house, with all these fucked-up people, dying of infection, with both of my fucking legs missing…" I raise my voice and tighten my fists with frustration. "*Please*, tell me, doctor, how the fuck do *you* think I feel?" sarcasm tinges my question as I lift my head and narrow my eyes up at him.

He's not as scary-looking as he once was to me. He's still huge, and hard-faced, stony-eyed, and constantly looks as though he's on a rampage… but it's as though his exterior has cracked. That big, evil tough guy shell has been chipped away, revealing the soft bag of blood and flesh inside.

I can see his human. And it's full of anxiety and fear. He's unsettled and lost. He doesn't know what the hell will happen to him if Faith leaves.

He's pathetic.

I blurt out a shrill chuckle. "You're fucking pathetic," I tell him.

Arlo stares back at me, somewhat bemused at my outburst. He sits back down onto my low, grimy death bed and cracks his knuckles- an irritating habit of his that I have not yet grown fond of.

"Sorry?"

I take a few breaths. Already, just stringing together a few sentences has sent my heart rate into overdrive.

His face blurs and flutters in and out of focus as my eyelids rise and fall. The bright red behind them stings.

"Look at your fucking self," I muster, "crying about a woman who clearly couldn't give a shit about you."

At that, his face drops. I sense a slight quiver, a nervous twitch in the side of his usually confident demeanour. It fuels the crackling flames that are now ignited in the pit of my stomach. Grim delight pulls at the corners of my mouth.

"What? You really think I feel sorry for you?" I continue, "think you're the poor, heartbroken man who'd do anything and everything for the love of his life? You've got to be fucking kidding me," I start to laugh; on a high as I watch his face crumple even further.

"Faith has been using you. Thanks to her, you're a criminal. A sadistic, torturous murderer. You know what they'll do to you in prison? You'll be gang-raped; they'll cut your fucking balls off…" I realise that I'm quickly descending into hysteria, tripping fast over my own words. "… and where will she be?" I stop to breathe and absorb the pitiful look on his face.

His small, dark eyes are glinting. Tears are welling up above his waterline.

"I'll tell you where she *won't* be," I whisper, groggily leaning forward, "she won't be saving you. She'll be running away somewhere to find some other schmuck she can seduce into doing her bidding. She'll leave you at the drop of a hat. You know why?"

Arlo blinks at me.

"Because you're all just pawns in her sick little game!" I hiss, "worthless little minions, brainwashed by some pretty girl into fucking your lives up."

"And now you want to cry about how devastated you are that she's fucking off and leaving you in this mess?" I smirk, shaking my head in disbelief. "What a liberty. For a doctor, you really are a stupid cunt."

Spent, I fall back against my soggy, stinking pillows and let my eyes close for the last time. I sigh a breath of relief.

He won't keep me alive now.

He can't handle the truth, and I've just delivered it to him first class on a shit-encrusted silver platter.

Silence falls upon us.

At first, it's empowering, and I feel as though I've won a battle.

However, my triumph is short.

Soon, the quiet and the bright redness behind my eyelids merges from peaceful to eerie, and I find my limbs tense.

What now?

I refuse to open my eyes. Instead, I hold my breath, hoping that soon he'll blow a bullet into my head or smother me with a pillow. I soothe myself in my mind, telling myself over and over that soon, the terrible pain convulsing in the bloodied stumps of my legs will be no more.

Everything will stop hurting.

Any moment now.

I must drift off because the waves beneath my little rocking boat somehow transition from choppy and nauseating to tranquil and relaxing. I float in and out of consciousness, and the stark red and orange blur that consumes my vision has faded to pitch black.

I wonder if I am dead.

I envision Bobby, my brother, walking towards me. I picture heavenly white clouds and a golden sun streaming through. A glorious pink and orange sunrise, a deliciously scented breeze, and the taste of fresh pastries on my tongue.

Then, it's like the cord from reality to imagination is severed in one swift chop.

"A stupid cunt, eh?" a low, rugged voice hisses in my ear.

Although I tell myself I am not afraid, the close proximity of his presence makes my blood run cold, chilling my veins.

"What?" I blurt out dumbly, rendered disorientated from the darkness.

A thick slab of warm meat slaps against my forehead, then holds it back hard against the headboard.

"You called me a stupid cunt," he spits, snarling underneath his breath. "But, now I'm going to *really* show you who's a stupid cunt."

Arlo

The bitch had it coming.

The intent was clear. She has made no secret of the fact that she wanted to die. But, she had her chance, and she blew it. Faith offered her death, and she declined. I didn't spend days reviving this fugly slut just for her to suddenly announce she has a death wish.

Once my work is done, I sit back and admire my project.

Faith is always going on about mindfulness, spirituality, and getting in touch with your innermost emotions. Fuck, maybe if Sundance had done that, the poor sod wouldn't be dead.

But alas, here we are, and now I have the perfect solution which will ensure that nobody in our family will ever suffer the mental turmoil that took Sundance.

Normal humans- normal people, spend a shit tonne on therapy. They pay a bomb just to sit and spill their guts to some smug, rich guy in an office who earns above average, just to sit and pretend they give a jot about someone else's problems.

Well, now, our family has its own in-house psychiatrist!

I frown as I notice a tiny bit of leakage dangling above her left iris. I gently pull the strand of gooey, dried super glue away from the lash line and grimace as I flick it away.

There.

Perfect.

"This will really benefit all of us," I tell her proudly. "Although, as my therapist, I can't just lie to you and say this is solely for the family…" I blush and give her a nervous smile.

"After all, I'm sure you already realised that I really enjoyed it."

She stares back at me, bloodshot eyeballs bulging from their sockets. Her eyelids are glued upwards to the brow bone, using an industrial-strength glue gun that we keep around the house- purely for mending things. See, our work is not so much about torture but about purpose.

It's just that sometimes, the torture is a bonus.

I lean forward and press a light kiss against her lips. She squirms, and I hear a tiny rip as she makes the mistake of attempting to open her mouth.

Now, it's my turn to laugh.

I stand up and give her a final once over.

She lays in the bed, her eyes now permanently open, her mouth permanently shut.

All she can do now is listen and look.

No more smart-arsed comments.

Now, she can be *really* useful.

I wiggle my fingers, waving her farewell before I plunge the room back into darkness.

I relish the pain and the indescribable fear that highlights all of the tiny red veins bulging from her eyeballs.

That's right; I think to myself as I turn and leave the room, savouring the desperate squeaks and murmurs that she makes through her mutilated lips.

No-one calls me a stupid cunt.

Faith

Already, it's been over a week since Sundance left me.

The way that the time is fleeting- dashing by at the speed of light seems incredibly sad and unfair.

Why should the world keep spinning when my baby brother is rotting?

I glance over at him and take another long drag of the thick, heavy spliff balanced between my fingers. I'm smoking only somewhat to numb the pain, but mostly in a vain attempt to drown out the horrific smell.

Nothing smells as bad as a decaying body.

Exhaling, I slowly rise from the polished, wooden chair at the foot of his bed and drift towards his rigid body, lying still and lifeless on top of the covers. His eyes have been closed, exposing white, waxy eyelids that glisten in the sliver of sunlight that creeps in through a gap in the curtains. Some of the girls have been maintaining him, keeping him presentable. But there's no concealing his death. It radiates off of him and seeps into my flesh, chilling me to the bone.

I stare at him for far too long.

My heart weighs heavily in my chest because I know that this must be goodbye.

A thick knot of pain congealing in my throat, I sink down to my knees so that I am level with his head. I balance my chin on the cold, fabric edge of the duvet and blink away more tears that cascade down my cheeks.

"I'm sorry," I whisper, my voice wretched with heartbreak. I stretch out an arm and place a hand over his cold, dead knuckles. I shiver at his touch. "I'm sorry I couldn't take care of you as I promised."

When I close my eyes, I picture the tiny, curious face of my darling, red-haired little brother gazing up at me with nothing but adoration.

My brother. The only one in the world who ever loved me, just because.

The cherished memory quickly fades and sizzles out to reveal a darker, more painful shroud from the past.

I was just a little girl.

Pounding through the house, heart racing, pulse drumming loudly in my eardrums. Searching frantically from room to room, tearing myself apart looking for him.

Not Sundance, but my other little brother. The little brother I had before him. The little brother he replaced.

I'll never forget the agonising bolt of devastation that struck me as soon as I'd crossed the farmyard and came to the slaughterhouse.

I'd been horrified to think that our piece of shit mother had been so thoughtless as to bring my little infant brother to a place where animals were being murdered and butchered.

If only that were it.

The bright, glistening blood. The stench of dead and mutilated flesh. The lifeless shape of my little brother's torso laying like a slab of raw meat over a butcher's table, whilst my mother cried pitifully in a corner and watched them cut him into pieces.

When I open my eyes again, the sheet is saturated with my tears. I failed them both. Both of my baby brothers.

I clear my throat and bite back the tears, determined to be strong.

After all, I'm all alone in this world now.

Now, it's just Beau and me.

She is my final chance.

My only reason to keep at this shit stain of a life.

"I'm going mad, Sundance," I tell him sternly, furiously rubbing tears from my cheeks. "The devil is in me. I feel it. I'm growing weaker and weaker. If I stay here, I know I'll go the same way you did."

Sundance, understandably, does not respond.

"So, I'm going away for a while," I say with a self-assured nod, although I am secretly quaking in my boots. "Probably for a few years, maybe even more. But I need you to stay here and watch over the family for me…" I pause and look at him expectantly.

"I don't want to make this any harder than it has to be," I whisper as I shakily get to my feet. "So… I'm just going to go. I have no idea where, but I'll send money back to this place to keep it running. I want you to take care of the family and make sure our work goes on…" I swallow the thick knot of pain in my throat. It feels like razor blades descending my esophagus.

I allow myself one final look at him before turning on my heel and purposefully striding away.

Goodbye.

Outside the door, lining the corridor as far as the staircase, family members stand with tears in their eyes. Some of them are sobbing, whilst others are silent, gazing solemnly into space as if contemplating their entire existence.

Unlike when I walked away from Sundance, no emotion whatsoever stirs inside my chest. I've been turned to stone. Hard and unbreakable.

Silently, I walk past them, ignoring each one until I reach the top of the stairs, where Arlo stands. As always, he towers above me, but his face is twisted and full of discomfort. In his arms, he cradles Beau, who's chewing messily on a small slab of meat.

At the sight of her, my face involuntarily breaks out into a smile, and I greedily snatch her from Arlo and cuddle her tightly to my chest.

Her odd, misshapen face puckers and gurgles up at me, and instantly I feel our bond intensify.

Just us two.

Us two, against the world.

"Faith," says Arlo, his voice higher, weaker than usual. "Do you really have to go? I know you're not feeling yourself, but just look at what I…"

"Arlo," I say in a throaty, darkened voice. "I'm going. That's that. I have to do it for the good of the family. Otherwise, I know that the devil will take me. He will kill me, just like he killed Sundance."

Wordlessly, he nods, too choked up to speak.

He sickens me.

Weak.

I turn briefly to address the congregation of my mourners.

"While I'm gone, Sundance is in charge," I tell them. "He will relay my wishes through Arlo. Just as long as you obey him and continue to carry out our work, you will be safe and loved."

No-one speaks.

"Goodbye. I love you all," I lie.

Then, that's it.

I turn my back on my family, the family that I was so proud of and that I worked so hard to build.

That's what death does.

Meaningful enough, death can change everything and anyone.

For me, Sundance's death was an extraordinary loss. And not just because I lost him and have been left with this gaping, painful hole in my life. But because, when he died, it made me realise that he was the only one I truly loved.

Everyone else is just a fucking accessory.

And what's an accessory?

I fit Beau into a car seat and pick up my large backpack of belongings from the front door. Without turning back, I exit the beautiful mansion I called home for so long and slowly pad across the gravel driveway. I fit us both into a car and take one last look at the house.

My family now stands outside of it, tearfully waving me off.

I give a grim smile before turning to my left to look down into Beau's rear-facing car seat. Her sharp, jagged teeth are yellowing and bloodstained, chunks of flesh jammed into cavities in her gums.

"Just you and me now, kid."

Abdul

It's been a few weeks now.
Since I watched my old boss be buried alive.
Fuck, that's something I never thought I'd say.
In actual fact, you could even say I helped bury him myself. After all, in the end, shovelling the wet dirt on top of his rigid, paralysed body was a group effort.
Part of me even enjoyed it.
Why wouldn't I want to bury the piece of shit that could've escaped this fucking place and gotten help? I often imagine where I would be right now if he'd just done the decent thing. Suppose he'd only just driven far, far away, and gotten some kind of help. Police, or ambulances, anything with flashing lights and a siren.
Probably, I'd be tucked up in my own warm, safe bed. My days would be spent attending intensive therapy sessions to combat the trauma. Friends and family would come and see me, and I'd probably get some kind of book deal for being a survivor.
But would I be happy ever again?
I doubt it.
It's true what they say; every experience changes you. And when you've been caged like an animal, forced to sleep crammed into a shit and vomit smeared compound, then coerced into cutting up dead bodies and watching your girlfriend die, to say it changes you is a big, massive, fucking understatement.
I'm coming to realise that maybe emotions aren't limitless. Maybe every human gets an emotional allowance, which is so great that it often can last a lifetime. But then, some unlucky fuckers, experience such pain, heartbreak, frustration, and turmoil, that they eventually burn out.
You become numb.
Wondering around aimlessly, a constant fuzz blaring in your head as you drag your feet and try to remember how distressed the

situation used to make you feel. Apparently, not being able to feel anything at all is worse than agony.

"Abdul…"

A quiet whisper in the night, so low that it is almost inaudible. I tense up and blink up at the gloomy ceiling that hangs above me. It's my turn on the mattress (Nancy and I take shifts of sleeping on the cold, hard floor that stinks of piss), although the sagging mattress makes my shoulder blades ache.

"Abdul!" louder this time. Now, there's no denying that it's Nancy's voice.

I roll over onto my side and strain my eyes until I can make out the black, fuzzy outline of her body on the ground beside me.

When she first got here, I wanted to fuck her. Now, it's like I have the libido of a castrated priest.

"You okay?" I whisper back.

I hear her scramble to her feet, and soon her face comes into view. Although it's gloomy, and she stinks, and her cheeks are smudged with dry blood, she's still pretty.

Wouldn't it be ironic if she tried to bed me now?

"Look what I've got," she whispers. I detect a tinge of excitement in her voice, which makes me somewhat uncomfortable. I shudder involuntarily.

Wordlessly, I watch as she holds up something. I make out the outline and at first think it's a gun.

It can't be.

But I blink again and realise that it is.

"What's that?" I ask.

Nancy giggles quietly like a schoolgirl. "It's a gun."

My heart begins to thud against the inside of my chest, barely able to believe it. "A gun?" I repeat.

She nods in the darkness.

"How?"

"That fucking clown from earlier," she whispers. "You know when me and him went outside?"

"Yeah," I lie because, honestly, I had zoned out. One of the men, Ziggy, was at the farm, giving us instructions. New recruits were being put to work out in the slaughterhouse. I was busy directing them, and as a reward, was being granted a night off from the circus. I was too busy to notice what Nancy was doing.

"I fucked him," she tells me excitedly, "the dumb prick didn't even realise I'd taken it off of his belt."

Sounds about right.

If any of the family members were a loose cannon, it was definitely that fucking guy.

"So… what are you going to do?" I ask.

I sense her pause and cock her head, arching an eyebrow at me in disbelief. "What am *I* going to do? What are *we* going to do? You and I are going to escape. Now."

A mixture of adrenaline and unease churn in my belly. Now, I'm sitting bolt upright, chewing my lower lip nervously. It tastes rusty, like old, stale blood.

"Now?" I ask.

"Right now," she tells me firmly. She gets to her feet and holds out a hand. Even though she's only a bit older than me, she has that warm, motherly presence that makes me do as she says. Obediently, I get up from the bed, and we press our clammy palms together.

"Let's go," she whispers.

Together, the two of us tip-toe to the doorway leading out of our grimy box room and glance across the dimly-lit slaughterhouse floor.

It's cold.

I shiver, and my skin breaks out in goosebumps.

My feet feel heavy, rooted to the ground; however, Nancy yanks me hard, pulling me across the stone floor. I pad after her. It feels like jumping into a nearly-frozen lake.

Aside from the gentle thudding of my chest and the sound of our feet slapping against the floor, it's silent. Eerily so.

Like thin, weightless shadows, we hurry out of the main warehouse, through the backroom, and before I know it, we are slipping through the double doors out into the sharp night's air.

"I don't like this," I whisper uncomfortably. "It's far too easy. Why isn't there anyone guarding the door?"

Nancy pauses, and we press our backs up against the wall, then slink down so that we are bathed in shadow, narrowly missing the strip of moonlight at our feet.

"Faith is gone," she says under her breath. "He told me. Apparently, it's non-stop parties back at the house now. With her gone, it's chaos."

This makes sense. But surely they wouldn't be stupid enough to leave us in the farm unguarded. I know that there must be someone nearby. Surely.

She pulls me up, and we continue skulking along in the darkness. The occasional whine of pain, the stench of suffering, and the rattle of a cage make my skin crawl, but thankfully I'm distracted from these unpleasantries by the pure fear and dread that cripples my spine with every step.

By now, the farmyard, even in the dense blackness, has become familiar to me. Instinctively, I know the direction to walk, and soon enough, we come to the back door of the farmhouse. Glass glinting against the white glow of the moon, it's obvious that all of the lights in the house are off.

"Let's go down the alley," Nancy says, pointing towards the side of the building.

I shudder again, remembering my last foiled escape attempt. We almost got away.

Prue and me.

But they found us. They hunted us like bloodhounds, and they killed her and made me their slave. The sound of her screams and the muffled movements of her struggle haunt me to this very day.

Naturally, I hesitate. Nancy blinks at me when she realises I am no longer trailing behind her. "Come on! What are you waiting for?" she hisses, impatience starting to tinge her voice.

"What if there's a trap?" I murmur, nibbling on the chewed nubs of my fingertips. "This is too easy…"

Without another word, she lunges forward and grabs me by the crook of the arm. When she pushes her face close to mine, her eyes are illuminated in the shine of the moon- they are wild and fierce, full of desperation and terror. Even though she keeps her lips firmly clamped shut, I find my feet comply.

I stumble along behind her, clumsy and heavy-footed, but she forces me to pick up the pace until we are both half-jogging along the perimeter of the house.

We aren't moving fast, but my pulse is racing; my heartrate screams alarmingly in my eardrums, and cold drips of sweat slither down my forehead.

Underfoot, the ground is marshy, damp. I can't help but imagine Kevin's body lurking somewhere in the soil beneath us. Surely he'd have suffocated down there by now. Would his flesh have already started to decay? Would tiny creatures be scrabbling about in the earth, nibbling and chewing at his rotting flesh? Nancy seems to be having the same thoughts. She speeds up so that we are now rashly stalking the length of the alley.

Soon, the tall, wooden fence at the end comes into view, looming over us like a dark, monstrous shadow, forbidding us from taking a step further.

"Here," Nancy presses the gun into my hand. It's heavier than I imagined, and the steel coating is hot and clammy against my palm, despite the freezing atmosphere.

I watch as Nancy stretches her body upwards and grips the top of the fence with her fingertips. Surprisingly, she manages to haul herself up halfway, her face red and contorted with effort as she kicks out a leg to steady herself against the wall. Once she has secured herself, jammed between the two sides of the alley, she starts to pant, as if she's just run a marathon.

"Are you okay?" I ask, sounding about as useless as I feel.

She doesn't respond and instead grits her teeth, resumes her tight grip on the top of the gate, and in one swift, difficult motion hauls a leg over the top.

Her shin collides with the hard wood with an almighty crack- so loud and so violent that it even makes my own leg bones ache and rattle.

"Fuck!" she hisses underneath her breath.

She tosses her blonde mess of greasy hair over her shoulder and appears to brave on through the pain. She maneuvers herself on top of the gate so that the sharp, thin edge is digging into the front of her chest. It must be painful, but she doesn't cry or scream. Her face remains scrunched up tightly. She'd holding it all in.

It's uncomfortable to watch as she attempts to gently coax herself off of the gate. At first, I worry that she's stuck there, just balancing in the icy night's sky. However, after a few tries, she disappears, tumbling down the other side of the gate. Apparently, the damp, marshy ground does not continue beyond it because I hear her body smack against concrete, and another loud gasp of pain follows.

I crouch down and try to find a tiny slither or gap in the wood so that I can see her, but the thing is solid.

"Nancy?" I whisper, shivering as a gentle yet harsh breeze slips over me.

She grunts back in response. Then, I hear her slowly compose herself and tap lightly on the other side of the gate.

"Come on- quick!" she grumbles.

"What?"

"You need to get over. Throw the gun first; I'll keep a look out."

Suddenly, there is a cold, wet squelch behind me.

I spin around, and my lower lip falls open, a gasp of shock stuck inside my throat.

A circular glow cast by a flashlight flits over the wet, muddy terrain, causing it to glint. I freeze. I can hear that Nancy is still talking to me; however, her voice fades out to an inaudible fuzz in the back of my head.

I feel my eyes widen as a tall, broad figure squelches into view, revealing a dark, haggard face with disorientated, bloodshot eyes. As he comes further forwards, I notice that his stocky, sturdy legs are quivering slightly, stumbling almost in the thick mud.

"What are you doing, Pig?" he spits at me, each word slurred, exposing the fact that he is clearly inebriated.

What was it that Rowan had told me about Arlo? That the man was a recovering alcoholic. Had killed a kid or something because he was drunk on the job as a doctor. Then Faith had found him on the run, taken him in, and helped him to turn his life around (and by turn his life around, that means become a torturous, murdering machine).

But yet, he is drunk. The more I focus, I realise that I can even smell the strong, pungent scent of some kind of spirit radiating off of him. Whiskey or rum, perhaps?

Apart from the torch in his beefy, worn hands, he appears to be unarmed. He's swaying on his feet, and his eyelids are swollen and jutting over his eyelids. I wonder what the fuck he's doing out here. Maybe he was in the house, and he heard us. Although it seems unlikely. The longer I stare at him, the more apparent it becomes that he isn't just drunk- he's absolutely shit-faced.

There's a mad, crazy flash that goes through me then.

Maybe I could take him.

He's twice my size, probably even more, but he's defenceless, and his senses are numbed and delayed. I've got a gun, and I've observed them being used enough over the last half of a year to understand how to work one.

Swallowing, I rest my finger on the trigger. My wrist wobbles as I try to hold it up, to point the barrel at Arlo's monstrous, wobbly shadow.

"Nancy… r-r-run…" I bleat, unable to conceal the fear that wracks my voice.

"What?"

"RUN!" I shout, giving the door a sharp kick and then poising the gun in front of me. I stretch my arms out as if somehow creating a kind of force field between him and me.

When I hear the distant, muffled sounds of Nancy scrambling away down the front driveway, a small sigh of relief escapes me.

"Come on then, Pig," Arlo chuckles, taking another step forward. "Let's have it. You couldn't kill. You haven't got it in you."

The unpleasant stench of stale booze intensifies then. Bile creeps up into my throat.

Rooted to the spot, I continue to stand there, hands gripped so tightly to my weapon that I can see my knuckles are turning white.

"That's what I thought," smiles Arlo, "fucking pussy."

He's about to take another step forward when I cock the gun. My brows knit tightly together in the middle of my forehead. "Stay where you are," I growl under my breath.

The intoxicated slump of his face stiffens then. He freezes.

For a few seconds, just the cold night air and a quietly murmuring chill hover between us. My brain races and my wrists are trembling so much that I fear I will drop the gun into the dirt.

I'm just about to open my mouth again when there's a loud blood-curdling crash, and before I can even absorb what is happening, I'm knocked clean off of my feet. Like the thick trunk of a falling tree, I collide hard with the ground, face-planting the sludge of dirt.

The gun skitters out of my hands.

Arlo laughs. I begin to haul myself up when a hot spike of agony shoots down the right side of my body. He is kicking my shoulder with the toe of his boot, amplifying the force with every swift movement. "That'll teach you to pull a gun on me!" he snarls.

Tears flood down my face, and I resolve to just curl up there in the damp, stinking shit on the floor. After all, that's what I am now. Or what I might as well be.

I hear Nancy crying too. When I chance a fearful look upwards, I see that the wooden gate is open, and Rowan is standing in the doorway, holding Nancy tightly in a headlock. Although he holds her tightly, his familiar eyes are trained intensely on me, glaring down at me like a disappointed parent lecturing an insolent child.

"Oh Pig," he groans irritatedly, shaking his head in disbelief. "What did you go and do that for?"

Arlo kneels down beside me, and with a shaky hand, retrieves the gun from the floor. He wipes each side on the fabric of his trousers, then hits me hard in the side of the face with it.

"Which one first do you reckon?" he chuckles, licking his lips, his dark eyes glittering hungrily. "Or shall we just put them in the cages?"

I find that, at this point, I'm sort of relieved. The end of my suffering is finally in sight.

Just then, a pattering of rain begins to fall in icy, sharp pelts from the inky sky.

Rowan clears his throat, "don't you think we should give Pig a chance? To redeem himself?"

Arlo scowls and turns to look at him. "What?" he demands incredulously.

If my mouth wasn't so jammed full of mud and blood, maybe I'd tell him not to bother. I'd rather be dead than be put back to work in that slaughterhouse.

"Remember Faith's rule?" Rowan says, coughing nervously. I sense that he is afraid of Arlo. "People can change. If they prove themselves, they should be given a chance. Otherwise, it's just as bad as murder."

My skin sizzles. I cringe at what a spectacularly ridiculous logic this is and expect Arlo to kick the shit out of me in response. But, to my surprise, he pauses. He actually looks as though he's thinking about it.

"Alright," he agrees finally. He looks down at me and gives me a particularly nasty smile that makes my stomach churn. Involuntarily, my lips fall into a frightened grimace. He reaches into the side of his belt and swiftly withdraws a small but sharp-bladed pocket knife. He holds it out to me.

"You want in, you've got it. You can be in the family. As long as you do your share and you don't eat each meat, you can have your own room, all the drugs you like, all the women you like, and more. You'll be protected by the police, and you'll be rich."

Somehow, his pitch doesn't exactly thrill me.

"But, you've got to prove you're one of us," he jerks his head towards Nancy, who is still quietly sniffling in Rowan's vice-like grip. "Kill her," he says simply, shrugging his shoulders as if it's no big deal. "Kill her now, or you go back in the cages."

It's as though my brain momentarily switches off.

All of a sudden, I'm no longer in control.

I'm an entity, hopelessly trapped inside the confines of my own skeleton, unable to stop the horrific scene that I sense is rapidly approaching.

Numb all over, I drag myself out of the mud and clutch the knife so tightly in my palm that the blade slits open my skin, and fresh blood congeals with the mud.

Inside, I scream and scream, begging it to stop, yet my eyes won't shut or allow themselves to be torn away.

Like a zombie, I stumble slowly yet purposefully over the mud, jabbing the air with the point of the knife in Nancy's direction.

She squeals and struggles, twisting her body inside her headlock, but there's no way in hell she's getting out of Rowan's muscular arms.

Sobbing now, her face convulses, and a string of snot shimmers in a vile paste down her chin. She's begging me. With her eyes, and in between pain-filled sobs of horror, she pleads for me to stop. For me to spare her life. To give her mercy.

I continue to stare back at her, wishing desperately that I could feel some kind of sadness, or hesitation, or even a passing flutter of emotion... anything.

But, nothing comes.

Instead, I lunge the knife forward and jam it straight into her stomach, ripping through her clothes and burying into her flesh.

The knife goes in easy, like a needle into a pin cushion, and after I've done it once, I find that my arm is on some kind of automatic motor, and I am unable to stop it.

Again and again, I stab her, penetrating her with the knife's edge. The rain intensifies, causing the blood to streak and smudge down my hands and arms. It's almost soothing, in a way.

Nancy throws her head back and lashes out in agony, but I must sever a vital artery because soon she is slumped over, her head bowed forwards, lulling lifelessly on her neck.

Yet still, I keep on mutilating her, wondering if I will stab her so hard that my knife will come out of her back, snapping the tendons in her spine as I go. But, before I can find out, there is a hand on my arm.

The touch brings me back.

Suddenly, my arm is aching. The knife falls from my fingers, and arm is just left hovering in the air, hurting and dripping with Nancy's crimson fluid. I bend over and vomit, all over my shoes and all over Nancy's flimsy, dead legs. At the sight of them, I puke again, and afterwards I'm left retching uncontrollably, my meagre diet having left me with not a great deal to regurgitate.

Staggering backwards, I glance from Arlo to Rowan, vomit dripping from my lips, a huge bloody stain covering almost every inch of my upper body.

Even through the slashes of rain that now fall all around me, I can see the soft, smiling expressions that fill their faces.

Rowan drops Nancy so that she lands in a broken heap at his feet, her face smacking into the pool of her own blood mixed with my puke. He steps forward and pats me hard on the back.

"Well done, Pig," he grins. "You passed the initiation."

Even Arlo is staring at me, apparently impressed. "Didn't think you had it in you," he admits.

I zone out, partially out of shock, partially out of guilt, but mostly because I've never been so fucking exhausted in my entire life.

I don't know what they do with Nancy's corpse. I don't even know how I get into the car. It all goes by in a thick, fast rush, and before I know it, I'm strapped into a car, driving back to the main house. When I get there, they give me decent food, I'm allowed a shower, and then they show me to a new room which I'm told is now mine. People pop their heads in, even though it's late, and they're nice to me.

It's fucking weird.

As I twist about in the thick bed covers, I reminisce how much I used to love lying in a warm bed on a cold night, listening to the rain patter against the window. It was soothing. It would almost always get me off to sleep.

But, as I say, your experiences change you.

And now, for as long as I live, every time I hear the rain, I know that that very moment will always come flooding back to me, harder and harsher than ever.

It's ironic. I'm so tired, but I can't sleep. I've been deprived of rest for so long, sleeping in that manky bedroom.

But now, even in this luxurious, fresh-smelling four-poster- I can't sleep.

Not anymore.

Why?

Because your experiences change you.

And because now, every time I close my eyes, all I can think of is the image of Nancy doubling over forwards into a deckchair, slowly bleeding out of stab wounds.

Stab wounds that *I* inflicted.

Stab wounds that maybe… I *enjoyed* inflicting.

BEFORE YOU GO!

Thank you so much for reading Circus. I really whole-heartedly appreciate it *so* much, and I hope that you enjoyed it.

I'd love to know what you thought of the book, so an Amazon book review would truly make my day. Good or bad, I want to hear your thoughts. It's also a great help to me as a writer because every review boosts the book in the algorithm and helps other readers to find it.

Also, let's connect! I'm on Twitter, Instagram, and Good Reads, and I love to hear from people who have read my books.

https://twitter.com/SianRoseAuthor

https://twitter.com/SianRoseAuthor

Thanks again.
Sian Rose x

Printed in Great Britain
by Amazon